He meant only to thank her with a kiss on the cheek, to make up for the words he couldn't find.

But she turned her head just then, her lips brushing his, and it became something much more.

She was staring at him, looking a bit as if she were in shock.

Of course she is. You had no right!

"Ali, I'm sor—"

She put a finger to his lips, stopping his apology. "Don't you dare say you're sorry. Not for that."

"But—"

"I understand. It was impulse. Unexpected." He thought he saw a faint rise of pink in her cheeks. "I liked it." His heart seemed to take a little leap. "But right now...we have to focus on Grace, don't we?"

That easily, and so very gently, she brought him back to earth. Back to reality. He couldn't look at her when he nodded.

"So, we put...that on hold. But, Colby?" He did look at her then, because he had to. "Just on hold, okay? Don't bury it."

Dear Reader,

Some time ago I met the most amazing kid on a ferry ride across Puget Sound. I was sitting and reading when she climbed into the seat next to me, even though there was nobody else in the row except her father, who was several seats down and on the phone. When I looked at her, she smiled and whispered, "You're reading so you'll be quiet so I can read too." As often happens in life, the best-laid plans...

The ride turned into a conversation with the smartest seven-year-old I've ever met. This kid was simply brilliant, beyond her age both in her thoughts and the way she spoke. Her father ended his call when he realized she'd moved, and came to see if she was bothering me. I asked if she was really only seven, and he smiled as if he'd been asked a hundred times, and nodded. And he was so proud of her he practically glowed with it.

That girl—and her dad—has stuck in my mind for years. I'm glad to have finally let her out and hope that her real life was much easier than the fictional one here. But judging by the way he looked at her, I'll bet the real-life dad would have done just what my hero here does...whatever it took to save his precious girl.

Happy reading!

Justine

OPERATION PROTECTOR

JUSTINE DAVIS

ROMANTIC SUSPENSE

If you purchased this book without a cover you should be aware that this book is stolen property. It was reported as "unsold and destroyed" to the publisher, and neither the author nor the publisher has received any payment for this "stripped book."

Recycling programs for this product may not exist in your area.

ISBN-13: 978-1-335-47188-8

Operation Protector

Copyright © 2026 by Janice Davis Smith

All rights reserved. No part of this book may be used or reproduced in any manner whatsoever without written permission.

Without limiting the exclusive rights of any author, contributor or the publisher of this publication, any unauthorized use of this publication to train generative artificial intelligence (AI) technologies is expressly prohibited. Harlequin also exercises their rights under Article 4(3) of the Digital Single Market Directive 2019/790 and expressly reserves this publication from the text and data mining exception.

This is a work of fiction. Names, characters, places and incidents are either the product of the author's imagination or are used fictitiously. Any resemblance to actual persons, living or dead, businesses, companies, events or locales is entirely coincidental.

For questions and comments about the quality of this book, please contact us at CustomerService@Harlequin.com.

TM and ® are trademarks of Harlequin Enterprises ULC.

Harlequin Enterprises ULC
22 Adelaide St. West, 41st Floor
Toronto, Ontario M5H 4E3, Canada
www.Harlequin.com

HarperCollins Publishers
Macken House, 39/40 Mayor Street Upper,
Dublin 1, D01 C9W8, Ireland
www.HarperCollins.com

Printed in Lithuania

Justine Davis lives on Puget Sound in Washington State, watching big ships and the occasional submarine go by and sharing the neighborhood with assorted wildlife, including a pair of bald eagles, deer, a bear or two, and a tailless raccoon. In the few hours when she's not planning, plotting or writing her next book, her favorite things are photography, knitting her way through a huge yarn stash and driving her restored 1967 Corvette roadster—top down, of course.

Connect with Justine on her website, justinedavis.com, at X.com/justine_d_davis or at Facebook.com/justinedaredavis.

Books by Justine Davis

Harlequin Romantic Suspense

Cutter's Code

Operation Whistleblower
Operation Payback
Operation Witness Protection
Operation Takedown
Operation Rafe's Redemption
Operation Rescue
Operation Protector

The Coltons of Owl Creek

A Colton Kidnapping

The Coltons of Alaska

Colton in the Wild

Visit the Author Profile page
at Harlequin.com for more titles.

Chapter 1

"What's he carrying?"

At his wife's words Quinn Foxworth looked up from the report he'd been studying. Hayley was leaning to look out the window beside the front door of Foxworth Northwest headquarters on the east side of Puget Sound. She was in the entryway, close enough for him to see, but he had no idea what to expect. He only knew it had to be Cutter, because only their dog could bring on that half-puzzled, half-"what now?" tone in his wife's voice.

Geez, dog, it's not even seven in the morning yet.

He was smiling as he thought it.

And then Hayley gasped, dropped the jacket she'd been about to hang on the rack near the entrance, and dashed toward the door. Instantly, knowing Hayley never overreacted, he followed at a run.

When he got through the door, Hayley was kneeling next to their sometimes too brilliant dog. Who was carrying a small, black-and-white puppy with his mouth, so very gently you would have thought it was his own.

At first Quinn thought the tiny creature was just wet. But the moment he got down beside Cutter and the dog even more gently set the puppy down, Quinn could see that it was indeed wet. But not with water, though it was raining hard enough to make even the thick-coated Cutter look soaked. Because the water running off the pup onto the sidewalk beneath him was... pink. And when Quinn touched him, then pulled his hand back and looked at his fingers, he was sure what the wetness was.

Blood.

"He's hurt," Hayley said urgently.

In that moment the little thing looked up at him, and he couldn't miss the fear and confusion in the big brown puppy eyes. Something snapped in Quinn.

"I don't see an obvious wound, but let's get him to Dr. Moore," he said.

As if they'd planned it out, they each started to move. Hayley ran inside and grabbed a small stack of towels, while he went and collected their jackets and the keys to their SUV parked in the gravel lot outside the building. Cutter stood guard until Hayley got there and began to ease the puppy with the jagged pattern of black-and-white patches of fur onto one of the towels. Then they both headed for the car, Cutter at their heels letting out an anxious whine.

"We've got him, boy," Quinn assured the dog. "But you might as well come along so Dr. Moore can say hello." He knew the reliable veterinarian would want to. He'd often told them that Cutter was his most remarkable patient in his thirty years as a vet.

Hayley made a phone call as they started down the long driveway. They knew the experienced Dr. Moore always left time in his busy day for emergencies, so their wait at the homey-looking white building was short. The presence of the blood—and the Foxworth name, for they'd become a little more than famous in this area—made it a priority.

The young vet tech who made the initial exam agreed with Quinn that there was no apparent wound, but they took the pup back for a more thorough check.

"Poor little guy," Hayley said as she paced the small room. "He was so scared."

"Leave it to Cutter," Quinn said, standing in front of the poster diagramming a dog's circulatory system, trying to focus on it instead of the trembling little creature they'd brought here. The dog he was referring to let out a soft woof. He was well-known here in the small veterinary hospital, and as a certified therapy dog, was the only animal other than the office cat who was allowed the run of the place.

"He's so polite!"

"He's so sweet!"

"He makes me feel so much better when I pet him!"

They heard at least a couple of those every time they brought their too-clever dog in, which was actually reassuring for both Foxworths, because it reminded them he was a pet, and not just the canine who had become such an integral part of the Foxworth team, be it at home or on one of their cases.

It had happened so fast that Quinn sometimes forgot about the time before. But coming to the vet reminded him, because of the deeply etched images in his mind, of when this dog had burst out of the trees and changed his life forever by bringing Hayley to him. And had risked his life to help them during that operation.

The dog had become the very heart of Foxworth, so often recognizing a case before they did, and knowing how to tell them in ways that were undeniable. He tried to imagine his life now if it had never happened. He could not. It made his throat tight just to try. Because without Hayley he would have no life, not one worth living anyway.

Something nudged at his knee. He looked down and saw Cutter, looking up at him steadily with those amber-flecked dark eyes. He knew the dog had sensed his emotions. Automatically he reached to stroke the soft fur, no longer surprised at the soothing feel of it.

He looked over at Hayley, who was sitting in one of the wooden chairs by the door. She wore her worried expression.

And that tightened his throat again, because it was so like her to be worried about this little puppy who had appeared out of nowhere, even if they knew absolutely nothing about him.

When the door from the back of the hospital, where they did all the routine procedures, opened and they saw Dr. Moore himself, Quinn knew Hayley had felt the same little jump as he had. They'd expected the tech to come back with the results. But they relaxed a little when he set the page he was carrying down on the exam table and bent to welcome Cutter, who had instantly gone to greet the kindly man who saw to his health.

"And how's my most clever patient ever today?" the man asked, and Cutter answered with a nudge of his nose and a happy tail wag.

After a moment he straightened and looked at the humans in the room. Quinn had learned a lot about reading people from the woman he so loved, and he had the feeling the good doctor was a stride or two beyond curious.

"Well, leave it to you folks to make my day interesting," he began.

"Is he all right?" Hayley asked, sounding a little anxious. "We couldn't see any injury that would have bled, but—"

"He's fine. No injuries internal or external. He's a good weight, clean and healthy."

"So, not a stray," Quinn said.

"No," Dr. Moore agreed. "He's well cared for. We're getting him all cleaned up now, and he should be out in a couple of minutes."

Quinn and Hayley looked at each other, and Quinn knew they were both thinking the same thing. "The blood that was on him," he began.

Dr. Moore's brow furrowed. "That's where it gets very interesting. As I told you, it wasn't his."

"Maybe his mom?" Hayley asked.

"No," Dr. Moore said. "So, knowing what I do about the Foxworth Foundation, I went a little further."

"Hit us with it, Doc," Quinn suggested.

Then, flatly and with a grimace, the vet said, "The blood wasn't canine. It was human."

Chapter 2

Ali Moran had only come home to get some dry clothes. The predicted rainstorm had arrived several hours early, and she'd ended up both soaked and more worried than when she'd started out on her search a couple of hours ago. That it was her own fault that her beloved new puppy, Zigzag, already shortened to Ziggy, had somehow slipped past the newly installed fence she'd had put in just for him, only made things worse.

She should have been outside when he'd started barking, right after she'd heard an unusual sound. But her phone had rung as she'd let him out, and it had been a client who would determine just how well they'd be living the rest of the winter, so she'd gone back to answer it despite the early hour. She'd cut the call short, but by the time she'd stepped back outside on her back deck, Ziggy was nowhere in sight.

She'd been outside ever since, searching. Every corner, behind every shrub in the yard, even crawling under the deck to be sure the little guy wasn't hiding. She'd only brought him home a couple of weeks ago, and while he'd seemed to adjust rapidly—probably more rapidly than she had since she herself had only been in this house for a week longer—maybe he hadn't been as happy as he'd seemed with his new home.

Or you.

It was true she'd never had a dog before, because her mother was beyond fastidious to the point of persnickety, but she'd read and studied and even taken an online course about new puppy life, and thought she'd had it down.

And then reality bites... Again.

She shook her head sharply as she traded her wet sneakers and socks for warm, dry rain boots. She straightened up, then slid her phone into her pocket, thankful she'd gone on a picture-taking binge when she'd first gotten Ziggy, so she had plenty of shots to show the neighbors and ask if they'd seen him.

But that would be the easy part. She was more worried about the woods behind the houses here on the dead end of the street. The long-untouched forest was why she'd chosen her cottage, the last in the small row, and the smallest on the street, especially dwarfed next to the big, remodeled-to-excess place next door.

She gave a mental apology to the residents, seven-year-old Grace more than her mother, Liz, a brusque, rather imperious woman Ali had quickly realized had been the one who simply had to have a bigger, grander, more impressive home than anyone else, to show off.

In a strange way, people like her were responsible for Ali doing what she loved. Because her interiors service—she refused to call it decorating, since that was exactly what she didn't do—catered to those who wanted attractive, functional homes, not showplaces that made you afraid to set down a glass or put your feet up after a long day. Which was why her website header was: It Doesn't Matter How Pretty It Is If It Doesn't Work for You.

She needed to check those woods first, she decided. Ziggy was just a little puppy, and no matter how big he might get later, right now he was easy prey for whatever predator might be living back there, from coyotes to bobcats to owls. At least the gorgeous bald eagles pretty much stuck to the abundant fish in Puget Sound, just a few blocks away.

She had to find him. She couldn't take another death. It had taken her a very long time to become even functional after she'd lost Josh. Even now her eyes teared up at the thought. They'd been supposed to have a long, happy life together, not merely a few years, ending in a flash of agony.

She shook off the too-familiar memories, pulled on her hooded slicker and braced herself for the wind and rain. She had the back door open when a knock came at the front. Her heart leaped. Maybe one of the neighbors had found Ziggy. Maybe it was Grace, who adored the pup and had come over several times to play with him.

She practically ran to the front door and yanked it open. There was a dog there, all right, but certainly not Ziggy. It was a big, partly reddish brown creature with shiny black fur over its head and shoulders. The eyes that looked up at her were dark, flecked with tiny bits of amber, and looked infinitely wiser than the eyes of any dog she'd ever seen.

Or most people.

He'd apparently brought his humans with him, because the man held the leash snapped to his collar. She'd just spotted the metal tag in the shape of a boat that hung from that collar when the woman spoke.

"Does this little guy look familiar?"

Only then did Ali realize the woman had been cradling a small bundle inside her rain jacket. A head poked out, and the moment he spotted her, the pup gave an excited little bark.

"Ziggy!" Ali yelped in relief.

The woman laughed. "I can feel his tail wagging madly. I guess that answers that."

"Thank you so much," Ali exclaimed as her visitor disentangled Ziggy from her jacket.

"Don't thank us," the man holding the leash of the much larger dog said. "Thank him."

He indicated the dog who was sitting calmly between them. Once she had her precious pup safely cuddled in her arms again and she could breathe normally, she gave the man a questioning look.

"He found your boy and brought him to us," he said.

"Our office is just down the road that way," the woman said, gesturing toward the sound.

Scrambling to regain her equilibrium, Ali belatedly realized they were standing out in the cold.

"Please, won't you come in? It's a little messy, I just moved in three weeks ago, so things are still in flux, but I have hot coffee on."

"Hot anything sounds wonderful," the woman said, with a smile that had Ali instinctively trusting her.

They stepped inside, Ali shut the door and ushered them into the living room, which was thankfully in good shape. All the clutter and unpacked boxes were elsewhere.

"I'm Ali Moran," she said. "And this little rascal is Zigzag, for obvious reasons." She'd named him the moment she'd seen the pattern of black fur running the length of his back from head to tail in a zigzag shape.

"And I'm Hayley Foxworth, this is my husband, Quinn, and this clever boy—" she reached out to pet the bigger dog, who was sitting politely at their feet "—is Cutter."

She'd heard the name Foxworth before—it was hard to live here and not be aware—but she had no idea if these folks were connected to those Foxworths she'd seen in the news. They seemed too…normal to be that famous, though.

"Well, I must thank you officially," she said, leaning over toward the other dog. "Is it all right?" she asked, pausing when she realized she was about to pet a strange dog she'd never seen before. And a dog who looked like a fluffier version of a lot of police and military dogs she'd seen on screen.

"Yes," Quinn said.

"And it'll be more all right when you do," Hayley added. Ali smiled at that, understanding because she now knew the happiness and pure stress relief she got from petting Ziggy.

But then, as her fingers stroked the dark head of the bigger dog, she realized suddenly she hadn't understood anything. Because the feeling of calm and ease she got, as if it were coursing upward from her fingers on that thick fur, was unlike anything she'd ever felt before.

Her gaze shot back to the woman, who was smiling. "See what I mean?"

"I...wow. What is he, some kind of therapy dog?"

"Among countless other things," her husband said, dryly but still lovingly. "We try to keep up, but he's always a few steps ahead of us."

There was something about the way Quinn Foxworth was looking at her that made her remember how this had all started.

"I honestly don't know how he got out," she said. "I've looked at the new fence and it's intact. I know it's short, but—"

"So is he," Hayley said.

"Yes," Ali said, glad she understood. She didn't want to get a reputation in her new neighborhood for being a negligent pet owner.

She explained how she'd come back in for her phone, had heard a string of barks from Ziggy, but then quiet so she'd assumed—which she would never do again, she swore—the pup had simply been barking at some passing squirrel or rabbit, since they were common here.

"He's not used to the wildlife yet, and everything seems to fascinate him," she said.

They chatted some more, and she couldn't help thinking she wished these were her next-door neighbors. Except for Grace, whom she'd miss. And so would Ziggy. And finally she felt comfortable to ask the question that had been hovering.

"Are you by chance connected to the Foxworth Foundation?"

Hayley smiled. "That would be us."

Ali's eyes widened. "Wow. You guys are amazing. I've read about you, and how you help the little guy. It does my heart good to know that you're out there, looking out for people who have been treated so unfairly."

"Whether they were treated that way by other people, or by life, we try to help," Hayley agreed.

"As long as they're in the right, the Foxworth Foundation is there," Quinn added.

Ali sighed audibly. "Wonderful. Thank you for…being."

They'd finished their coffee, and Ali noticed it was Quinn who stood and gathered all the mugs and took them into the kitchen, all without comment.

"At the risk of being clichéd, I love what you've done with the place. Welcoming, comfortable and functional."

Ali laughed. "That's practically my business motto."

"Business?"

"I do residential and business interiors, for people who want function over form, but still want to like what they're looking at."

Hayley looked around again, and slowly began to nod. "I can see you're good at it, just from this. Clean lines, but not cold."

"Thank you," Ali exclaimed gratefully. "That's exactly my goal."

"Ali?"

Quinn spoke from where he'd walked after dropping off the coffee mugs, over by a side window that looked out toward the house next door. Grace's house, as she preferred to think of it, since her mother seemed to have no desire to be on a first-name basis.

"What?" she asked.

"When you heard Ziggy barking, did you hear anything else?"

Her brow furrowed. "I heard something right before, but it was far away. So I thought he was just barking at the noise, or

I've got a family of rabbits living out there he always yips at, so I thought he'd seen one… Why?"

It was Hayley who answered her. "Forgive us for not telling you right away, but we wanted to check you out before we got into this. When Cutter brought Ziggy to us, he had blood on him. Quite a bit."

Ali gasped. "What?" She immediately looked back at the puppy in her lap, running her hands over him urgently.

"He's fine," Hayley assured her. "We took him to our vet to be sure. It wasn't his blood."

For a moment Ali felt as if she could breathe again, but then the implications of what Hayley had said sank in. "Then what…?"

"The blood," Quinn said from his spot over by the window, "was human."

She blinked. Human? How on earth? "But… I'm the only one here, and I'm not— I haven't—" She broke off, at a total loss.

"I believe you," Quinn said. "Because I think I know how it happened." He turned then to look at them. "I think that sound you heard came from next door."

"What?" She felt like she'd missed something in a complicated story she was reading. She got up, started toward him, wondering what he'd seen. When she got there, he pointed toward the back of the house across the side yard, where a window was clearly broken.

"You want my best guess," Quinn said, "Ziggy heard the breaking glass, barked at the person who broke it—and apparently cut himself up in the process—and who obviously didn't want to be discovered, so he ran over and grabbed your pup to shut him up."

Ali sucked in a harsh breath. And cuddled Ziggy even closer.

"But he didn't hurt him," Hayley, who had joined them now, assured her. "Our vet checked him thoroughly."

Ali looked at the broken window at the back of the house

next door. It did make sense, but if it was true… A memory hit her then of that time little Grace had climbed through a window to come over to play with Ziggy.

"Oh no," she said, staring, feeling more than a little stunned. "That's Grace's room."

Chapter 3

Ali hastily explained about her charming, dog-loving little neighbor, but then hesitated. Hayley, who had come up beside them, urged her on.

"Something's bothering you," she said. "Is it about Grace?"

Ali took a deep breath. She didn't want to spread rumors that were based only on her admittedly limited observation and assessment of her neighbors. She was the newcomer to the neighborhood and had no right to pass judgment on people she barely knew. But Grace...

She was thankful Hayley didn't push but instead gave her time to think. She remembered all she'd read and heard about the Foxworth Foundation, all the good they'd done, on a huge scale. Even taking down the crooked governor of the state. Surely they wouldn't get involved here, when she truly had no idea there was really anything wrong?

But she'd also read about them standing for the little guy in the right against the big guys in the wrong. Helping people who had no fame, no position, no influence to barter. She'd even read they had begun by recovering and returning a stolen locket to a little girl, the child's only memento of her dead mother.

In the end, looking at that shattered window, she decided. Because what if that blood had been Grace's, what if she'd broken that window to get out?

"Grace is sweet, loving, and adores Ziggy. I saw her climbing out a back window—that window—of the big house to get here once, but I accepted her explanation that the house was being cleaned and she had to stay out of the way. So it took me a while to realize that she was sneaking over here to play with him without her mother's knowledge. When I asked her about it, she said her mother would kill her if she found out she was coming over here. I assumed she was exaggerating, like kids do. I've met her mother, and while not the warmest person I've ever met, she seems okay."

"But?" Hayley prompted.

In for a penny... Ali went on, still doubting her own decision, but something about this woman made her trust. "But... Grace was shivering. Panicky. As if she were genuinely terrified. And all of a sudden I wasn't so sure—"

The other dog, Cutter, suddenly let out a rolling, almost demanding sort of bark. Both Foxworths spun around. The clearly revved-up animal was at her rear door, looking back over his shoulder at his humans. The bark came again.

"I guess he needs out?" Ali suggested. Before she even finished, Quinn had quickly gone over to the dog.

"That's his 'You need to see something' bark," Hayley said.

Things started to happen so fast Ali was a little boggled. The Foxworths were out the back door with their dog so fast it occurred to her perhaps that person who'd broken the window and grabbed Ziggy might still be around, and the dog had heard him or scented him somehow. Hastily she put the puppy in the playpen she'd set up for him, and followed their visitors outside.

She got through the back door just in time to see Cutter clear her four-foot fence as if it were no taller than Ziggy. Quinn was next, clearing it as easily with one hand on a fence post, as did Hayley. She had less faith in herself, and headed for the gate.

They were into the trees and out of sight by the time she got out of the yard. She paused to listen but heard nothing, not even the dog who had trumpeted the announcement that had made his humans leap into action. They knew him, she thought as she ran, they must be sure this meant something.

Maybe I was right before, thinking he looked a little like those well-trained enforcement dogs.

She went carefully, slowly, not knowing what might be ahead. She at last caught up to them in a small space between some towering evergreens. They were standing facing one of the largest trees, Quinn and Hayley behind their dog, who was a yard or so in front of them.

Their dog, who was staring at the man sitting at the base of the tree, cradling a bloody arm against his chest.

The window. He *was* still here. And Quinn had been right—this was the source of the blood that had ended up on Ziggy.

"Guess your burglary didn't go too well," Quinn was saying.

"I'm not a burglar." The man said it flatly, wearily.

Feeling it was safe now—somehow she knew that either the dog or Quinn Foxworth would stop the man if he tried anything—Ali picked up her pace. She supposed she should be grateful the guy hadn't actually hurt Ziggy, but—

Just as she got close enough to take in the entire scene, the strangest thing happened. The Foxworth dog's demeanor shifted entirely. He went from bristling and on guard to something altogether different. His head came up, he stretched his neck out, his nose aimed at the bleeding man. He tilted his head, as if curious. The man was looking at the dog in turn, warily.

Cutter walked toward him. The injured man shifted, starting to get to his feet, as if he expected the dog to attack.

"Don't think about running," Quinn advised, but made no move to call back the dog.

And then Cutter reached the man, sniffed at him closely, gave a little whuff that sounded oddly like the animal had made a decision. The man was still edgy with the dog right there, but the dog himself seemed different. Calmer, yet no less…determined?

She sighed inwardly. She had a lot to learn yet about dogs, if she was imparting human thoughts and emotions to this one.

And then Cutter turned around, facing his people, and sat at the bleeding man's feet. He stared up at the Foxworths steadily, unwaveringly.

"Oh?" said Hayley, as if the dog had somehow spoken.

Quinn grimaced. "Really, dog?"

Whatever Cutter had been trying to communicate, clearly the couple understood it. Ali had the feeling this was far from the first time this had happened. Maybe she hadn't been so wrong after all.

"Apparently so," Hayley said.

Quinn let out an audible breath. "Well, we had December off at least."

"And a lovely December it was." Hayley was smiling now, and Ali was a little boggled by how relaxed they both suddenly were, when the man who had tried to break in next door was sitting right there. Not to mention they'd just had an entire conversation that made no sense to anyone else.

She stifled the pang she felt, thinking of when she, too, had had a relationship like that, and shifted her gaze to that man on the ground now. He looked as puzzled as she felt.

He also looked familiar. He was a big guy, she could tell that even as he remained crouched there. Long legs, muscular arms—the left one blood-soaked even wrapped in what looked like a strip torn from his plaid shirt—slightly shaggy dark brown hair, and bright blue eyes.

Her pulse jumped. She'd seen those eyes before.

Grace's eyes.

The image captured in the photo Grace had once shown her, a clearly precious thing to the child, flashed through her mind. She remembered the girl pulling it out of her pocket, whispering that she had to hide it or her mother would take it away and burn it.

It showed a couple-of-years-younger Grace, a delighted grin on her face, getting a ride in a wheelbarrow pushed by her equally grinning father.

By this man.

"You're Grace's dad," she said, staring at him.

The man stiffened. "You know my girl?"

She nodded. "I moved in next door three weeks ago."

His expression cleared immediately. "You're Ali?"

Surprised, she nodded again. But she was even more surprised by the utterly and unmistakably grateful expression that came over his face then. And when he spoke it was with a sincere tone that matched that look. And surprised her even more.

"Thank you."

Chapter 4

Colby Kendrick had known he was in trouble the moment that puppy had started yapping. He'd had no choice at the time except to grab it and try to quiet it. His ex-wife slept like a log—usually a drugged one—but he couldn't risk it. So he'd picked up the dog, who had wiggled so much it hurt his bleeding arm to hang on to him, and then he'd put him down on the ground back here in the trees so he could try to stop the bleeding. And as he'd hoped, the territory outside his fenced yard fascinated him enough he'd just started sniffing and exploring.

But now Colby was obviously in more trouble than he ever had been in his life.

That was what he got for sitting here in the rain for what, a couple of hours? But Liz had been so furious about the window he had been worried about his little girl. He heard the whole fight from here in the trees. His brave, courageous little girl who had immediately told her mother she had broken the window accidentally.

He didn't think Liz would physically abuse her, but at this point he wasn't certain of anything. And he wasn't about to leave Grace alone, even if he was bleeding.

And that was when everything had changed. When that other dog had arrived. He'd looked like a police dog or something when he'd first come racing out of the trees at him, and Colby had wondered if he was about to get bitten on top of everything.

But it all changed again, and he was acting like a well-behaved pet. Well-behaved and...friendly.

"We need to have a discussion," the tall, powerful-looking man who had come up beside the dog said.

That was when a sudden thought struck him. "Did she call you? You work for them?"

"Them?" The woman who had come with the man spoke now. He assumed they were a couple, presumably the owners of the dog. There was something about the way they were together...

He nearly laughed aloud at himself, for thinking he had a clue. After all, he'd thought Liz loved him, too.

"Who?" the man asked, and there was an edge in his voice that said he wasn't a guy to mess with. And that instinct Colby trusted. So he answered.

"The Hollens."

He saw recognition of the name cross both of their faces. But unless he was completely wrong—entirely possible—he also saw a tinge of distaste.

"Hollen? Grace told me that was her mother's last name."

Colby's gaze snapped to Ali. And it happened again, just as it had the first moment he'd looked at her, before she'd explained and he realized she was that new friend Grace had told him about. That hair, the color of the reddest leaves in autumn. And her eyes, green like the other woman's but different, lighter, like the first growth of spring. And that voice, low and deep and rich, sending an oddly shivery sensation down his spine. He hadn't had a reaction like this to a woman in...forever.

Never let it be said your timing doesn't suck, Kendrick.

"Yeah. She never changed it when we got married. She was on the outs with the family then, but the name was...socially significant, she used to say."

"They are kind of...famous around here," the other woman explained to the new arrival. The man beside her snorted audibly, and he knew he'd been right about the distaste. "We're not a densely populated county, but if there's a family that is known by most residents, one way or another, it's them."

"You mean they're…a big deal?" the redhead asked, an undeniable emphasis on the last two words, as if she were quoting them.

"So they think," the man said. "Big real estate moguls, who like to buy up beautiful parcels of rural property and turn them into concrete canyons. Never mind the trees or the wildlife. Or that the roads and local facilities can't handle it." His tone matched that snort, and Colby felt a spark of hope. If that was how they felt about the Hollens…

"That's what Grace said about her mom. That she thinks she's a 'big deal.'"

"And I'm not," Colby said wearily. "And don't want to be. Never did. Which is why the divorce." He grimaced. "She thought I'd want to take advantage of the connection and move up—way up—in their world."

The woman called Ali hesitated, those lovely eyes looking troubled. "Her mother wants to change her last name to Hollen, but Grace doesn't want to. They fight over it, apparently."

Colby bit his lip but couldn't stop the moisture from welling up in his eyes. They'd fought over her first name, too. Grace had been his choice. She'd won that one, and the name on the birth certificate was Brianna, after her father, Brian. Well, she'd sort of won. Until Grace got old enough to choose for herself, and refused to respond to anything but Grace.

The redhead moved suddenly, crouching down as if she wanted to be on his level, eye to eye. The big dog nudged her, gently, and she looked at the animal. And Colby would swear, if it wasn't crazy, that the dog nodded.

Then she looked back at him and said, very quietly, "She told me she loves you, very much, and she wants to keep your name."

He lost the battle this time, and had to swipe at the tear that was starting down his right cheek. He didn't dare try to speak. Was sure nothing could get past the knot in his throat her words had caused. He felt a touch on his left hand, and his gaze shot back to her face.

And then, somewhere out of left field, she asked in a normal voice, "Did you and Grace really build that birdhouse? Or should I say, bird apartment complex?"

He knew he was gaping at her, but he couldn't seem to help it. But his throat loosened up enough that he thought he could get some words out.

"Yes. Yes, we did. Last summer, at my place." Then his brow furrowed. "She still has it?"

"No. I do."

He blinked. "What?"

"It's in my garage for now, out of sight," she said, nodding toward the cottage-style home he'd always liked better than the overdone thing Liz had insisted on. "Grace said that's what you do. Build things."

"Yes. I'm a carpenter," he said, a little defiantly. "A good one. It's what I love to do. I never wanted to build skyscrapers or industrial parks. Just things for…people."

"And birds?" Ali asked gently. He nodded. "She asked me to hide it for her. To keep it safe."

His eyes closed. He had to suck in a deep breath. And couldn't keep the note of bitterness out of his voice when he said, "Yeah. Her mother wanted to burn it."

"And she tried to. It's a little scorched on one side, but no real damage that couldn't be fixed, I think."

He jolted upright. "Tried to? Who stopped her?"

"Grace pulled it out of the firepit in the backyard."

He swore, harshly, not even trying to keep it under his breath. "She could have been hurt."

She was looking at him now as if what he'd said had decided her somehow. She looked up at the couple, who had been oddly silent through this exchange. And then the dog moved, reaching out to gently nuzzle his hand. The uninjured arm, he noticed, although the dog couldn't possibly understand that. His instinctive response was to pet the dark head, but he did so warily, given how the animal had first approached him.

The moment his fingers stroked over the dark fur, he felt an impossible wave of calm go through him, a reassuring kind of feeling. That he could feel that now, in the midst of near-panic about his baby girl, the pain in his arm and the specter of the Hollens hanging over him, was a little unsettling. As was the fact that it was coming from this dog he'd just moments ago feared was going to rip his throat out.

"Question," said the man towering over him. Colby looked up, waiting. "You broke the window?"

He hesitated, decided trying to lie wasn't going to do him any good, since he sucked at it, as Liz had often told him. And there was something about this guy, some air of authority or something, that told him it wouldn't be smart to lie to him anyway.

"Yes. It was locked, and Grace was in there, curled up on her bed crying really hard. Screaming, in fact. I was afraid maybe…it had become physical."

"Has it been before?" the woman asked, her tone sharp. The man's wife, judging by the ring on her finger, sounded oddly concerned for someone who didn't know him, or Grace, although they apparently at least knew of Liz's family.

"Not that I've seen any sign of, and believe me, I've checked."

"What happened then?" Quinn asked.

"Grace got up and came running to the window when I broke it, but then Liz stormed in. I ducked just in time, when I heard her stomping down the hall."

He shrugged, wincing as it tugged on the cut on his forearm. He also felt a splat on his nose, as rain began.

"So she didn't see you?"

"No." He closed his eyes, and gave a slow, aching shake of

his head. "Grace…she screamed at her that she broke it, trying to get away from her."

"Quick thinking," the man said.

His eyes snapped open and he looked up at the man again. "My Grace is a very, very smart kid."

"Her mother could have called the police. You could have been caught. You're hurt and bleeding. Yet you're still here. Why?"

"I couldn't leave Grace here alone with her when she was that angry." He nodded toward the big house, which was visible through the trees. "Here at least I can still hear what's going on, and see if she leaves with her." He lowered his gaze again. "She's always threatening to vanish with her, to keep her away from me."

"Is there a custody agreement?" the woman asked.

He laughed bitterly. "Sure. But when your name's Hollen you don't have to worry about those little details."

"May I suggest," Ali said, "that we take this inside before the rain really gets going again? I have some first aid supplies, we can take a look at your arm, too."

"Good idea," the other woman said.

"Very," said the man, as the skies opened up again.

Colby didn't move. Looked toward the big house. "It's okay," Ali said gently. "You'll still be able to see the house from inside."

"And there will be four of us to watch," the other man said briskly.

Colby got to his feet slowly, warily. He looked from Ali to the other man, then back to her. For some reason she was the one he trusted, if only because Grace trusted her, and as he'd said, his girl was a very, very smart kid.

He nodded toward the couple. "They're friends of yours?"

Ali smiled, and it was breath-stealing. "I think they will be, although we just met. They brought my puppy home, after he—" she nodded at the big dog "—brought him to them."

Colby winced. "I'm really sorry about that, I had to quiet him or Liz would have seen me. Then while I was trying to stop the bleeding, I lost track of him."

"He's home safe now, thanks to Cutter, here." She seemed to be watching him rather carefully when she added, "And these are Cutter's people, Quinn and Hayley Foxworth."

He blinked. "Foxworth?"

"Nice to meet you," the man said blandly. "Now can we get inside before we're all drenched?"

Colby followed the trio toward the cottage. The dog, however, stuck to his side as if he were his owner, not the couple ahead of them. Maybe he was a herding dog or something, making sure the straggler stayed in line.

Foxworth?

It couldn't be, could it? But it would certainly explain why Ali had been watching him so intently when she introduced them. Because Foxworth was a name well known in these parts. He knew it, not just because of the headlines when they'd toppled their twisted governor, but because of a job he'd done last year. Was this just coincidence, them showing up here? He'd known they were based in the area, but had no idea they were this close. He—

His racing, tumbling thoughts broke off as the dog at his side nudged his hand. He automatically reached to pat the dark head, and felt it again, that soothing, somehow reassuring rush of sensation he couldn't even begin to explain.

He gave his head a sharp shake, trying to clear it. He was all tangled up with the emotions he'd felt when he'd heard Grace wailing, when he'd seen her tearstained face. Plus, he hadn't slept last night, nor had he eaten, so he knew he couldn't think straight just now.

Maybe that was why he just numbly followed these people he'd never even met before.

Or maybe it was that reassuring dog.

Chapter 5

My dad's the best. He loves me more than anything. My mother keeps trying to scare him away, but he promised he'd never give up.

Ali remembered Grace's firm statement, spoken with utter conviction. She remembered hoping the child was right, that it wasn't some idealized image of her father she clung to.

Now she was certain.

She'd gotten her first aid kit from the cupboard she stored it in, and at Hayley's suggestion gave it to Quinn.

"He's had to deal with worse," she'd said.

"Military?" Ali guessed. At Hayley's nod and questioning look she explained, "I did a job for a retired commander in the Navy. They have that air…"

Hayley smiled widely. "Yes, they do."

Now they were standing by the window with the best view of the house next door, while Quinn had Colby's arm stretched out on her kitchen counter, already cleaned up with the antiseptic she kept on hand. She remembered the feel of his hand when she'd touched him. Not soft, office-bound hands, but tough, roughened hands. A working man's hands.

"Could go either way," Quinn said. "Stitches might help, but not sure they're really necessary. It's long, but not too deep."

"I can't leave until I know Grace is okay."

"I figured as much," Quinn said, clearly unsurprised. "There are some butterfly bandages in here that could hold things. You'll likely have a righteous scar, though."

"Won't be the first," Colby muttered.

Ali watched him as Quinn worked, saw him wince once, but otherwise remain expressionless.

It wasn't until his arm was cleaned and bandaged and Colby had flexed it slightly that he looked up at the man who had been efficiently doing the work. He seemed to hesitate, then asked, "You're not…those Foxworths, are you? *The* Foxworths, I mean?"

One corner of Quinn's mouth quirked upward. "Depends on what you mean by that."

"Ogilvie. Flood."

So he did know, Ali thought as he named the disgraced politicians Foxworth had helped bring down. Their disgustingly crooked former governor, and the even more disgusting senator turned powerbroker—or at least that had been his plan before Foxworth had uncovered that his wife's death, which he had milked for all it was worth, had been a murder contracted by him.

Ali glanced at Hayley, who was smiling. "Read the news, do you?" she asked in a cheery tone.

"When I think I can stomach it," Colby said sourly.

Quinn laughed. "I'm with you there."

"But I only paid attention to that because I'd already heard of you. From a guy I've done some work with."

Fascinated, Ali watched the exchange, getting the feeling there was more to this than just recognizing a well-known name.

"And that would be…?"

"Local building contractor. Guy named Drew Kiley."

Ali blinked. She knew that name, had seen signs for Kiley Construction at sites in the area. He'd built a couple of buildings in town that had become gathering places, because they were beautiful, well designed and constructed. She'd even read that he'd been offered some very big projects but had turned them down, because that wasn't what he wanted to do.

She also knew she hadn't mistaken the sudden change in demeanor in both Quinn and Hayley at the mention of that name.

Nor, apparently, had Colby.

"So you are that Foxworth," he said. "The ones who helped him."

"He was our third case, after Hayley and I met," Quinn said.

"He told me his life was a mess, and then it got worse, but you guys stepped in and saved it all. Him, his wife and their little boy."

"Drew," Hayley said, "understated his part in saving it all. As usual."

Colby smiled slightly, and nodded. "Sounds like him. He's a good guy. And great to work with. We kind of see eye to eye on things."

Quinn nodded, then tilted his head slightly. "So, if we call him and ask about you, he'll have good things to say?"

Colby blinked, pulled back a little. "Yeah. I think so. I hope so. But why—" He stopped abruptly when Quinn pulled out his phone, clearly intending to make that call right now. "Say hello for me," he added, sounding a little bemused.

Ali was a little surprised at how quickly Quinn had the head of the company, Drew Kiley himself, on the line. After a quick moment of greetings exchanged, Quinn asked to put him on speaker for the rest.

"We're here with someone who says he's done work for you. Colby Kendrick."

"Colby?" came a deep, male voice from the phone. "He's there?"

Quinn nodded at Colby, who answered. "I'm here, Drew."

"You okay? Grace okay?"

"For now, I think."

"But there's a problem?"

"We're still assessing," Quinn said. "I just wanted your take."

"My take is that Colby Kendrick is a great guy. And one of the best carpenters I've ever worked with. That Village Center project you guys like so much? He's the one who saved that undertaking."

Ali kept watching, fascinated by all of this. "It was just an idea that worked," Colby said, sounding almost embarrassed by the praise.

"A genius idea," Drew corrected. "Turning that narrow breezeway into a full, covered patio with a play area not only made it a better community center, it solved the problem of how and where to run the power and plumbing lines to the new building."

"It worked," Colby repeated.

"That it did. You made us look really good. And I'd hire you full-time in an instant, you know that, right?"

Ali saw Colby swallow as if his throat was tight. "Thanks, man."

"Quinn, anything I can do?" the man on the other end asked.

"We'll let you know, Drew. Thanks."

"Any time, you know that," the man said. Then he added, rather vehemently, "He really is one of the good guys, I promise."

"Thanks for confirming it." Quinn ended the call.

Confirming it, Ali thought. So Quinn had already thought so? She wasn't surprised. You didn't run an organization like the Foxworth Foundation without being a pretty good judge of people.

Only then did she notice their dog was staring at Quinn, and when Quinn looked back, he gave a short, sharp little yip.

"Yeah, yeah," Quinn said with a wry smile. "I know, you told us so."

"Told you...what?" Ali asked, fascinated by this dynamic. And the more time she spent around the Foxworths and Cutter, the more she wondered if she had the knack at all to deal with a dog.

Hayley was smiling when she answered her. "That look he gave us when we first found Colby here? That's his 'fix it' look."

"Fix it?"

"As in there's something wrong that we can fix," Quinn said.

"And," Hayley added, "that he's decided this person deserves our help."

Colby tilted his head, a thoughtful look coming over his face. "Drew's kid, Luke... I remember him saying you had a magic dog."

Both of the Foxworths laughed.

"Seems that way sometimes," Quinn said. Ali found that fascinating, since she never would have guessed the tough-looking guy had a fanciful streak.

"Is he ever wrong?" Colby asked, looking at the dog a little warily.

"Hasn't been yet," Quinn said. "Besides, how could I ever doubt the dog who brought Hayley to me?"

Colby looked bemused again, so much that Ali wondered if he'd quite absorbed what had just happened here. She felt the sudden need to make it clear.

"So...you'll help him, and Grace?" she asked.

"Looks that way," Quinn said.

She looked at Colby, saw it register. He drew back slightly, looking from the dog to Quinn to Hayley. "You mean...?"

"You've got the Foxworth Foundation behind you now," Hayley said gently. "And we'll get this sorted out, whatever it takes."

Colby swallowed, staring as if in disbelief. Ali had the thought that his ex had belittled him so much that he couldn't quite believe an organization on the level of Foxworth would actually help him. She'd convinced him he wasn't worth that kind of help. Ali felt a little nauseous. She knew people like

Liz Hollen existed, but so far she'd managed to keep them out of her life.

And she was seized with the urge to help Colby get this one out of his.

"Yes, we mean it," Quinn assured him when Colby didn't—or couldn't—speak. "So you need to mean it, too. We'll have to probe, ask questions you might not be comfortable answering."

"Just remember," Hayley put in, "that we're not them, and we won't hold anything against you short of maybe murder."

"Not yet," Colby said dryly.

"We'll need to know it all. And you need to answer any questions honestly, even if you can't see the reason we need to know."

"I...all right."

"We'll need to keep a close eye on Grace. Do you live nearby?" Hayley asked.

He shook his head. "I'm a few miles away." He lowered his gaze. "It's just a little place but I like it."

Ali didn't doubt that "little" was in comparison to the place next door.

"Okay," Quinn said. "We can set up and work from our headquarters, which is a lot closer."

"Why don't you stay here, to keep an eye on things?" Ali said.

Colby's head came up sharply, but it was Quinn who answered. "We're used to working from anywhere, but it could get a little chaotic. Coming and going and all."

"I don't mind. I already like Grace so much. It would be an honor to help."

Colby sat there at the kitchen counter, staring at them all for a long, silent moment. Then he slid off the barstool to his feet. He looked at Ali. "Where's your pup?"

Her brow furrowed. "He's in his playpen. Why?"

"I want to go thank him. If he hadn't started barking and I hadn't grabbed him… I'd still be facing this alone."

And in that moment all Ali could think was what a fool Liz Hollen was.

Chapter 6

"Lay it out for us," Quinn said. "Just be honest, that's all we ask of anyone."

They were sitting around Ali's dining table, a nicely built piece with cushioned chairs that invited longer stays. Colby had a feeling they were going to be very glad of that before this was over.

"Do you want me to leave?" Ali asked.

"No," he answered instantly. "Unless you want to. You've already helped Grace…"

"And I'd like to help more. So I'll stay, if it's all right with you."

He was a little surprised at how all right it was. How much he wanted her to do just that. Because from the moment he'd set foot in this place, it had felt…welcoming. And he hadn't missed that while there were some unpacked boxes in the far corner of the living room, the bookshelves along the wall opposite the big windows were already stocked. And stocked with every kind of book he could imagine, heavy, hardbound tomes, paperbacks, large books of photographs of all sorts of places and things.

It felt like home.

It was a moment before he could shift his attention back to the Foxworths.

"Where do you want me to start? The beginning, the end…?"

"How about the beginning of the end," Hayley suggested.

His mouth quirked at that. He was still having a little trouble believing this was really happening, that he had this operation, with the incredible reputation for helping people trying to fight the bigger behemoths around today, on his side.

On Grace's side.

"Liz and I got married young," he began. "That was the first but not the biggest mistake. The biggest was that neither of us had any idea of who the other really was. I knew her family was—" he glanced at Ali "—a big deal, but she insisted she had nothing to do with them, so it didn't matter."

"A bit of youthful rebellion?" Quinn suggested.

"Yeah. But after Grace was born they patched it up. Which I thought was a good thing."

"But it wasn't?" Hayley asked, as if she already knew the answer.

"Not for me. Because it came with a lot of mistaken assumptions."

He started to lift his hand to shove back that stubborn lock of hair that always fell over his forehead, but the cut on his arm twinged and he stopped the movement. He took a deep breath. He could only hope they'd understand. Drew's story encouraged him to go on.

"She assumed that I would immediately grab at the chance her family offered, to become part of their…empire. Become an executive, leave the dirty business of doing actual, physical work with my hands behind."

He hadn't meant to sound so bitter, but apparently he didn't quite have that leashed yet.

"Because of course who wouldn't rather be trapped in a high-rise office rather than being out here in nature, among the peons, creating things," Ali said, her tone nearly as sharp as his had been.

Colby's gaze snapped to the woman sitting at one end of the table. He'd been a little surprised at himself when he'd realized that for some reason he didn't mind that she was going to hear just how stupid he'd been. But now she was jumping in to defend him. To defend him more than his then wife ever had, when Ali didn't even know him beyond what Grace might have said.

"And what was your mistaken assumption?" Hayley asked.

His mouth twisted wryly. "That she knew me. That she understood this was who I was, and I was doing what I wanted to do. And... I assumed she understood me. Enough to know I wouldn't be happy doing anything else."

"And loved you enough to let you do it?" Ali asked, her voice soft now.

"Yeah," he said, his jaw tightening. "My biggest mistaken assumption. When the truth was, I embarrassed the hell out of her. I made decent money, it wasn't like she had to do without, but she was embarrassed when she had to introduce her husband, *the carpenter*, to their ritzy friends."

He'd tried to put the same tone of distaste in his voice that Liz had used, and thought by Ali's look of utter disgust that he'd succeeded. He glanced at Quinn, who he thought wore an expression that seemed just as disgusted. Which was proved right when the Foxworth man muttered a description of women like Liz that made the tension inside Colby ease a bit. It even made the two women here and now smile, although he could see them try to suppress it.

They saw it. They really did. They weren't at all impressed by the Hollen name, or their status and standing in the county. But then, after what the Foxworth Foundation had accomplished in the last few years, they had no reason to be. They were, in fact, a much bigger name than the Hollens themselves.

And there was nothing guaranteed to make ol' Brian Hollen, Liz's father, madder than that.

"So what happened after she reconciled with her family?" Hayley asked.

He shrugged. "She got madder and madder at me for not following her plan. Then one day I came home to an empty house.

She'd packed up herself and Grace and gone. I wasn't home more than five minutes when a guy knocked on the door and I was served with divorce papers."

He'd never forget that horrible day. Staring at his little girl's room, stripped of everything that made it Grace's. Except, he'd noticed through numbing shock, the things he'd gotten for her. Those were left behind in garbage bags.

He tried to describe the next steps in the grim journey, but he wasn't sure he'd gotten it all through the gray, light-dimming curtain that descended in his mind every time he thought about Grace, his poor little Gracie, caught in the middle of a battle she couldn't understand.

"Then I made yet another mistake," he said grimly. "I assumed—that damned word again—that Liz just wanted to be rid of me, that she still loved Grace and wanted her to be happy."

"And instead she used her as a weapon," Hayley said gently. At his startled look she gave a sad shake of her head. "We've seen it before. Too often, sadly."

He sucked in a deep breath, so relieved at this immediate understanding of—and belief in—his situation that for a moment he couldn't go on.

"When I hired a lawyer, I didn't realize I'd need the most bloodthirsty shark around. So it was the full cadre of Hollen attorneys and all the Hollen money against me. I ended up with the right to three hours a week and one weekend day a month with Grace."

"Ouch," Quinn said.

"Bad enough if Liz would have abided by it. But she didn't. She was always finding things to take up the whole weekend, things that were for Grace's benefit, so she said. And the last time I confronted her about it she told me to back off or I'd never see my girl again."

This time he did shove that hair back, deciding he needed that little jab of pain to keep him on track, and not spiral into the morass of regret and sadness that tried to swamp him every time he tried to deal with losing his little girl. And it did help him focus, enough to go on.

"The local sheriff's office doesn't have the staffing to come out and stand by every time I go to pick Grace up, but I know damned well that if I even accidentally lay a hand on Liz trying to get Grace away from her I'll be in jail faster than I can blink. And then I really might never see her again."

"What's your worst fear about all this?" Hayley asked gently.

He didn't have to think about his answer. "That she'll make good on her threat to disappear with Grace, to go somewhere her family has access to but that I'd never be able to set foot, lowly being that I am."

He thought he heard Ali say something, but it was too low for him to make out the words. The tone, however, was perfectly clear, and it steadied him.

Quinn and Hayley exchanged glances. "I'll call Gavin," Quinn said, in the same moment that Hayley said, "I'll call Carly."

Colby blinked. He thought about the accounts he'd read of the big scandal a few months ago, wondered if he was remembering right. "Gavin...?" he began.

"De Marco," Quinn confirmed.

Colby went still. Very still. Having a good lawyer was one thing. Having world-famous Gavin de Marco on your side was an entirely different atmosphere. He did okay financially—at least he thought so, as long as he wasn't compared to the Hollens—but a guy who could probably charge a thousand dollars for a three-minute phone call was beyond heady, it was downright absurd for a common carpenter.

"I...could never afford him," he said, feeling oddly as if he was watching a ship leaving the dock, a ship he'd hoped—however briefly—to be on.

"That's not your problem," said Quinn briskly. "Gavin works

for Foxworth now. And we foot the bill. Because when we take on a client, it's not for money. It's for what's right. And the only thing we ask of you is to help us help someone else down the line."

"What a wonderful rule to live by."

Ali's voice was soft, but still full of awe when she said it. And Colby certainly couldn't disagree. Still…

"I did break that window," he said. "Grace was…" He had no words for how seeing his little girl nearly hysterical had affected him. "I had to get to her somehow, and I knew if I just knocked on the door Liz would do her worst."

"You didn't try calling the sheriff?" Quinn asked.

"I…" He grimaced again. It was becoming a habit. "I don't have a working phone at the moment. I just this morning discovered Liz was tracking mine, and monitoring my calls and messages, so I bricked it. I don't know how she got the spyware on there, but she did. Probably one of the Hollen tech people did it for her, she's not that tech savvy."

Hayley's brows rose as she spoke. "And location tracking?"

Damn. He hadn't thought of that. "Probably," he said wearily. "That's why she came raging back to Grace's room so quickly. In fact, that's probably why Grace was crying in the first place, now that I think of it. Her mother must have known I was in the area, and gloated that she was going to get me thrown in jail. That's her usual approach when Grace gets stubborn."

"Where's your car?" asked Quinn.

"Around the corner, so Liz wouldn't see it." He groaned inwardly. "You think she's tracking that, too?"

"Possibly." Quinn glanced at Hayley.

"I'll call Ty as well," she said.

Quinn looked back at him. "Let's get this started," he said briskly.

And for the first time Colby felt a jab of a feeling he'd thought lost long ago.

Hope.

Chapter 7

"Okay, we've got the basics set," Quinn was saying as Ali brought the fresh pot of coffee she'd brewed out to the table. They'd made those phone calls they'd mentioned, and results were already happening.

Ali was feeling much more cheerful now. Foxworth, *the* Foxworth, was going to help. In fact, their clever dog already was; he'd been playing with Ziggy and keeping him out of the way while they organized things.

Quinn was looking at a rather sizable laptop he now had open on the table. A young man with a trace of a Texas sort of accent had dropped it and some other things off ten minutes ago, pausing only for a brief introduction as the local Foxworth tech guy, Liam Burnett. He was also apparently helping orient a new hire—from what Ali heard, a man who had helped them on that big-headline case with the senator last year.

"How's Cort doing?" Hayley had asked.

"About as well as he could be. But he says he'd rather be working and learning than sitting at home grieving. Rafe's taking him on for the next stage as soon as we wrap this case."

Ali gathered the man had been widowed shortly after that headline case had wrapped, and she had felt an all too familiar jab of empathy for someone she'd never even met. Then Liam had headed back out to deal with the other case they were handling.

"You do a lot of multitasking?" Ali asked now.

"We've often got more than one case going," Hayley said. "Liam's in the final stages of his, so he'll be available later if we need him."

"And by the way," Quinn said, looking over at Colby, "he noticed a crew installing security cameras next door."

Colby sighed audibly. "I'm sure I triggered the rush, but she has been telling Grace she would. Saying it was for her sake."

His expression made it clear he didn't believe that. And frankly, at this point neither did Ali.

"Liam said just be aware, that the models they're installing have an extremely wide angle of view."

Colby went still. "Meaning they'll cover down to Grace's room?"

"Probably. And probably recording 24/7."

"I guess I should be thankful she doesn't have a video of me breaking that window. I shouldn't have, but Grace…she was screaming, I thought maybe she was hurt—"

Quinn held up a hand. "We'll deal with that, if we have to."

"You mean if she has me arrested for trespassing or something," he said sourly.

"Gavin's up to speed," Quinn said. "He'll be standing by."

Ali saw the look of awed wonder cross Colby's face. She didn't blame him, she'd feel the same way if she was looking at potential trouble and had Gavin de Marco on her side.

"And," Hayley said, almost cheerfully, "we've got a counter ploy. Liam also dropped off a couple of similar cameras for us to set up, so we don't get caught staring out the window at them all the time." She glanced at Ali. "That is, if you don't mind us putting them up outside."

"No, of course not," she said.

"Good. We can stream the feed from here to our headquarters as well. You can watch from there, Colby. I presume her employee over there would recognize you?" Colby nodded, but said nothing. "Then at this point we don't want you being seen anywhere near the house. We don't want her making any connection between you and Ali that might make her pull Grace back."

Colby nodded again as Quinn picked up the devices Liam had left and headed outside.

"And," Hayley said, picking up something else Liam had left behind, a box with two cell phones that looked rather heavy-duty, "you each take one of these. They're our own phones, with links to each of us and headquarters. The red button here is the emergency call out to anyone close by, if you need it, or if you need a fast answer to something."

Ali nodded as she and Colby both took one. Then he turned his head to look at Ali. She saw him swallow as if his throat were tight. And there was a warmth in those blue, blue eyes of his that told her he meant what he said next, deeply. "I...thank you. Again. For worrying about Gracie. For helping out now. For...everything."

"I'm pretty fond of that little girl of yours," she said with a smile. "And," she added pointedly, "I trust her judgment."

And I trust those eyes.

She couldn't help thinking of the last time she had gone with her instincts on that particular thing. When she'd looked into a man's eyes, trusted. And with that man she'd found love and an all too short three years of happiness before fate and illness had stolen it all from her.

And now in Colby Kendrick's eyes she saw all she needed to see, the love and worry for his daughter, the desperation, the gratitude he was feeling. It was all genuine, there was no wall around it, and it was no facade put up to fool others. This man was for real, and even if all this was only visible because of his near panic about Grace, it was still real.

His heart was real.

Some part of her mind tried to point out that she'd met the man all of a couple of hours ago, and she didn't disavow it entirely. Just mostly. Because it was outweighed by the memory of the pure adoration in little Grace Kendrick's face as she spoke of him.

Judging by how quickly he was back, Ali guessed this wasn't Quinn Foxworth's first time installing security cameras. He went back to the laptop and worked on it for a moment, then nodded.

"All right," he said. "We've got the entire back side of the other house on one, and the front and driveway on the other." He looked out to her great room, then back up at Ali. "And if you don't mind, we can cast this to the TV so we don't have to always be in front of the little screen here."

She nodded immediately. "Any movement would be more obvious, too, on the big screen, wouldn't it?"

Quinn smiled at her. "Exactly."

Moments later they were settled in the great room, on the couch in front of the fireplace and TV. The previous owner of the house had included the rather complex setup in the sale, thankfully, since that was not at all her forte. And actually, the evergreen framed view of the big house wasn't unpleasant. In fact, it could almost be an acceptable screen saver, if you were into that kind of thing. She herself preferred mountains and wilderness, and this time of year, snow. But then, that was why she lived here in the first place.

"When's your next scheduled time with Grace?" Hayley, who had been reading things on her phone for a while, finally looked up and asked.

"Friday, after she gets out of school."

"Do you pick her up there at the school?"

He laughed, and there was that bitter undertone again. "She won't allow it. Wants me to come to the house to get her, so she can be there."

"To remind you she's in charge?" asked Ali with a grimace, starting to truly dislike the neighbor she'd barely met.

His gaze snapped to her when she spoke, and he looked both surprised and…grateful? What, that someone saw his side? Or was it perhaps simply that someone was listening to him? And actually wanted to help? Obviously it was taking him a while to get used to that, to having help.

"That's our first step," Quinn said. "We make sure someone is always with you when you pick her up. As a witness. We've got Liam, and Teague if he gets back from Oregon when scheduled."

"I could help with that," Ali suggested.

Hayley smiled at her. "I don't think so. If Colby shows up with a woman, I'm guessing it'll really set her off. And you being a neighbor might make her suspicious."

Ali looked at him. He shrugged. "Yeah. No one could possibly replace her. Besides, she doesn't want me, so of course nobody else would either."

"So she lies to herself, too?" Ali asked, making her tone as saccharinely sweet as she could.

Colby blinked. He averted his gaze in an almost shy way. But slowly, a smile curved his mouth.

Sure, nobody would want to kiss that gorgeous mouth, Ms. Superior-to-us-all.

"I'm thinking maybe I should make solo contact," Hayley said to Quinn. "We can come up with some pretext, so I can get close enough to feel out the situation. Get her to trust me with whatever plans she might have."

"Pretext like what?" Ali asked.

Hayley shrugged. "We'll have to think of something."

"Or not," Ali said. "Let me do it. I already have the perfect in, the new neighbor thing. I can make a downright nuisance of myself, when motivated."

She was smiling now, liking the idea. Not just of helping Grace, but helping her father. She glanced at him. He was shaking his head, as if in wonder.

"Why would you do that? Why are you doing any of this? You don't even know me."

"Yes, I do. From everything Grace has told me about you. From that picture she showed me, of you pushing her in a wheelbarrow."

"She has that? And showed you?"

"She's saved it from her mother's purge. And yes, she showed me. And she's told me stories."

He let out a compressed breath. "I'm sure she has. My girl's a storyteller. She writes them all down. I think she'll be a writer someday. She—" He stopped abruptly, paling a little.

"What?" she asked, aware that both Quinn and Hayley were listening to them.

"I...that's how I first knew how bad it was. The last time I was in that house, when I got there before Liz, Grace let me in before the housekeeper could stop her. I saw a story she'd written back before the divorce. About a little girl who lived with a monster and had to hide all day until her daddy came home and she was safe."

Ali gasped aloud. Hayley reacted visibly, and Quinn's gaze narrowed into a stare Ali thought would intimidate anyone.

It took Colby a moment to go on. "That story showed me I'd never had the happy family I thought I did. And it made me worry about Grace. About her safety. Enough to fight for custody even though I knew I'd lose." He let out a long, weary sigh. "Enough to risk breaking that window today to get to her."

"What were you going to do?" Hayley asked, sounding merely curious.

"I'm not sure." Colby gave her a wry, almost embarrassed look. "I wasn't exactly thinking straight just then."

"Who would be?" Ali said quickly.

"Then we'd better get rolling," Quinn said.

And from across the room Cutter gave a short bark that sounded oddly like "About time."

Chapter 8

"Colby Kendrick, meet Juvenile Detective Carly Devon."

Colby shook hands with the tall, obviously fit woman with the cropped, tousled blond hair. Despite the chill, she was wearing a short jacket that he belatedly realized was so she could easily get to the weapon on her hip.

He'd been a little nervous about them calling in law enforcement, and a bit more afraid that a female juvenile officer would lean toward Liz's side. But Quinn had insisted she was a straight arrow, and it didn't matter who she had to stand against, she'd proven she'd stand for the right.

And if he went by the way the dog, Cutter, greeted her, he'd have to believe it.

He cast a glance toward the kitchen, where Ali and Hayley were planning out her approach to Liz. He had the feeling he was going to be thankful Ali couldn't hear them, given the questions he was likely about to be asked.

"I heard you built the new veterans' meeting hall out at Douglas Rockford's place," she said after petting the dog.

That unexpected observation startled him as much as that steady, assessing, bright blue gaze unsettled him. Together they made him feel as if he were being tested somehow.

"Where'd you hear that?"

"My husband. Parker Ward."

Colby blinked. He remembered the man on Drew Kiley's

team, and the stories of how he'd nearly destroyed his life by turning whistleblower on his evilly corrupt boss. "You're Parker's wife?"

"Yes." She smiled. "I kept the old name because it was too big a pain to change all the legal and badge-related stuff, and Parker didn't care."

"He's had...bigger things to worry about," Colby said.

It was coming back to him in a rush now, how Foxworth had helped Parker, too, in the end hooking him up with Drew's company. Had this woman helped in that?

"Indeed he has," she agreed, and pride echoed in her voice. The kind of pride he'd never heard in Liz's voice, talking about him. "But he told me how much all of Drew's crew liked working with you. And that you'd volunteered for the veterans' hall project."

"I...yeah." It was starting to hit him, all the people he knew or had worked with who had Foxworth to thank for the better lives they had today. He knew they'd also helped a guy who had ended up at Sarge's encampment for veterans. Plus, they'd helped Sarge himself when setting up the refuge for vets who needed a place to get their feet under them again had run afoul of some bureaucrat.

"He also said that you did it for materials cost only."

He shrugged. "Sarge is doing a great thing there. I wanted to help."

He saw the woman nod as if she'd heard what she'd expected to hear. Then she looked at Quinn and said, "So, that...theoretical situation you wanted to discuss?"

Colby's jaw tightened nervously at the "theoretical." Quinn had promised him they'd stay in what-if territory, that they would not reveal anything that would make the detective feel as if she had to step in. At least, not yet. He had to trust them, these people he'd only met hours ago. And when it came to Grace's welfare, it was hard to trust anyone. But the Foxworth name was as unassailable as any name could be, at least around here.

"Seven-year-old child. Divorced parents. Father, working guy, clean record and clearly loves the girl. Mother, wealthy family, with influence she uses like a sledgehammer. Also uses the girl as a weapon against the father. No physical abuse that we're aware of."

The detective shifted her gaze to Colby. "Let me guess, she's also making the father seeing his daughter as difficult as possible?"

"Yes," Quinn answered for him.

The woman's gaze never left Colby. Clearly she knew he was the father in question. "And how far has the father had to push, to see his child?"

"So far just the broken window I mentioned," Quinn answered, "to check on the girl who was locked in her room, nearly hysterical."

Detective Devon nodded, still looking at Colby. And then she shifted her focus to Cutter, who had walked over and sat at—in fact on—his feet, but turned to face her. The dog looked up at her steadily. And as if that had been the deciding factor, she looked back up at Colby and said, very quietly, "I won't step in officially unless I absolutely have to. Unless I'm ordered to. Does she have that kind of influence?"

He let out a weary breath. "Afraid so."

"Mostly local, though," Quinn put in. "Not so much on the other side, or down in Olympia."

"All right," the detective said. "That tells me who not to ask for information, if I need it." That caught Colby off guard and his eyes widened. And then Carly Devon smiled, widely, and shifted her gaze to Quinn "Guess I'll stick to Brett."

"Always a good plan," Quinn said with a grin.

Under the circumstances it took him a moment to put it together, that they were referring to the other local detective who had been instrumental in that takedown of the crooked governor, Brett Dunbar. And once more he felt that wave of wonder, that he had people like this on his side.

"I checked as you asked, Quinn, and as of half an hour ago, no reports on a broken window from that address," she went on, snapping him out of his reverie.

"Figured," Quinn said. "So she's not playing by the common rules."

"She doesn't think she has to," Colby said before he could stop himself. He had to remind himself to word the rest carefully. "Plus...she's the type who might keep that as a secret weapon. Her family's big on that."

"Tell her about the story you found," Quinn said,

It was difficult, sharing how wrong he'd been about the life he'd foolishly thought he had. But that story Grace had written, those two and a half pages of her surprisingly well-formed printing, had been the thing that changed everything, the thing that had opened his eyes.

"You know," the blonde said when he'd finished, her tone carefully neutral, "a lot of people would have shined that on as just a kid's vivid imagination, maybe after watching some movie with a monster in it."

He shook his head. "Not Grace. When I talked to her about it, she said it was real, that she only made it a monster in case Liz found it. So she could pretend just that."

The detective's brows rose. "Smart indeed."

"Yes. And she doesn't lie." Surprising himself, he smiled. At the detective's questioning look he explained. "Once when we were in a hearing, the family court officer asked her if she liked her home. She said yes, but it would have been better if I'd built it. Then they asked her if she had her own room, and had enough clothes and things. And she said yes, after her mother got her own stuff. So they asked her if she had everything she needed, and she said no."

His throat tightened, and he couldn't go on. But it appeared he didn't have to, because Ali had come up behind him and said quietly, "And I'll bet she said it was because she didn't have you."

He nodded, not even surprised at her accurate guess. He was remembering that hearing so vividly now his eyes began to sting all over again. He looked up at Ali, marveling anew at how she had stepped up on his side when they'd met less than— he glanced at the time stamp in the corner of the camera feed on the flat-screen—five hours ago.

He didn't realize he was shaking his head until the detective asked quietly, "Problem?"

"No, I just… This morning I was dealing with this alone, with my gut telling me I was going to lose and be lucky if I didn't end up in jail. And now…" He gestured toward Ali first, then Quinn and Hayley as they came out to join them.

"They do have a way," Detective Devon said after being introduced to Ali. Then, smiling widely, she said, "I owe them—and their boy Cutter—for my current state of delirious happiness. And I'm just one in a long line."

"You met Parker on one of their cases?"

She nodded, confirming his earlier guess. "And the team matchmaker," she said, nodding toward the dog, "decided then and there Parker and I needed to be together."

Ali laughed at that. "The team matchmaker?"

"You laugh now, but just you wait."

Colby wasn't sure what that was supposed to mean, but he was too transfixed by the delighted look on Ali's face to speak.

The detective got to her feet, looking at Quinn and Hayley now. "All right, I'll do a bit of research, find what you asked about. If anything changes, you need more, or need me to step in, you've got the number."

"Thanks, Carly. Say hello to Parker for us."

"Oh, I'll do more than hello," she promised with a wink.

"That," Hayley said with a grin after she'd gone, "is a happy woman."

"And Parker's a happy—and lucky—guy," Colby said.

"What was that about Cutter being a matchmaker?" Ali asked.

"He just knows when two people should be together, like she said," Hayley answered.

Colby was sure he looked as doubtful as Ali. Enough that Quinn grinned at them. "He started with me and Hayley, and he hasn't let up since."

If there was anyone Colby would have thought wouldn't buy into that kind of fanciful idea, it was Quinn Foxworth. And as if he'd read the thought, the man laughed.

"Yeah, I know. And I was a very, very tough sell. I mean seriously, a dog? But if you still don't believe after nearly twenty times without a miss, you're not hard to convince, you're blind."

He shifted his gaze to his wife, who had walked over with Ali. The wife he so clearly loved and apparently would not have were it not for that dog who was now sitting watching them intently.

"You get a plan worked out?" Quinn asked.

"We did," Hayley confirmed.

"All right." He shifted his gaze to Colby. "Big question I have to ask. Do you know if there are any weapons in the house? Does she own any?"

Colby blinked. "Uh... I don't think so." His mouth twisted. "She considers herself above such things, but I know the Hollens have armed security when they need it."

"Typical," Quinn said, then shifted back to his wife. "So what's the plan?"

Hayley looked at Colby. "First of all, to ease your mind, Cutter is now acting as Ali's for the duration. He'll keep her safe, and Grace."

He couldn't deny he was relieved. But also puzzled. "But he hasn't even met Grace."

"But he'll have her scent," Ali said, "and Hayley says that's enough."

"How…?"

"I have a sweater she forgot last time she snuck over here."

"We'll give Cutter a good sniff," Hayley said, "and that with the command 'protect,' he'll know what to do." She smiled. "Not that he wouldn't even without that. The 'protect the children gene' is built in, from what we've seen."

"So I'll go over with him, pretend he's mine. She doesn't hate dogs, does she?"

"No. As long as they don't track dirt into her house, she doesn't react much to them."

Ali wrinkled her nose. Colby almost smiled. "I'll still try to make nice with her," she said. "Grace told me she likes fancy wine?"

Colby smothered a snort. "Yeah. Top-of-the-line stuff. French, mostly."

Ali smiled. "Hayley says they can handle that."

Colby looked at the other woman questioningly. Hayley nodded. "We have a couple of bottles that were a gift from a client. Very high-end. Not to our taste, so now it can be put to good use."

"Anyway," Ali went on, "I'll take her the wine, and if I can get her to drink some and relax a little so we can…talk. And since I know nothing about conducting an inquiry or investigating—" she held up what looked like a pair of pearl earrings "—I'll have Foxworth in my ear, guiding me."

He should have guessed, given what Foxworth had accomplished around here, but somehow it was only now registering just how sophisticated and well-equipped they were. But was it enough, when his little girl was involved?

"But if she finds out Grace has been sneaking over here—"

"We're going to send Grace a message to stay quiet about that. Cutter will deliver it."

He blinked. "What? How?"

"He'll manage. He always does," Quinn said.

"Will she recognize your writing? In a note?" Hayley asked. "We need her to be sure it's you."

"I always put a star after I sign it. Because…she's the star of my life. So she'd know if it wasn't there, that it wasn't really from me."

"Brilliant," Ali said approvingly.

He smiled at her, but it was a bit wry. "Not feeling it, at the moment."

"Then we'll fix that, too," she said, with a certainty he wished he could feel.

And he'd like a lot more of that look she gave him, too. After years of Liz's haughty looking down her nose, he definitely liked Ali's smile and, even more, her obvious approval.

Whether he deserved either, he wasn't sure.

Chapter 9

Ali clipped on the second earring, glad that they were a subtle style. They looked so normal she was almost startled when she heard Hayley's voice in her ear.

"Copy?"

"You're loud and clear," she told her as she came out of the bedroom and into the great room. The time was getting close. Her new neighbor had returned home from work or wherever she'd gone for the afternoon—did women on her level really work?—and Grace was ensconced back in her bedroom, according to the new camera aimed that way. Everything was in place. While Quinn would also be listening, they'd decided Hayley would take the lead in the communications.

"She's the best at picking up the subtle stuff," Quinn had said. "And she understands women better—" he'd thrown his wife a loving glance "—much better than I do."

"Your biggest problem," Hayley said now, "and I speak from experience, will be not automatically answering verbally when I say something. I'll try to keep it to a minimum, so you don't get too distracted. I'll feed you background info we've gathered, if it seems appropriate, and might help."

"And I'll feed her ego," Ali said, remembering their earlier discussion.

"Yes. And play up to her, like you've heard of her family

and you're impressed." Hayley shifted her gaze to Colby, "Any goals or causes she'd be particularly receptive to?"

He let out a short, sharp laugh. "Anything that makes her feel more important. Her family supports a few charitable causes, but it's all for the PR. She doesn't really believe in any of them. In fact, it annoys her to have to pretend she does. Even her grief organization to help widows and orphans is about making her feel she's better, stronger than they are."

That jabbed Ali deeper than she wanted to let on. Colby had no way of knowing, of course, so she kept her gut-level reaction hidden.

"Interesting," Quinn put in. "We have a contact who dealt with that organization say much the same thing, that Ms. Hollen seems to be in it for the photo ops, that when it comes down to actually dealing with or even talking to the people she's supposedly trying to help, she's mostly absent."

"What about close women friends?" Ali asked.

Colby turned his head to look at her. "She doesn't trust anyone, male or female, who might be…tougher than she is. Doesn't want them around her."

"Because they might show her up?" She was guessing, but from what she'd heard so far it seemed to fit. And Colby nodded.

"And then she'll go to any length to take them down."

Ali thought for a moment, then looked at Hayley. "I'm thinking maybe Cutter's my therapy dog? Emotional support dog? He's certainly got the knack."

"That he does," Hayley agreed. "And that's a good idea, especially since he's actually certified as a therapy dog, with clearance to visit hospitals and rehab facilities."

Colby moved suddenly, leaning forward to put his elbows on his knees and his head in his hands. He'd been looking decidedly edgy about this from the beginning, but now he was slowly shaking his head.

"Colby?" Ali asked gently.

He looked up, and the concern in those eyes of his touched her to the core. "Just be careful," he said in a pleading tone. "If you got hurt somehow trying to help us, I…"

He let out a long breath that sounded exhausted. She sat down beside him. He clearly cared, so much, and was worried. And she knew now that it wasn't solely for Grace, but for all of them. He truly was not used to this kind of help, or maybe any help that could or would stand against the Hollens, and that alone made her even more determined.

She wanted to hug him. To hold him, to reassure him. And it had nothing to do with the fact that, to her eyes, he was gorgeous. Yes, physically, tall, built, obviously strong with that thick dark hair and those brilliant blue eyes, but for her it was the caring that did it. The risk he'd taken for his little girl. Now the worry for her, for all of them. That was what appealed to her on the deepest level.

Cutter walked over to him and nudged his right hand. Seemingly automatically he reached down and stroked the dog's dark head. Then he went still, staring into the dog's dark eyes.

"I think," Ali said very quietly, "the therapy dog thing will be an easy sell."

He looked up at her. "It's…amazing."

"Between him and a bottle of this ridiculously spendy wine, how can we go wrong?" she asked lightly.

She saw him let out a long breath, and he closed his eyes for a moment, with his hand still on Cutter's head. Then he looked up at her.

"Can you drop he's also a guard dog, please?"

"I can do that," she promised, and gave in to the urge to put her arm around those broad shoulders. Shoulders that had carried this unpleasant load alone for too long.

But he wasn't alone anymore, and she was going to see to it that he knew that.

And in the end, Liz Hollen would know it, too.

It went much more easily than she'd expected. From her purposely hesitant introduction at the door—"I hope you don't think I'm imposing, I know someone like you probably doesn't have much time, but when I heard your name I couldn't help but want to meet you."—she seemed to hit the right notes.

And when she introduced Cutter as her emotional support and guard dog, she saw something flash in the woman's dark eyes that told her Colby had been exactly right. Liz Hollen liked women who were, in her eyes, weaker than her. And Ali knew from the way she took charge of the meeting at that point that she'd found the right way in.

Her mind was racing to assess, with too many brain cells searching for how and why Colby had ended up with this woman in the first place. But when Liz went over to her well-stocked wet bar and was focused on opening the bottle she'd brought, she remembered to slip the note Colby had written to Cutter. Amazingly, the animal took it carefully in his teeth and kept his wet tongue away from it—how on earth did you teach a dog to do that?—as she bent and whispered "Find."

Cutter's nose had been twitching since they'd walked in, and Ali guessed he knew his goal, Grace, was here. She had also noticed him watching Liz like the guard dog she'd said he was, as if he knew without being told that this was someone to be wary of. The enemy, even.

The instant she whispered the command, the dog quietly headed down the hallway. A moment later she thought she heard a slight sound that could have been a door opening. Then an exclamation that she tried to cover as her own with an exaggerated "Oh!" as she walked over toward the wet bar, acting as if she were fascinated with the framed print that hung on the wall above it.

"Is that a Hector?" she said.

"Well done," Hayley said in her ear.

Liz, who had looked up at her words, set the now open bottle aside as she got two glasses out of the cabinet.

"Yes," she said, "it is. An original. I met him at an exhibition in LA, and he practically gave it to me."

It took all she had to say with what she hoped was the right level of admiration, "I'm sure. It would be great publicity for him to be able to say someone like you had one of his pieces."

Ali had to physically stop the eye roll she wanted to make. She was familiar with the current fad of cartoonish drawings turned into what the man called art, and privately thought he likely had to give them away, because who'd want to buy them? But she knew she was thinking too logically, and that with a fad like this, the desire was to be in the crowd that treasured trappings more than reality.

Then she heard the slight sound of Cutter returning, and the dog came back to her side. Mouth empty, she thought, just as he gave her what she would have sworn was a nod, indicating mission accomplished.

And apparently Grace both understood and accepted her assignment. She could just imagine the child reading that note.

Gracie,
Your friend Ali is helping us. Her puppy brought us some friends, including this dog, Cutter. Ali is pretending Cutter is hers, and you need to pretend you don't know her until you meet her now, okay? Just wait a few minutes after you get this, then come out.
   We're going to make it better, sweetie. I promise.
Love, Daddy ★

"What was he doing?" Liz asked, a little sharply.

"Cutter? Oh, I hope you don't mind. He likes to look around, but he's done now," she said, hoping Hayley got the message.

"Message delivered," Hayley said on the other end, confirming her hope.

Liz shrugged. "I don't mind dogs. People tend to trust people with pets."

Well that's an interesting and ice-cold assessment of the benefits of dogs...

Ali went on, gushing a bit but trying not to go over the top. She was already a little amazed at how the woman seemed to eat it up, or rather, take it as her due. "I can't blame him. Your home is so beautiful."

"Thank you," Liz said. Then, in what Ali guessed was, for her, a polite tone, she said, "Your place is rather cute, in a diminutive way."

Zap!

This was where she normally would write someone off. *No, be honest*, Ali told herself, *you would have written her off the moment you walked in this overdone mass of fakery.*

"It's nothing compared to this," she said, again trying to judge just how saccharine to get. She had a feeling the woman's ego required a lot of feeding.

Now that a few minutes had passed, Liz poured a bit of the wine into her glass and tried it. She nodded in approval, and looked at Ali with what she thought was a bit of surprise.

Because of course us peons know nothing about good wine.

Then the woman picked up the bottle and looked at the label. "I didn't realize they'd come this far," she said. "I'll have to let my father know. He might want to invest."

"Subtly letting you know how bucks up they are," Hayley said in her ear, her tone so dry it was all Ali could do not to laugh.

Liz topped off her glass, and filled one for Ali. She gestured out toward the grand salon—*she really, actually called it that!*—and they went to the big, luxurious couch and sat. Frankly, she thought her own was much more comfortable than this overstuffed, polished leather thing you slid all over every time you moved.

Cutter came and sat politely at her feet.

"He seems very well-behaved," Liz said, sounding as if she were still reserving final judgment.

"He is. And very tidy."

"You mentioned he's also a guard dog?"

"Yes, he is. A good thing for a woman living alone, I think?"

She went with the uptick at the end, as she had been doing, since it made it sound like everything was a question, which in turn made her sound more uncertain and less of a threat.

"You may be right," Liz said, studying Cutter more intently now.

"And I just love him," Ali gushed. "He's so good with my new puppy. And you should see him around children, he's a great playmate. And he makes sure nobody bothers them."

Liz's head came up. "So he's protective of kids?"

"Very."

"Would he warn you if…someone he didn't know was around?"

"Absolutely. He wouldn't even let them get close. Sometimes I—"

She broke off at the sound of footsteps in the hallway Cutter had vanished down earlier.

Grace had not missed her cue.

Chapter 10

Quinn had given Colby an earpiece to wear so he could listen, although the transmit function was disabled. The Foxworth man had started to explain why, but Colby shook his head.

"I get it. I'm liable to explode if I have to listen to her for long."

Quinn nodded in approval. Colby settled the tiny device in his ear just in time to hear Grace's voice.

"Who are you?" Bless his girl, she was playing it perfectly.

"I'm your new neighbor," Ali said brightly. "I just moved in next door a couple of weeks ago. And this is my dog, Cutter. I thought you should meet, so he knows you're friends. I have a puppy at home too, but he hasn't quite learned how to behave yet."

He thought he heard the sound of movement, as if the dog were walking across the hard floor. Toward Grace, if he had to guess.

"He's pretty," Grace said, and he could tell from her voice she meant that sincerely.

"And he's very sweet. Go ahead and pet him," Ali said, then added with the same sort of obsequiousness he'd heard so many use with Liz, "Assuming it's all right with your mom."

"Mother?"

Colby saw Quinn's glance. "She always calls her 'mother.' She told me that one of her friends said 'mommy' was for a mother you loved."

Hayley's head snapped around. She covered the small mic that came around in front of her mouth. "She put that together on her own?"

He nodded. "I never said anything about it. I try never to say anything bad about Liz in front of her." His mouth twisted. "Probably for my own sake as much as Grace's."

"Wise decision," Quinn said. "Cuts down on the 'He told Grace this or that' claims, if and when it comes to that."

"Exactly."

"That," Hayley said as she uncovered the mic again, "is one smart girl."

Colby only nodded.

"Could I come over and play with him sometimes?" Grace asked. "If it's all right with my mother?"

"Of course you could," Ali said. "What a lovely idea."

"Why on earth," Liz asked, "would you want to have her over there bothering you?"

There was a second-long pause during which Colby guessed Ali had shifted to look at Liz. It also gave him that time to rein in the surge of anger at his ex's dismissive words about the child he so loved. *Her* child, who she clearly did not love. Not like she should, anyway.

"You have raised a wonderful daughter, Ms. Hollen," Ali said, somehow managing to give Liz the credit, which Colby knew would go over well. "I'd be delighted for her to come over any time to play with the dogs, since I work from home anyway."

"What's your work?" Liz asked.

"I'm an interior designer," Ali said.

They'd talked about that, and how even though she hated the title, it was more likely to impress Liz. And it would also make her reaction to that ridiculous painting more believable, he thought now.

"And I know Cutter would love it," Ali added. "She'd be totally safe, with him around."

"He would…protect her?"

"He would protect her against any threat," Ali said.

Colby saw Hayley nod approvingly, and gathered they must have discussed that exact response. Judging by her satisfied expression, that they'd chosen it to include Liz herself, although Liz would never interpret it that way. The only threat she ever saw was him.

"So I can go?" Grace asked.

She sounded as if she were holding her breath, waiting for an answer that would determine…everything. She was handling this so well, as if she understood exactly what was going on. How on earth had ordinary him managed to father the most brilliant seven-year-old in the world?

"I think that would be all right. As long as you don't make a nuisance of yourself. And tell Irene where you are." A pause, then an explanation. "Irene is my housekeeper and child minder."

Colby heard a tiny sound he was certain was Grace suppressing a squeal of delight.

"She knows not to act too happy," he said at Quinn's look. The Foxworth man gave a short shake of his head, and Colby saw that his jaw was tight.

"I'll make sure she knows when Grace comes to visit, Ms. Hollen," Ali said.

"I think," Liz Hollen said slowly, "you should call me Liz."

Colby sat up straight.

"Damn," he said under his breath. Hayley turned her head to look at him. "She's got her," he explained. "She doesn't give first-name rights to anyone she hasn't decided she can trust."

He got to his feet then, because he had to. He could feel it swirling inside him again, that feeling of hope. He was pacing when Liz started what he'd figured would be coming.

"It's only fair to warn you, Ali," Liz said, "Grace's father is a good-for-nothing slacker who thinks he still has rights, and he may come looking for her."

There was a soft whuff it took him a second to recognize as coming from Cutter. To his surprise Grace said nothing, so there was a brief silence before Ali said, "Oh, dear."

"If he does while she's there, just call me and I'll handle it."

"What if you're not home?"

"I'll still see to it. I have people."

"Well, that's a relief, that you have it handled."

"Ask if she has a photo of him," Hayley said quickly into the mic, and Ali did so. Colby wasn't sure what that was for, but he was sure there was a reason.

"Here," Liz said. "Be on the lookout."

"His driver's license?" Ali asked. Liz had a copy of his DL? How had she managed that?

"I snuck a photo of it one time when he was here to visit Grace. I thought I might need it one day."

Always planning ahead, that was Liz.

"Does he still look like that?"

Colby blinked at that, wondering why she'd asked when she knew perfectly well he didn't. Well, not much.

Liz let out a rather unladylike snort. "Hardly. He's much... scruffier now. I held him to a certain standard, and he was quite handsome then, but he quickly reverted to type once we separated."

Colby rubbed a hand over his stubbled chin, but resisted shoving his hair back again. She just never stopped, never passed up a chance to slam him, even to, in essence, a total stranger.

A stranger who's helping you for no reason other than kindness and liking Grace.

A stranger who had gotten past Liz's considerable walls in less than an hour. Speaking of brilliant females...

He heard a sigh that he knew had to be Ali because Liz would never betray that much emotion. "I hate it when men do that. Appear to be one thing, or pretend, but turn out to be something else altogether."

Instinctively Colby winced, even knowing those words weren't an accusation of him, but part of the plan.

"Exactly," Liz said, with a firm sort of approval. And then she turned to Grace—he could tell by the change in her tone to an irritated sharpness—and began to instruct her.

"You may visit, if and when Ali says it's all right. You may pet the dog, but I don't want you coming home dirty or muddy or covered in dog hair, do you understand?"

Grace's tone was sour. "How about if I don't—"

He heard that small whuff of sound again, and his girl stopped abruptly. That had to have been Cutter. There was a sound of movement before Liz repeated her demand.

"Do you understand?"

"Yes, Mother."

Quinn looked at Colby. "What do you think she was about to say?"

"Probably 'how about if I don't ever come back,'" Colby said. "Which would have made Liz beyond angry."

"Then that's what Cutter sensed. And stopped." Colby looked at him curiously. "Just like before, he could tell whatever Grace was about to say would likely set Liz off. Don't ask me how, he just knows when things are about to go sideways."

He was still looking doubtfully at the obviously tough, experienced man who was saying something that seemed ridiculous about a dog, when Hayley spoke into the mic.

"Go ahead with our plan, Ali. Just make sure you bow down first."

Then he heard Ali speak again. "I have an idea, Grace. You

know that big window on the side of my house?" There was a pause, and he guessed Grace must have nodded because Ali went on. "How about if I put a big blue piece of paper in the corner, maybe with your name on it, whenever it's okay for you to come over."

"That would work."

He could hear the excited undertone Grace was trying to suppress. He doubted Liz would; she never paid that much attention.

"You must always, always check with your mother or Irene first," Ali cautioned, and he gathered that was the bowing part. He was a little amazed at how thoroughly Hayley in particular had grasped exactly what kind of woman Liz was, and what she would require in the way of sucking up. But then, Foxworth had dealt with several people of an even higher echelon than the Hollens.

Ali went on, and there was a lighter, almost teasing note in her voice now. "And if I put a red paper in that spot, please come over as soon as you can, because Cutter really needs someone to play with."

Grace couldn't smother her gleeful squeak at that, but to his relief Liz didn't react or call a halt to the whole thing.

"I'll have a friend from school visiting for a while," Ali added, "and poor Cutter may feel neglected. So if he really, really needs to play, he may come looking for you."

Colby went still. Had they worked that out, too? He looked at Quinn. "Is that a way to get her out of there if necessary? You send the dog over?"

Quinn nodded. "And if we do, he won't leave without her."

This dog of theirs was starting to sound like some Special Ops guy or something. Maybe he was, maybe he'd been a military or police dog or something. He was still boggling over that idea when he realized that Ali was saying goodbye.

"See you soon, Grace."

"Okay." His little girl was making a valiant effort to hide her excitement. It was something he knew all too well.

"That sounded pretty uninterested," Hayley said with a glance over at him as she straightened up from her intent, monitoring position.

"She has to hide anything she really likes or wants. If her mother finds out she'll use it against her."

"Well, we were convinced before, but doubly so now," Quinn practically growled.

Colby looked back at Hayley. "I'm guessing you're the 'friend from school' she mentioned?"

"Yes. So Ms. Hollen won't be surprised to see another person here."

Ali came in through the back door, Cutter at her side. Automatically Colby got to his feet. The redhead bent to stroke Cutter's head.

"You are *such* a good dog," she crooned. "And so smart!"

She straightened up to look at the Foxworths, who were smiling at their clever pet. Or fellow operative. Probably both.

Then she walked into the room, shifting her gaze to Colby.

"And I don't ever use this word, but your ex," she said with a sour twist of her mouth and an eye roll, "is a bitch."

He couldn't help it—he let out a snort of laughter.

"I know, you warned me," Ali said, "but holy cow, she's…"

She waved her hand as if there were no way to describe the woman she'd just left. Colby couldn't argue with that, so he merely nodded.

"And you," Hayley said, coming over to take the earrings Ali removed, reminding him to pull out the earpiece they'd given him, "handled that perfectly. You got more than we'd hoped. So now that we have the groundwork laid, we have to plan what's next."

She sounded so confident it filled Colby with hope all over

again. And he couldn't stop himself from taking that half step between them and giving Ali a heartfelt hug.

"Thank you," he said, his voice more than a little hoarse.

"Grace is a treasure. Thank you for trusting me to be a part of this."

He no longer had any doubt that slicing up his arm on that window was the best thing that could have happened.

Chapter 11

"I have only one question," Ali said as she took a seat next to Colby on the sofa, her last—truly it was—slice of pizza in her hand.

He was wiping his fingers with the napkins that had come with the delivery—albeit it had been another Foxworth man called Teague, not the guy from the actual pizza place—and now stopped to look at her. She had the feeling he hadn't been eating well lately, or maybe at all, judging by how much and how fast he'd bolted that down.

"Only one?" he asked, with a half laugh that was clearly self-directed. Lord, that woman had done a number on him.

She glanced from where they were seated at the counter back toward the table, where Quinn and Hayley were working out whatever planning they had left to do, although she couldn't imagine what they could possibly have overlooked. But once certain they wouldn't be overheard, and because she genuinely wanted to know, she asked her question.

"How did you end up with her?"

He took in a deep breath and let it out slowly, audibly. "I claim ignorance. I met her my freshman year in college. I had no idea who her family was. All I knew was she was a couple of years ahead of me, she was…well, gorgeous, and she took an interest in me. Much to my surprise."

She tilted her head as she looked at him. "I don't find it surprising at all."

His eyes widened. He stared at her for a moment, opened his mouth, then closed it again, as if he could think of nothing to say. He lowered his gaze to the crumpled napkin in his hand.

How could such a simple thing flummox him so? He had to know he was a good-looking guy, who would catch any woman's eye. Even Liz, bi—she caught herself, she'd meant what she'd said about not liking to use that word—witch that she was, had seen the appeal.

"So she was gorgeous, practiced, a little older, more experienced in manipulation... No wonder you fell for her."

"If that's your way of saying I was a gullible, naive idiot, then yeah." He grimaced. "I was stupidly happy that she wanted to get married. But it was...miserable. I knew it wasn't working. But then she got pregnant with Grace. After telling me she was on the pill."

She knew she hadn't mistaken the bitter tone that had come into his voice. She remembered the call Quinn had made, to the contractor whose name she'd seen on such beautiful work.

My take is that Colby Kendrick is a great guy.

Then, even stronger, what Colby himself had said hit her...
She was embarrassed when she had to introduce her husband, the carpenter, *to their ritzy friends.*

A fierce sort of anger began to bubble up inside her. The impression she'd gotten in person added fuel to it. It was quite clear Liz Hollen was the kind of woman she had to try very hard not to hate.

"She really did a number on you, didn't she?"

He let out a long sigh. "I was supposed to join the family firm. Rise to the top and all that. But I had no interest in that. Which is why she divorced me."

She thought again of what Drew Kiley had said, about his

idea that saved one of her favorite places. "Why would someone who can do what you do want to become a paper pusher?"

He blinked. And again his mouth opened as if he were going to speak, then closed again as if there were no words to be found. She wished he'd stop doing that. Not just because she didn't like the idea of him being too wary to talk to her, but because darn it, it made her keep looking at his mouth. And that was something she was not used to even thinking about.

But something in the way he was looking at her, something in those blue eyes, made her add, "Paper pushers who deal with other people's products or property are a dime a dozen. People like you who can build or make those things, now, they're worth something. A lot, because it seems like we have fewer of them all the time."

She saw him swallow as if his throat was tight. He looked away then, but she heard a low, rough-sounding, "Thank you."

A phone across the room rang, and when she looked over, Quinn was pulling his phone out yet again. She wondered what it must be like to run an operation with as many threads and connections as Foxworth obviously had. He listened for a moment, then said, "Thanks. Nice to know."

She felt a little nervous suddenly, because when he'd said that he'd been looking at her. And when he slid the phone back into his pocket he came toward them.

"Seems you two have a connection," he said, looking from her to Colby.

She shot a glance at the man sitting on the stool beside her, just in time to catch him doing the same to her. For a moment the only kind of connection she could think of was the one she'd been pondering before, when she'd caught herself watching his mouth a little too much.

Had she been that obvious? True, she was out of practice, focusing entirely on her work now, and building her business. But—

Quinn looked at her. "The name Doug Rockford ring a bell?"

"Yes," she said.

At that, Colby gave her a startled look. "You know Sarge?" he asked.

She nodded. "I designed the interior of his new building at the veterans' camp."

Colby was smiling when he said, "I built it."

"And both of you did it for nothing," Quinn said.

"I love it," Hayley said, beaming as she came up beside her husband, "when we're proven so thoroughly right about our people."

Quinn grinned at his wife. "You mean when he is," he said, nodding at Cutter, who was lounging near the fireplace.

"That, too," she answered cheerfully. Ali saw Hayley realize both she and Colby were looking from her to the dog and back, and she laughed. "You'll get used to it. We had to. Because he's never been wrong. Confused once, but never wrong."

"Confused?" Ali asked.

"That was the first time he met my brother," Hayley said, still smiling, "whom I was very angry with at the time. So Cutter was a bit torn."

Ali found herself smiling again. And thinking about what the woman had said about "our people." As if, once they'd decided to help you, you were family. She glanced at Colby. He could use that kind of support. And so could adorable little Gracie. And helping them help him was making her feel better than she had in a very long time. Since Josh's death, in fact.

"Now," Hayley said briskly, "we need to work on timing and details. Colby, it's clear your daughter is a very smart young lady, but—and we need the most honest answer you can give—how good is she at keeping a secret?"

He took in a deep breath and let it out slowly. She could almost sense him turning from the lighter topic of Cutter's apparent skills back to the matter at hand. She wondered briefly if the Foxworths had lightened things up for those moments intentionally. She wouldn't be surprised; they were obviously very good at what they did.

"She can do it, as long as she understands why," Colby said, sounding cautious. Then, in a more depressed tone he admitted, "But if she gets mad enough, sometimes she'll blurt something out before she thinks."

"Why, you'd think she was human!" Ali put all she could of mock astonishment into her voice. Colby's gaze flashed to her, and one corner of his mouth twitched.

"Can't picture you getting that mad," he said.

A chill went through her at the words. "Oh, I can," she said, and now her voice was grimly level. "Unfortunately uselessly."

He tilted his head slightly, clearly wondering, but Hayley called them back to the current situation and Ali silently thanked her for it.

"If you think she'd let it out that Ali's helping," she began.

"She just needs to understand," Colby said. "How important it is not to tell her mother…anything. Then she'll keep it secret forever if necessary."

"We need to lay out some boundaries," Quinn said, clearly on his wife's wavelength. "Grace coming here doesn't necessarily mean you'll see a lot more of her."

Ali frowned. "But he could be here." She glanced at him again. "You could come any time. Or stay."

And again he looked a little stunned, and she wondered what it must be like to feel so beaten down, so abandoned, that the concept of someone willingly helping was utterly foreign. Even in the worst days after Josh's death she'd never felt that.

Hayley's tone was understanding but firm as she explained. "It would be nice if you could see more of her while we're working this out, but if she might let it out at an inopportune moment, it could blow everything."

"But she already knows I'm involved," Colby said. "That note…"

"Yes, but keeping a note quiet versus seeing her beloved daddy in person are two very different things," Hayley said. "Plus, we don't want Ms. Hollen or her helpers to see him here."

Hayley was still watching Colby, and Ali knew she was sensing the same current of tension in him.

"We'll get there, I promise," Hayley said to him, "but we have to start slow. We have a lot of work to do, and some of it will be dead ends, until we find the right path. Are you okay with that?"

He grimaced. "You mean can I keep it reined in?" He looked from Hayley to Quinn and then to Ali. She thought she saw something flash in his eyes then, something she could only label as hope.

Then he looked back to Hayley. "I think I can. Now."

Chapter 12

Colby took the mug of hot chocolate Ali handed him. It smelled luscious, and he'd noticed while she was making it that it was more than just heating up some milk and a mix. His first sip woke up every taste bud and seemed to warm him to his toes. She smiled, and he guessed his was the usual reaction to the chocolaty, cinnamony with-a-touch-of-marshmallow concoction.

He'd also noticed, as she'd handed him the mug, something he'd missed before. The lighting hadn't been right, or his mind had been so totally otherwise occupied. But now he'd seen it, that slight indentation or line on her left ring finger. Like from a ring long worn but only recently removed. He wondered if perhaps that was why she was so understanding. Maybe she'd just been through a divorce of her own.

Hayley and Quinn were back on their phones again, arranging who knows what. He was still stunned at the evidence of the size and scope of Foxworth, and their apparent resources.

And it had all started with Ali and her pup, who was currently playing a futile came of tug-of-war with Cutter, who held the rope toy so carefully it was like he knew his playmate was younger and more fragile. As he obviously did, from their description of how he'd brought Ziggy to them.

Who would have ever thought bleeding all over that little mutt would have led to…this?

She came around the counter and sat on the stool to his right. Without really thinking about it, he looked down at that finger again. He'd been right, he could see the faint indentation and tan line. He doubted she got very tan, with her complexion that fit with the red tones in her hair, but it was still there, just barely.

He wanted to ask, even though he told himself it was none of his business, really. He could make up some reason, like asking if they needed to worry about her ex showing up, but he didn't want to do that. But he couldn't seem to quash his need to know.

"There was a ring there for a long time," he finally said, making sure it wasn't a question so she could ignore it if she wanted.

She turned her head to look at him. "Yes. Nearly ten years."

"You did a lot better than I did," he said wryly.

"If you call being a widow better."

His eyes widened, and he felt his gut tighten as if she'd punched him. "I... I didn't... I'm sorry. And I'm just going to shut up now, before I say something worse."

"It's all right. You had no way of knowing."

He stared into her vivid green eyes, and even he couldn't miss the pain there. But she didn't seem on the verge of tears or anything, so he risked asking, "When...?"

"He was killed in a car accident four years ago. But I only took the ring off when I moved in here."

"Is that...why you moved?"

She nodded. "I spent those years in the home we made together, unable to let go. But I finally realized I had to, or I was going to stay mired in misery forever."

He tried to imagine what that would be like, to have a woman love you so much she couldn't get past losing you. He couldn't. He'd never even been close to that.

He tried to choose his words carefully, not wanting to step in it again with her. "While he was here, he was a lucky man. To have you, I mean." He shook his head, that still sounded bad. "That was stupid, too. Shutting up now," he muttered.

"To the contrary, Mr. Kendrick. That was a lovely compliment."

Before he had to come up with some stumbling response to that, Quinn rescued him.

"All right, let me run this by you both. Hayley will stay here a few days to get a feel for things, under the cover of being your friend from school, Ali. She'll be open about it, and if at some point it feels right, you can introduce her to your charming neighbor."

Quinn's tone was beyond sarcastic on those last two words, and it made Colby almost smile.

"We'll use my maiden name, Cole, in case she might recognize Foxworth," Hayley said.

Quinn went on. "Also, in shifts, another of our team will be here—not necessarily inside, Ali, so don't think you have to have houseguests the whole time."

"It would be fine if I did," she said. "And by the way, there's a door into the garage—" she gestured toward the side opposite Liz's place "—and then into the house, so you can come and go as needed out of sight. I'll get you my extra key and door opener."

Colby stared at her again, boggled anew at her willingness to trust what were basically strangers to her.

"We don't want to interfere with your work any more than necessary," Hayley said.

"I'll be fine," she insisted. "I can close the door to my office, and put my headphones on. That way I'll never even know you're here unless you pound on the door. And I'm a little light right now anyway, my next big project doesn't start for a couple of weeks."

He wondered whose life she was going to make comfortable, organized and functional. Lucky people, whoever they were. A while ago he'd gone back to look at the place he'd helped build for Sarge, and had been amazed at how whoever had done it had managed to make it a welcoming dining hall, meeting room, office space and functional kitchen all in one.

Now that he'd met her, he wasn't surprised at all.

"All right. Colby, one of our crew will be going with you when you go to pick up Grace for your scheduled visitation." The man glanced at his wife, and Colby got the feeling they'd discussed this at length. "It would be me, except Hayley thinks I'm a bit...overkill."

Colby couldn't help chuckling at that. "You do have the air."

Quinn shrugged, and it was Hayley who, grinning, went on. "We'll start with Liam. He's more the lean, wiry type, not quite as imposing. And that drawl of his distracts people from seeing just how strong he is."

"Perfect," Colby said, remembering the man's accent and his lazy grin. "Because Liz will take that twang as meaning he's stupid. To her, anybody from certain places she would never set foot must be."

"Her mistake," Quinn said flatly.

"I'll bet," Colby said. "He didn't strike me as the least bit stupid."

"He's at the top of the tech tier at Foxworth Northwest," Hayley said. "And smart as the proverbial whip." She grinned again. "Smart enough to use people's misperceptions to get what we need."

"He'll be wired into us so you don't have to wear an earpiece," Quinn went on. "Unless you make a habit of it?"

"Actually, I do. Loud power tools and all. I don't think she'd wonder about it."

"All right," Quinn said. "Then you can be live with us too. We'll get you set up with one of ours."

"Does that mean I don't get to wear the pearl earrings?" He put all the innocence he could muster into his voice. Ali, who had been taking a sip of hot chocolate, nearly spit it back out again, laughing. Hayley laughed as well, and even Quinn chuckled. And it all made Colby able to genuinely smile.

Hope, he thought, was a powerful antidote to despair.

"Careful," Ali said after she swallowed. "She might like that enough to take you back."

"More likely she'd slit my throat and steal them," he said dryly.

"Did I mention we have a prize-winning ex-military sniper on our team?" Quinn said, just as dryly.

Colby blinked. "Uh…no, you didn't."

"But he's about to get married," Hayley put in, "so we'd rather not call him in if we don't have to."

Colby wasn't sure how to take the cheerful yet apparently serious tone. He had the feeling that, even with what he knew of them from people they'd helped, he'd vastly underestimated the Foxworth Foundation.

Chapter 13

Ali couldn't imagine what it was like, having the woman who supposedly loved you enough to marry you and have your child use that child to manipulate you from the day she was born.

She stood looking out the front window at the garden, which had been one of the big selling points to her. The garden where Grace loved to play because of all the little places to hide. She gave a sad shake of her head at the thought.

Hayley came up beside her, having spent the night as planned. Cutter had stayed with them, which delighted Ziggy and made Ali feel wonderfully safe. It was quite a knack that dog had.

"You don't look happy," Hayley said.

"I just feel like I should have realized," she said. "When Grace came over here, I didn't realize she'd had to sneak out. But she loved to be—" she gestured to the window "—out there, because of all the little places to hide among the bushes and behind where the tree branches brush the ground. I thought it was because she and Ziggy made up a game, she'd hide and he'd find her. But now I wonder…"

"If she's just learned to hide whenever possible?"

Ali nodded sadly. "There were other hints. I see them now looking back."

"But you'd only just moved in, only just met Grace, so you couldn't know for sure, at least not yet."

Ali looked at the other woman. "Are you always so tactful?"

Hayley smiled. "Not always. But I do try."

"You make me wish you really were my friend from college," Ali said.

"And that is the nicest compliment you could give me. So let's say I am, we just got a late start."

Ali smiled back at that.

"Quinn just texted me," Hayley said, nodding at the phone in her hand. "He and Colby are on their way. And Liam finalized his case, so we're set for him to be with Colby tomorrow when he goes to pick Grace up."

Ali couldn't deny the spark of…something that ignited at the thought of Colby being here again soon.

"And for what it's worth, if you had any doubts, our top tech guy in St. Louis did some digging. To the upper crust of the county, Colby's known only as Liz's ex she's well rid of. But to just about everyone else he's an honest, hardworking guy who gives back. Did you know the local fire department gave him a civilian medal?"

Ali drew back a little in surprise. "No."

"He was working up on Cedar Hill Drive when a residential fire broke out a couple of doors away. Propane leak. There was an explosion, and a fireman was trapped, and seriously injured. The others were all on the other side of the building, so Colby went in and brought him out."

"Wow," Ali said, meaning it. "I didn't really have any doubts, but still…"

Hayley smiled and kept going. "And then the fire department turned up info that he'd been a hero twice before. Once he was doing some late-night emergency repair work at a house in a neighborhood out on the peninsula. He spotted something at the house next door. Turned out there'd been something miswired there, and a fire had started. He called it in and got over there and got it put out before the truck even arrived. There was a family of six in that house, and they could have all died. Third time it was a medical call, where he did CPR on a neighbor until the medics arrived. They said the man would have been dead if not for him."

Ali was smiling herself now. Widely. "So what you're saying is, to Liz and her ilk, he's a nobody, but to the people who matter, he's a hero."

"Exactly." Hayley grinned at her then. "I knew I liked you."

"Ditto," she said back to her.

Cutter, who had been delicately wrestling with Ziggy on the floor, suddenly scrambled to his feet. Ears up, he trotted toward the door into the garage, even though as far as she knew the dog had no idea where it led.

"Ah," Hayley said. "The guys are here."

Ali hadn't heard a thing, but she was already learning not to doubt either the dog or this woman. And when, a minute or two later she heard the sound of a voice coming from the garage, it verified her instincts.

Quinn greeted his wife as if he hadn't seen her in a week rather than just overnight. Ali found herself studying Colby, who watched them for a moment with a look of almost sadness before he turned away as if he couldn't watch the two who so obviously adored each other any longer. She and Josh had been like that once. Teased by their friends for the constant displays of affection.

But Colby Kendrick clearly had never known that feeling at all, which left her wondering which was worse, having it and losing it, or never having had it at all. She had thought Tennyson had it right, and seeing Colby's expression in that moment confirmed it for her.

"Irene took Grace to school at the usual time," Hayley said, in the tone of someone making a report. "And we are going to have to be careful. Grace was looking over here the whole time. I would guess she was wondering if you were here, Colby."

He nodded, and when he spoke he sounded resigned. "And if Liz figured it out, she'd unleash holy hell."

"About that," Quinn said, "Liam did a little digging last night." A brief grin flashed across the man's face, and changed him from the very imposing former military Special Ops guy Hayley had told her about last night into a handsome charmer. "He's very good at it, enough to compete with Ty in St. Louis. But he also knows a lot of local lore, so that helps sometimes. Anyway, after Colby mentioned there had been a change of venue in the middle of their custody case, from here locally to over on the other side in the city, Liam got out his virtual shovel. Turns out the Hollens have…let's say a lot of influence over the judge it was transferred to. Which explains why it went so hard against him."

Ali stiffened. She looked at Colby. "So they bribed somebody, or coerced somebody, into making that change happen?"

"Our judicial system, fair and balanced," he said, and she couldn't blame him for the bitterness in his tone.

"This," she said, not caring that the *s* came out like a hiss, "is seriously making me angry."

"Can I interpret that as you're still willing to help?" Quinn asked, looking mildly amused.

"You can interpret it as meaning that as long as Grace isn't hurt in the process, whatever it takes to bring Liz and her family down a notch, I'm in."

As if she'd felt his gaze on her, she looked back at Colby. He still seemed astonished at the simple fact that she wanted to help. After a moment he said quietly, "I like the order you put that in."

"Grace is the most important thing, obviously."

He sucked in a breath and let it out slowly. "To me. To her, not so much. Winning is the most important."

"And she's used to winning against you?" Quinn asked.

He nodded. "She knows I'll back off because of Grace. That I can't fight her."

"It's more important to outthink your enemy than to outfight him."

Ali saw Colby blink, draw back slightly at Quinn's words. "Quoting Sun Tzu?" he asked.

Quinn smiled. "Former occupational hazard. You're familiar, I gather?"

"Yeah. My dad became a big fan when he was in the service."

Ali thought she saw something change in Quinn's expression, as if finding out Colby was the son of a veteran had confirmed something for him.

"What branch?" Quinn asked.

"Army," Colby said. Then, sadly, "He died five years ago. But at least he never had to deal with…this."

"So we will," Quinn said, his voice showing the sympathy he didn't mention in words. Men indeed had their own ways, Ali thought. "With the aid of our ancient strategist."

Colby smiled, gave a short nod as if shaking off the grief that had to still linger. "But if you're going to talk about waiting to take the enemy unprepared, I've got to tell you, she never is."

Quinn smiled back. "I was thinking more along the lines of 'The whole secret lies in confusing the enemy so that he cannot fathom our real intent.'"

Colby looked thoughtful. "All warfare is based on deception?"

"Exactly."

"You have something in mind?"

"A few things. And so does Liam, and so will Teague. Plus we have a lot of former clients who dealt with custody situations we can call on."

Ali sat watching the two men, taking an enjoyment she didn't quite understand in the conversation. And judging by the slight smile on Hayley's face, she was, too. "It's a good thing you two are in charge, getting all philosophical about it," Hayley said, obviously teasingly.

"A very good thing," Ali said. "I'd be planning to grab Grace and run. Which obviously, with her family's pull, would not go well."

"Don't think I haven't thought about it," Colby said, looking at her rather curiously. "But I wouldn't have expected you to feel that way."

Ali shrugged. "Neither of my parents were prizes, but given the choice, if my father had been half the man you are, I'd have gone with him gladly."

He stared at her, looking almost stunned. And that made her ache inside all over again.

And she had the delicious thought that someday, eventually, when all this was over and Grace was safe, she'd like to put Liz Hollen on her expensively clad butt.

Chapter 14

"Don't worry, man. I'll put on my stupid hick suit, and she'll barely even see me. I know her type."

Colby looked at Liam Burnett, who was grinning at him. Friday had arrived, and they were prepping to head over to get Grace. "I'll bet you do," he said. "At least you're smart enough not to have married one."

"Me? Nope. My Ria's the best thing that ever happened to me, along with Foxworth." He gave Colby a sideways look. "But hey, we're all blind about some stuff. And it took me a darn long time to understand what really matters. And your little girl really matters."

"Yes," Colby said, his voice suddenly rough. "Yes, she does. For me, she's all that matters." He meant it more than ever. And felt stronger saying it now, with Foxworth on his side.

He looked around the building where he'd met up with Quinn and Liam this afternoon. He'd been a little surprised that there was no signage, no indication that this was the headquarters of one of the most well-known operations in the northwest. Quinn had said they kept a low profile, but not even a sign? Just a long gravel drive winding among trees, ending in a parking area next to a three-story, rectangular building painted nearly the same color as the evergreens that surrounded it except for a large, open meadow to the rear, spreading out to where the trees began again.

There was a large, hangar-style building to the right of the main one, with a concrete pad in between.

"A helipad?" he'd asked.

Quinn had smiled. "For Igor."

It had taken Colby a moment to get there. "As in… Sikorsky?"

"Seemed fitting."

"Don't get him started on Wilbur," Liam warned with a grin, "or we'll be here all day."

"Let me guess…you've got a plane, too?"

"We do. But Liam's right. We need to focus, so I'll shut up about it."

And so they had gone inside, where he was again surprised, this time by the homelike atmosphere. It had looked like an industrial type of building from the outside, but inside was welcoming and warm. There was a fireplace with a large sofa and some chairs gathered in front of it, around a large coffee table. Then a small kitchen in one corner, and in the opposite corner what appeared to be a bedroom and bathroom.

"I don't think we need the meeting room upstairs, at least not yet," Quinn said, "so let's get comfortable."

Once they were seated, the gas fire had been turned on, adding a pleasant visual to the room along with some needed warmth. It was a comforting, inviting place, and he couldn't help smiling.

"This looks like Ali could have designed it," he said.

"I think she and my wife have very similar tastes in that area," Quinn said. "If she'd left it up to me this'd be a lot less… nice."

He said it with smile and a very satisfied expression. The kind Colby had noticed Quinn got every time he saw, spoke to or apparently even thought about his wife.

Liam was in the small kitchen, apparently prepping a large pot of coffee. Which was a good thing for Colby, because he'd had a very disturbed night. He would have thought having all this help all of a sudden would have made for a more restful night, but as usual before his afternoon with Grace he'd been restless.

He was taking his first sip, wondering what kind of preparations Quinn had in mind, when the front door opened.

"I'm spoiled," said the man who came in and paused to shed his rain-dampened coat and hang it on the rack just inside. "I'm used to the butler opening the door for me."

Liam laughed, then explained to Colby, "He means Cutter. He's really who that handicap button is for. He hears you coming and has the door open before you even get out of your car."

"I think I believe that," Colby said, remembering what he'd already seen of the clever animal.

"Don't ever underestimate that critter," Liam said, then excused himself to go upstairs, saying he had some setup work to do.

Colby wasn't sure what setup work was, but the thought was blown out of his mind as the new arrival turned and walked into the main room. And Colby gaped. All the photographs and newsreels he'd seen of the man over the years hadn't done him justice. Hadn't been able to capture the sheer presence of the man. With eyes as dark as his hair, his gaze was intense and penetrating.

Colby remembered seeing a clip of him talking about his first big break, having to step up from assistant counsel to lead when the senior attorney had died of a heart attack mid-case. He'd called himself the understudy who made good, which Colby had thought rather modest, given the worldwide fame he'd achieved after that.

"Colby Kendrick, meet Gavin de Marco," Quinn said.

They shook hands, and even with the forewarning he might be involved, Colby wasn't prepared for the feeling he was under the close scrutiny of a very, very perceptive man. But what he was prepared for even less was the man's first words.

"I gotta say, Colby, at first I thought you had the biggest pile of bad luck. Yours is the worst parenting plan I've seen in a while, especially with no proof of abuse."

Colby blinked. Then seized on the most important words. "At first?"

"Then I remembered who you were dealing with. I assume you had no idea both your attorney and the judge who heard your custody case were in the Hollens' back pocket."

He stared at the famous face, unable to even respond.

"I didn't think so," de Marco said. He shifted his gaze to Quinn. "No concrete proof of that yet, but it's undersurface knowledge among some circles that they've got a nice mutual support system going."

"I'm curious," Quinn said. "Did they always have that family law judge, or only after Grace was born?"

"After," de Marco confirmed. He glanced back to Colby. "But right after."

Colby's brow furrowed. "She was planning this that early? Back when Grace was a baby?"

De Marco gave him a sympathetic look. "I don't know if your ex herself was involved at the beginning. From what I've learned about her parents, it could well be they decided to cover that base early, just in case."

"That sounds like her mother," Colby said sourly.

"So how did they acquire this influence over both lawyer and judge?"

"Again, only rumor, but strong ones. The attorney has a drug problem—" he again looked at Colby sympathetically as he added "—albeit a well-hidden one."

Colby groaned. Maybe Liz was right, he truly was too stupid to live in her world.

"As for the judge," de Marco went on, "rumor has it he has

a penchant for young boys. That that's why he went into family law because it brought him...possibilities."

Colby recoiled in disgust. He stared at de Marco. "And you think the Hollens have proof of that?"

"That's my guess. But," he cautioned, "it is only a guess."

"And a guess from Gavin de Marco is worth five from anybody else," Quinn said.

"I don't know whether to thank you or throw up," Colby said sourly.

De Marco smiled understandingly. Then he looked back at Quinn. "You want me to keep probing on that?"

"Yes, keep digging, while we stay focused on Colby's situation. If we get the chance to take all of them out later, after Grace is safely removed, then we'll do it."

Colby stared at the man who spoke as if something like that was all in a day's work. "All of them?"

Quinn met his gaze steadily. "The lawyer, the judge...and the Hollens." He said it like a man with full confidence it could be done.

But then, he was sitting here with Gavin de Marco, so that alone sort of implied anything could happen.

They talked a little longer, but Colby wasn't sure how much of it he took in. By the time de Marco left, he was still reeling a bit.

"He'll give you his best," Quinn said as the door closed after the famous attorney. "Especially now."

"Now?"

Quinn smiled. "Gavin just got back from his honeymoon, and I have a feeling kids are on the agenda soon."

Colby wondered what it would be like for a kid to have a father famous around the world. A father to be proud of.

My daughter needs to be proud of her father, not ashamed because all he can do is pound nails.

Liz's words, which he had only later realized was her last-ditch effort to get him to change his mind, his life, echoed in his head now. He was glad when Liam came downstairs to rejoin them.

"All righty, I've got my background into the system, in case your ex or her kin get nosy."

Colby never would have thought of that, but realized he should have, because he knew Liz made a habit of investigating anyone and everyone she had even a passing interaction with. She'd told him she was always looking for talent, but now that he knew the truth he had the feeling she was also looking for dirt.

"Let's get this show on the road," Liam said. "You ready?"

Colby nodded.

"Remember who I am?"

"The kid I took on as an apprentice."

"Yep. Just another dumb carpenter."

Colby's mouth twisted. "She's the dumb one, if she buys that."

Liam's tone became suddenly very serious. "If she bought it about you, she's worse than dumb." Then a grin flashed. "Heard you were trading Sun Tzu quotes with the boss."

"I...yeah, sort of."

"I don't know much about the man, but one of the boss's favorites really rang my chimes. About defeatability and undefeatability."

"'Undefeatablility lies with ourselves. Defeatability lies with the enemy.'"

"Yeah, that one," Liam said. "You oughta keep that one in mind. We're in the right, Colby. That's our strength and power. And it makes them defeatable."

Somehow hearing that from this guy—who had no other reason to help than that "we're in the right" belief—made that burgeoning hope grow even larger.

Chapter 15

It was very strange, Ali thought, to be sitting here at the Foxworth headquarters, watching the camera feed on the big flat-screen and hearing the words spoken through an earpiece, while the scene was actually happening live right next door to her house.

It was also fascinating. The Foxworth man, Liam, had dressed the part, at least what was probably the part in Liz Hollen's mind. A worn, rather ragged shirt and a pair of equally worn khaki cargo-style pants. Hung in a loop sewn into the side seam of the right leg he had what Quinn told her was a nail puller. It looked to her like it could be a rather effective weapon if necessary. He also had a utility knife in one pocket, which could serve the same purpose if you didn't mind getting up close and personal. Yet they were logical things a carpenter would have handy.

As for Colby, he looked…nice. Really nice. As he probably normally would try for when he came to pick up Grace for their precious hours together. Clean, new-looking jeans and a lighter blue long-sleeved Henley, with a flannel-lined jacket half-zipped against the chill. Oddly, she found herself fixated on how he moved, how he walked up to his ex's front door in long, graceful strides, although he'd probably be embarrassed by the word graceful.

They had just driven up the Hollen driveway in an older

pickup truck that also fit the image, a vehicle Quinn explained they kept on hand for just such situations. The excuse they were going to use was that Colby's car had broken down and Liam had offered the ride.

And as she sat watching and listening with the Foxworths, she was a little amazed at how accurately they had pegged her neighbor. Colby had told them she always had Irene, the woman she called her child minder and housekeeper, answer the door, so she could keep him waiting on the porch.

"Have you even set foot inside that place?" Ali had asked when they'd been planning.

"One," Colby had answered dryly.

"One-foot distance, or one foot?" she asked, smiling despite herself.

"About both. She threatened to call the cops if I went any farther."

"Lovely."

"I didn't mind. Place is as cold as a winter storm in the Cascades. Not like your place."

She'd been glad Hayley had interrupted them at that point, so she didn't react and speak out of the sillily warm feeling his words had given her.

So now she sat watching, rather nervously, what Quinn had called the first phase of the operation. Cutter padded over and sat beside her. Ziggy was quietly snoozing in the bigger dog's bed, worn out from all the playing the two dogs had done this morning. She automatically reached out to stroke the dark fur on his head, and felt again that odd sense of calm. And remembered how the dog had raced ahead when she, Hayley and Ziggy had arrived, how she had laughed when he'd raised up and batted at the large, square handicap door switch, opening it for them.

"Here we go," she heard Liam say as the front door was pulled open.

Ali watched as Irene looked curiously at Liam, then at Colby.

She said something, so quietly it came through as an unintelligible murmur. Her expression was too neutral for Ali to read. Even as she thought it, Hayley confirmed her feelings.

"She either doesn't care, or she's experienced enough not to show her own feelings while at work."

"Colby said she's always been civil to him at least," Quinn said as the woman closed the door, leaving the two men on the porch.

A couple of minutes ticked by, and Ali was growing more and more irritated on Colby's behalf as he was, clearly intentionally, kept waiting.

"She's quite the manipulator, isn't she?" she muttered.

Hayley nodded. "Frequently used way to remind people you're in charge is to keep them waiting."

"Because of course your time is more important than theirs."

Hayley gave her a sideways look. "You have some strong feelings about this."

She let out a sigh. "I hate people who play power games all the time. It's one of the reasons I left the city and came here."

"Well, there's a lot fewer of them here, I promise," Hayley said.

As distraction Ali looked around the room again. It had the air of a comfortable great room in a well-designed house, which had been a surprise to her because of the commercial look of the outside. If someone had hired her to take the utilitarian building and make it feel like a home, it might well have ended up something like this. Which made her like these people even more than she already did. And now it was personal, not just by reputation.

"And who is…this?"

Liz's voice, with more than a little undertone of distaste in it, came clearly through the earpiece, and Ali's gaze shot back to the screen. As predicted, she was looking at Liam as if he were some sort of insect that had found his way too close to her door.

"Liam," Colby said. "New apprentice."

"Really." It wasn't a question, and her undertone was one of disbelief. Probably that anyone would want to learn a trade that was actually useful.

"My car broke down, so he gave me a ride," Colby explained.

"Too bad you can't afford a decent one," Liz said.

"Pleased to meet you, ma'am." Liam had apparently had enough of being ignored. Ali drew back, smiling because she couldn't help it. He had truly poured on that Texas drawl. And it made Liz's nose curl and go up even farther.

And then she spotted the truck. The truck that was so obviously a working man's vehicle, with racks above and a ladder and a tool box in the bed.

"You expect my daughter to ride in…that?"

"I cleaned it out, ma'am, I truly did," Liam said earnestly, still with the exaggerated drawl, as if trying to impress in a job interview.

"We're not leaving town," Colby said.

"You'd better not."

"Yeah, yeah." He was sounding weary now. Or better, bored with dealing with her. She couldn't help smiling at the difference Foxworth had already made in his outlook. His voice had the same tone when he said, "Will you call Grace, please?"

Yes, bored, especially the almost blatant insincerity of the politeness. And she guessed there was nothing that would insult someone like Liz more than being found boring.

There was a moment of silence, and Ali got the definite impression Liz was weighing whether a battle now and over this was worth it. Apparently she decided it wasn't, because she then turned her head and yelled toward the back of the house.

"Grace, now."

So quickly Ali knew she had to have been anxiously awaiting the call. Grace appeared in the doorway, looking up at her father excitedly. She gave Liam a puzzled look, but clearly getting away with her father was more important than any questions she had. She grabbed Colby's hand and started for the porch steps.

"You have until 6:03," Liz said loudly as they headed for the truck. "And don't ruin her dinner."

Grace didn't look back, but now that she was close to her dad Ali heard her mutter, "It's already ruined if she's there."

She had to smother a sharp laugh so they could hear anything else, and she saw Hayley was also chuckling, and Quinn was grinning.

"I like this kid," he said.

They heard the vehicle doors slam shut, and then Colby making sure Grace was belted in. The motor fired up, and they started to back out the long driveway.

"That woman's like crossing a mule with an alligator," they heard Liam mutter, in his real voice now. "Not a critter I'd want to ride."

They heard a giggle, clearly from Grace. And Ali wondered yet again how Colby kept himself from just grabbing the smart, adorable child and running to somewhere, anywhere, his ex couldn't find them.

Judging by the change in background noise, they were on the street. The cameras showed only the empty porch now, front door closed, so she focused entirely on the vague sounds of a vehicle driving coming through her earpiece.

Then came Grace's voice, with a worried note.

"Are you okay, Daddy? The man who came to fix the window said it was bloody."

"I'm fine, sweetheart." Ali felt her throat tighten at the pure love that rang in the man's voice. "It was just a cut, and... I think it turned out to be worth it."

"You're funny. How could a cut be worth it?"

"You'll see in just a minute," Colby promised.

Ali knew it was true, because she'd just driven that same route about an hour ago. She remembered them saying their headquarters was just down the road, but she hadn't expected it to be this close. She'd noticed the entrance when she'd gone by before, but had thought it was to a house nicely hidden back in the trees.

An idea struck her, but she only made a mental note of it when Cutter got to his feet and trotted to the door. Once more he hit the door switch with a well-directed paw, and it began to swing open. The dog squirmed through the moment it was open far enough.

"They're here," Hayley said.

Ali hadn't heard a thing, but obviously Cutter had. She got to her feet. She felt a little anxious, but at the same time glad the Foxworths had included her in this. They all needed to be on the same page, Quinn had said.

"What is this place?" Grace asked with lively curiosity evident in her voice.

"This is where I hang out," Liam answered her, sounding like he was grinning.

Then, almost simultaneously, Ali heard the sound of tires on gravel, and Grace's exclamation. "There's Cutter! Is Ali here? Is that why we're here?"

She felt a burst of inner warmth at the hopefulness in the child's voice. It was a new feeling for her, and she couldn't deny she liked it.

When the door swung open again, Cutter was the first through, with Grace beside him, stroking his back. Then the child looked up and spotted the humans in the room.

"Ali! You are here!" The girl ran to her and threw her arms around her in an energetic hug. Ali hugged her back, beyond moved at the child's open trust. Especially having heard the difference in her while speaking of her mother.

"I am," she said, smiling widely.

A small yip drew Grace's attention. "Ziggy is here, too!"

"I didn't want him to feel abandoned. He and Cutter played until he needed a nap."

Ziggy ran excitedly toward his friend, tail wagging madly. Grace dropped down to her knees to hug the puppy to her.

"Shall we all sit, and we'll work out our plan of action?" Hayley suggested.

Grace's head came up at that. She looked as if she wasn't quite sure what it meant. She looked at her father, who smiled warmly back at her. He took a seat on the big couch and beckoned her over. She hesitated, then decided, and scooped up Ziggy before she ran over and climbed up beside him, the puppy on her lap. Ali noticed that Colby immediately reached out to pet the dog as well, as if it was the natural thing to do.

Funny what small things tell you.

She took a seat on Grace's other side, delighting in how the clearly deliriously happy Ziggy couldn't stop squirming, trying to collect pets from all three of them. Her gaze met Colby's, and for a moment seemed to lock in place. For an instant she was surprised she hadn't heard a click, because it felt as if two parts had connected somehow.

She wasn't sure what that meant. Or didn't mean. All she knew for certain was that she wanted to help these two, and that she was happy Foxworth was going to let her.

Chapter 16

"Do you remember that movie we saw last summer, about the kids who fought off the bad guys?" Colby asked his daughter.

Grace nodded immediately. "I remember. They won!"

"Yes, they did, in the end. But it took a long time, remember?"

She nodded again. Then she looked around at the adults in the room, as if she were trying to figure out what that movie had to do with any of them being here, or with anything else.

"Remember why they nearly lost?"

"Because that little snitch Mitch couldn't keep his mouth shut," she said, sounding disgusted.

"You told me you never would have spilled the beans no matter what."

"I wouldn't have," Grace exclaimed.

"You ready to prove that, Gracie?" he asked softly.

Her brow furrowed as she stared up at him. She was very good at reading him, and he knew she'd realized he was dead—and maybe deadly—serious. "What? What's happening, Daddy?"

Colby took a deep breath. "We're going to fight, baby."

"Fight?" She looked puzzled. "Fight what—" She broke off and her blue eyes, so like his own, widened. "Mother?"

He nodded. "And her whole family, if we have to. Just like those bad guys in the movie."

He saw eagerness bubbling up in the child's expression. He also saw the moment when she tried to tamp it down. She glanced over at the Foxworths. "But...who are they?"

"They're friends," he said. "They're Cutter's people."

"Oh."

Grace relaxed a little, as if that was all she'd needed to hear. As if in her book, anybody who owned a dog like Cutter had to be all right. He wasn't sure she was wrong.

Then she shifted her gaze to the woman sitting close beside her. "You, too, Ali? Like Daddy said in his note, you're helping us? Really?"

"As much as I can," she said.

"I knew you were good. Cutter said so." Grace looked thoughtful. "That's why you're letting me come to your house?"

"I'd want to do that anyway," Ali assured her. "But yes. If you ever need a place to go in a hurry, you can come to me. And if I'm not there, we'll figure out a way you can get inside."

"I can do that," Liam said, almost lazily. "We'll rig up a handprint lock. I'll show you how it works."

Grace studied the young Texan for a long moment. "You're with them, aren't you?" she said, pointing at Quinn and Hayley. "You don't really work with my daddy."

Liam looked surprised, but he was smiling. "Well, now, aren't you as bright as a new penny," he drawled.

"You're talking funny again," Grace pronounced, and Liam laughed.

"And you're bein' smart again," he retorted.

Grace giggled.

At that sound Colby felt such a rush of feeling, of gratitude, of thanks, and so many other tangled emotions that he couldn't get a word out past the knot in his throat.

"You really can keep this secret?" Ali asked, leaning down to look Grace in the eye. "Because that's very, very important."

As if she sensed the truth of this, Grace sat up straight. She gently put Ziggy on the floor, then looked directly into Ali's eyes. "I can," she said firmly.

"Your mother's pretty sneaky," Colby warned. "She'll get you talking about something else and try to make you slip up."

"I know. She does that all the time. I've heard her. It's how she gets secrets out of people."

Ali gave a wondering shake of her head. "Are you sure you're only seven?"

Grace grinned suddenly. "I'm a smart seven."

"That you are," Colby said fervently.

The first day after their meeting at Foxworth, Ali put up a blue piece of the construction paper she sometimes used for mock-ups in the window. Within ten minutes Grace was racing across the yard. She and Hayley met her at the back door, where Cutter was already waiting.

Since it was a Saturday and they hadn't seen Liz leave, she was careful to ask the child, "You talked to your mother?"

Grace made a sour face. "Yes. She said I could come."

"Okay, Grace," Hayley said. "Now we need to call your mother."

That startled the child. "Why?"

"Not because we don't believe you, we do. We know you wouldn't lie to us. But you know how your mother wants everyone to obey her?"

"Daddy calls it bowing down to her."

Ali couldn't help smiling. "And I'd agree. But she needs that. I think…" She hesitated, but telling herself the child had more than proven herself smart enough to understand, she went on. "I think she likes it when people are a little afraid of her."

Grace simply nodded. "I know. I see her sometimes when she's yelling at somebody on the phone. She sounds really mad, but…she's smiling."

Ali felt a jab of repulsion at the twisted mentality that would take. But it vanished in the wave of admiration that followed, for just how smart Colby's little girl was. The emotion was touched with a bit of sadness, however. No child this bright and precious should have to deal with a mother like she had. Her own had been no mother-of-the-year nominee, but she hadn't been vicious.

Ali had to steady herself before she made that call.

"It's Ali next door," she said with all the bright cheer she could muster. "I wanted to double-check that Grace cleared her visit over here with you, like she promised."

"She did," Liz said. "But good for you for checking. Wise decision."

Gee, thanks, Your Highness.

"Just wanted to be sure," she said.

"If she gets to be a nuisance, send her home."

"Cutter's tolerance level is pretty high," Ali said, managing a fairly credible laugh. "But I'll make sure she's home in a couple of hours."

For a moment after the call she stared at her phone. A nuisance. Nice.

"It's supposed to start raining in about an hour," Hayley was saying to Grace. "Until then you and Cutter and Ziggy better play out here in the backyard, where you'll be visible. Then when it does start to rain you can come inside and she shouldn't think a thing of it."

Ali reached into the basket that sat beside the back door. "Here," she said, handing the girl a rubber bone.

The girl looked at the slightly gnawed-on toy. Hayley laughed and explained, "I think Cutter is trying to teach Ziggy to fetch, but he needs somebody to throw it so he can show him what to do."

"I can do that!"

Grace looked deliriously happy. Ali wondered how much of that was simply because she didn't have to hide it over here.

She and Hayley sat on the back porch. And after about ten minutes, she was looking at Hayley in amazement. "He really is trying to teach Ziggy how to fetch."

"That dog," Hayley said, "could teach just about anybody to do just about anything."

"You've obviously trained him well."

Hayley looked back at the girl and the two dogs. "Wish I could take the credit, but he came that way. At a time when I desperately needed him." Then she looked back at Ali. "He showed up on my doorstep shortly after my mother died."

Something in the way the other woman was looking at her told Ali what she wasn't saying. "You know. About…my husband, I mean."

Hayley nodded. "Foxworth does our research."

Ali thought about that for a moment. About the idea of being "researched" by an organization the size and scope of the Foxworth Foundation. It was intimidating, and a bit scary. But that was outweighed by something else.

"You checked me out because you wanted to be sure I truly wanted to help Grace."

"Yes," Hayley said simply.

Ali let out a long breath. "All right."

"You're okay with it?"

She nodded. "Grace deserves that kind of care."

"Yes."

Ali gave the woman she was starting to wish really was a longtime friend a sideways look. "I assume you did the same with Colby?"

Hayley smiled. "We did. You'll have to trust us as he did about you, he's all he appears to be. A good guy to the bone."

She blinked…*as he did about you?*

As if she'd guessed what had rattled Ali, Hayley said, "Understandably, he's not completely confident of his own judgment about women. The reason is right over there, and by the way, she's looked out the window toward us at least twice since we sat down here."

Ali let out a long breath. "I'm really glad you're here. This… undercover stuff is so not my milieu."

"Yet you're doing it so well," Hayley teased, making her both smile and relax a little.

The first drops of rain hit the roof over the porch in almost the same moment that Ziggy finally seemed to grasp the concept of fetch. At least, he brought the rubber bone back to Grace, with a proud Cutter trotting behind.

"A good note to end on," Ali called out to them as they neared. "It's going to open up so get inside before you get soaked. I think some hot chocolate is in order."

Grace gave a happy little whoop, and the trio trekked inside.

She had only known the child for a short time, but the change in her demeanor seemed both blatant and wonderful.

Almost as wonderful as being a part of this.

Chapter 17

Colby told himself he liked meeting with Ali because she told him things about Grace, things he sorely missed, things he didn't know because he wasn't allowed enough time with her. He liked meeting with her simply because she was spending afternoons with Grace and freely shared every aspect of that. She told him everything his girl had done and said in those five days so far, and he could convince himself it somehow made up, in part at least, for the huge hole in his life.

Especially when she told him how Grace talked about him, and he knew the child understood that even when he wasn't physically there with her, she was always first in his thoughts.

This was their second meetup here at the Foxworth headquarters, marking exactly a week since he'd made that surprisingly great decision to punch out the window of Grace's room. Ali didn't seem to mind at all spending time talking about her time with Grace, and he seized on that gratefully. That was the big reason he looked so forward to meeting with her.

He even almost believed that was the only reason.

"—Hayley amazed me, pulling that off."

He snapped back to the moment. "What?"

Ali looked at him. "When Liz came over and started quizzing us about our days in college together. I was terrified, we hadn't really talked about it, but she had me believing it." She looked up at Hayley, who had just topped off their mugs of coffee with that delicious blend he kept meaning to ask about. "Made me understand exactly what you meant when you said Foxworth did their research."

"Oh." He wasn't sure what else to say.

"She not only knew I'd gone to Washington State, she knew my major, and tossed off that we were both in about three campus organizations together."

"That you were really in, I gather?" he asked. Ali nodded.

He glanced at Hayley, who nodded at him. "And Ty—he's our head tech guy out of St. Louis—had me planted on the rosters within the hour," she said, "so if she checked, or had someone check after she got back home, there I'd be."

"And she would," he said. "She never trusts anybody completely."

"It makes me wonder how she trusted enough to even have a child," Ali said.

Colby let out a disgusted breath. "That was her last shot."

"At what?"

"She thought since nothing else had in nearly five years, that having a child might wake me up."

Ali drew back. "Wake you up?"

He nodded. "Make me realize I needed to give up this silly idea of what to do with my life and take what her family was offering. For the sake of the child."

She seemed to go very still before saying, with a note of near-disbelief, "So she used your sense of responsibility against you."

"From what we've found," Quinn said as he sat down opposite them, "she—and the rest of her family—use any tool at hand against anyone who's not following their plan."

"Pretty much," Colby agreed. "I'm sure that's why she... picked me. She figured I'd jump at the chance to be on their level. I was supposed to leave my stupid, useless life behind and grab the opportunity I didn't deserve but they were going to give me anyway."

"Because of course, anyone would," Ali said, and he felt a kick of warmth at the utter disdain and sarcasm in her voice. And for a brief second he wondered what it would be like to hear that low, husky voice under other circumstances. Intimate circumstances.

He reined it in and went on. Admitted something he rarely did, even to himself. "If I had it to do over again, knowing what I know now, knowing Grace and the kid she would become... maybe I would have done it."

As if the dog had sensed the change in his voice, Cutter came over and sat at his feet, resting his head on Colby's knee. He reached out to stroke the dark head, and oddly, felt a sort of calm, as if it were radiating from the dog through his fingers. He looked up, a little disconcerted, to find Ali staring at him.

When their gazes locked, she said quietly, "I'll bet you would. For the sake of the Grace you know now, you'd have given up your life. Figuratively...or literally. You'd die for her, wouldn't you."

It wasn't really a question, but he answered as if it had been. "I would. To save her I wouldn't hesitate a minute."

"And deep down, even though she might not think of it in those words, she knows it. What a gift to give your child."

Her words warmed him in a way he hadn't felt in a long time. The kind of warmth he'd felt the first time his baby girl's tiny hand had reached up to touch his face as he held her, the first time she'd piped out "Da-da," the first time he'd made her laugh in delight. Something deep, deep down and glowing, some sense of value and worth he'd lost.

Or Liz had trampled out of him.

"But think about this," Ali said quietly. "If you had given in, if you hadn't had the courage to fight and had gone down that Hollen road... Grace very likely would not be the girl she is now. They would have smothered her with their wealth, power and attitude just as they tried to do with you. The child you love so much, and who adores you, probably wouldn't exist."

He had never, ever thought of it that way. He stared at this woman who had, in the space of a week, become an integral part of his existence, part of the operation that gave him, for the first time in so long, hope.

Even the usually brisk, businesslike Quinn seemed to have been moved by her words. "And there you have it, Colby. The wisdom of the world, given to you on a platter."

Colby nodded slowly, unable to speak. Then Liam came down from what he'd gathered was their meeting and computer level upstairs, and Quinn was back to his usual job of solving problems.

"I think we can get away with Liam going with you again tomorrow," he said.

Colby shifted his brain to the issue now at hand. It was an effort. This emotional crap drained him faster than anything else.

"Agreed, given her opinion of my work vehicle, which is only a bit higher than her opinion on the one Liam drove. And only that because it's an SUV, not an actual pickup."

"And her opinion of me," Liam put in cheerfully. "I'm too stupid to be a problem to her. We can nurse that for a while, I think."

And the next day it worked just as Liam had said. This time the Foxworth man stayed in the truck, and as they'd planned, Colby told Liz he was too intimidated by her to get out. He could tell she liked that idea, enough that she didn't seem to question that it had been a full week for him with no vehicle of his own.

After the usual quiz about where they were going and what they were doing—"Local, as always, and for a walk in the nature park"—they were permitted to leave.

What he hadn't mentioned was what was happening before that stroll in the nature park. Which was a stop at Foxworth, where Hayley, Quinn and—he hoped—Ali would be waiting.

And when they turned onto the gravel drive to the big Foxworth building and he saw her car, his pulse took a little leap.

As they pulled to a stop the door swung open, apparently triggered once more by that clever dog. Cutter raced along the walkway, and Grace called out his name in delighted greeting. Colby hurried to let her out to greet the dog, who had been followed by the little wiggle-butt, as Ali lovingly called her pup.

"Ali's here!" Grace crowed, and raced toward the door as if she was as eager to see her neighbor as she had been the dogs. She looked back over her shoulder. "Hurry up, Daddy! Ali's here."

Which was reason enough for him. He just didn't know how Grace knew that.

Colby couldn't describe how cheering this was, sitting here with people who saw the real Liz, the liar and manipulator. Not to mention Cutter's rather amazing knack for giving comfort with just a touch on his dark head.

Hayley brought a tray with coffee mugs, and one filled with hot chocolate for Grace. They sat sipping for a moment, and Colby felt himself relaxing now that Grace was safely with him.

"I don't know how I can ever repay you for all this," he said, looking from Hayley to Quinn.

"Oh, we'll think of something," Quinn said.

"Already did," Hayley said, grinning. "That is, if you'd be willing to take on a real apprentice or two, later, when this is all wound up. We have a couple of outreach programs run by former clients, and they can always use willing employers. We foot the bill for it, of course."

"Deal," Colby said instantly, knowing he'd do anything he could for these people who were doing so much for him, and for Grace.

"I've been thinking," Ali began after a moment, sounding a bit hesitant.

"Do you ever not?" Colby asked, not bothering to hide the

note of appreciation in his voice. Ali smiled at him, quick, bright and heart-stopping.

"We're open to all ideas," Hayley said encouragingly. "What?"

She looked at Colby. "What's your work schedule these days?"

"My work's on hold at the moment," he said brow furrowing, not sure why that mattered to Ali. "My girl's much more important. Why?"

"Just… I was thinking about some dog walks. And that maybe after a bit longer, when Liz is used to Grace coming to my house, we could convince her to let Grace come with me on those walks."

"That would be nice," Colby said, still a little uncertain where she was going with this.

"And now that I know how close this—" she gestured at the building around them "—really is, Grace and I and the dogs could be here in maybe ten minutes at the most."

It hit him then. A meeting place. She was offering a meeting place. For him and Grace.

"But I…" He glanced at the Foxworths. "The family court order…"

"There is that," Quinn said. "We'll get Gavin's opinion on it, to see how much of the coincidence defense could apply."

"But if I keep meeting her here—"

"We may have to limit the encounters," Quinn said.

"Or," Hayley said thoughtfully, "what if you had to get out of your place for a while. Maybe it needs work done, and you had to temporarily vacate. So your friends offered you a place to stay." She nodded toward the bedroom and bathroom he'd noticed the first time he'd come here. "That little suite is here for just that kind of reason."

He supposed he was gaping at them now, but he couldn't help it.

"We're what, about halfway between Liz's house and yours? So you'd be close, but not so close it would make her suspicious if she spotted you," Quinn said. "It would be a lot easier to pass off as coincidence if you happen to…run into Grace outside your allotted visiting hours."

Grace had been looking from one speaker to the other, her brow furrowed, as if she weren't sure she was getting this right. But it only took her a moment to figure it out. She stared at Ali. "You mean you and I could walk the dogs here and Daddy would be here already?"

"Yes," Ali said quietly.

Grace turned sharply toward him, got up on her knees and threw her arms around his neck.

"Daddy! We could see each other every day!"

"Well, not quite that often. But…more. If, I mean really if, you can keep it secret."

"I won't tell her. I won't even talk to her!"

"Can't do that," he cautioned. "She'll figure out you're hiding something. Maybe just yes or no answers." He grimaced. "Make that yes, Mother, or no, Mother."

"Less said, the better," Quinn agreed.

Grace's brow furrowed. "She'll ask. Pushy. Like she always does. Not like she cares, but like…"

"Like she's the boss and you have to report in," Colby said, having been on the receiving end of that himself.

"Yeah," Grace agreed.

"Maybe," Ali suggested, "just three-words-or-less answers. Like 'I'm reading,' or 'I have homework,' or 'walking the dogs,' or most importantly, 'I don't know.'"

"And always, the last time you saw me was our last official time," Colby said, "when I came to pick you up and she knows it. Can you keep that straight?"

Grace gave him an eye roll. "Of course I can. I'm—" she slid a glance at Liam "—bright as a new penny."

All five adults in the room, including him, burst out laughing. Ziggy let out a string of happy yips. And Cutter looked at them all as if he were saying, "I told you so."

Colby thought maybe he'd underestimated the dog he'd already admitted was very, very smart. Then he realized Grace was staring at him. Then she threw her arms around him again and gave him a fierce hug.

"What, baby?" he asked, hugging her back.

"You laughed. Really laughed."

He lowered his chin to rest on her silken hair. "I love you, Gracie." It came out a little gruffly, his throat was so tight.

"I know, Daddy. I know she's wrong."

"Wrong?"

"When she says you only pretend to love me, to get back at her."

He felt every muscle he had tense. He heard a tiny sound he thought had come from Ali, and at the same time sensed the Foxworths go very still.

"That," he said, "is the biggest lie she could ever tell."

When he finally looked up again, he saw Ali looking at them, her eyes shining even in the indoor light. She was blinking rather rapidly, and he realized the shine was tears. And that made some deeply buried, frozen part of him begin to stir.

"Liz Hollen could tell me grass was green and I wouldn't believe her," Ali said.

Grace laughed at that. He felt it as much as heard it, that sweet, beloved sound, and it let him regain some kind of control over the emotions that were rocketing around inside his brain.

"I don't know how to thank you," he said to Ali.

She gestured toward them. "Seeing this is a pretty good thank-you."

"That it is," Hayley said quietly.

"I was also thinking, before," Ali said after a moment, "that

I should make a big deal about asking her permission for Grace to come with me dog walking. Kowtowing, and all that."

"She'll love that," Colby said dryly.

"Good idea," Hayley agreed.

"Keep in mind she might try to follow you," Quinn said, "until she's sure that's all it is. She seems the suspicious type."

"And then some," Colby said. "I think she has before, a couple of times."

"Then you and the dogs should stop out back," Hayley said. "They can play in our meadow out there. It's Cutter's favorite play spot, and he'll keep the pup in line. And you can say that's why you come here, because they can play off leash."

"And for now," Quinn added, "if asked you have no idea who we are, just that we let the dogs play here."

Colby realized Grace was listening intently, her gaze shifting to each person who spoke, as if trying to process everything. "I know it's complicated, sweetheart, but it's all to help us."

His little girl nodded. Then she looked at Ali. "You helped first."

Ali smiled. "And I'm going to keep helping."

Grace smiled back, warmly. Then she scooted over to give Ali a hug as well. "I knew you were nice. That I could trust you."

"And that," Ali said, "is the best start to the New Year I've ever had."

Colby sat there watching the two, thinking she wasn't the only one.

Chapter 18

Colby sat at the small picnic table, watching Grace attack her cinnamon roll in her own distinct way. She loved the concoction from a famous local bakery, with the slightly hollowed out center filled with even more of the luscious frosting. She carefully tore the soft roll into pieces as she went, dipping each one into the center to be sure each had its share of the good stuff, as she called it. And he knew when she was down to the last piece she would wipe it across the plate to catch any escaped drops, and then lick any residue off her fingers before finally admitting it was gone and wiping her hands with the napkin.

His girl did love these cinnamon rolls.

He took another sip of the strong, black coffee he'd ordered. Liam had dropped them off in the picturesque little town and gone about some Foxworth business, and would be back to pick them up for the unhappy trip back to "the mother," as Grace always put it.

He sat fighting down the usual ache he felt on these days, that in far too short a time he would have to take her back to that house and that woman. Which gave him another battle to fight, that of his own stupidity, and wondering how on earth he'd ever fallen for her mother. Especially when—

"I wonder if Ali likes these too," Grace said out of the blue.

Colby blinked. Because the thought she'd interrupted would have ended with "—when there were women like Ali Moran around."

"I…don't know. She hasn't lived over here that long. Maybe she's never had one."

Grace's eyes widened. "We need to get her one."

"I…"

"Let's buy one and take it to her."

"Honey, I can't."

"Why?"

"Because it has to be a secret that… I know her."

She frowned. Not in an unhappy way, but in that way that told him that agile mind was racing. "Oh. Because then *she'll*—" she didn't explain what she, just made it clear with the emphasis "—make me stop seeing her, if she thinks you and Ali are friends."

Yes, his girl was smart. And she'd had to learn to survive under the current regime. "Exactly," he said.

Grace frowned again, and this time it was the unhappy kind. And it ripped at him. He felt as if he were trapped in some cell made of unbreakable glass, where he could see the outside, could see his daughter and what she was having to live with, but couldn't do a damned thing about it.

He shoved it out of his mind. He only had an hour left with her today, and he didn't want it weighed down with his own frustration and unhappiness. But that became a harder task when, as they walked down to the harbor to look at the boats—and hadn't he sometimes thought about buying a nice big one and taking off for parts unknown with Grace—she spoke again, in as close to a sulky tone as she ever got.

"I don't want to go tomorrow."

He sighed. He knew Liz was taking her to the city for the weekend. And he was very much afraid he knew why.

"I won't get to see Ali or Ziggy or Cutter, for two whole days," Grace said.

"I know."

"I don't like it over there. There's nasty stuff painted on all the walls and signs and they cut down all the trees."

He couldn't argue with that, remembering his last trip over there, thankfully some time ago. He just wasn't a city guy at heart, yet another part of him he'd have had to crush to follow Liz's diktat.

"Maybe, if you ask right, when you get home she'll let you go over and say hello, at least."

Grace made a sour face at that, no doubt imagining what it would take to ask in a way that would get her the answer she wanted. Then she brightened. "Maybe Cutter will come over and get me. Ali said he might if he misses me."

"Now, that's an idea," Colby said.

But he couldn't help wondering how long Liz would put up with the dog interfering. He doubted she'd ever figure out it was planned, because she barely gave other humans credit for that kind of intelligence. Not when compared to herself, anyway.

Still, it might be worth a call to Ali, asking her if she could send the big dog over when she saw they were home. Actually it would be Hayley who would do it of course, he was her dog after all, but…he could still call Ali to ask.

That he wanted to do that so much should be a warning, he told himself. The last thing he needed right now was to get himself all tangled up over a woman, even if she was the first woman he'd reacted to like this in…maybe ever. With Liz he'd been blinded by the flash, the confidence, the demeanor he now knew was very well practiced to conceal the reality.

With Ali it was genuine. She was just as gorgeous, in her own green-eyed way, with that red hair that made him think of nights in front of a warm fire. And on the inside, she was genuine, honest, open and caring, everything Liz was not. Her insides were like that warming fire, not Liz's dark, cold, swirling, muddy evil.

"Daddy?"

"Sorry," he said quickly, snapping out of his reverie. "I was just thinking about calling and asking if they—" he chose the nonspecific word carefully "—could send Cutter over once they see you're home."

Grace lit up. "Would you? I know Ali would if you asked her."

"I will," he promised.

"I wish Mother would let me have a phone. Then I could call myself. And I could call you, too."

"Sweetheart, I have a feeling that's exactly why she won't let you. I'd buy you one myself, except if she found out, it would make things worse. Much worse." At the look on her face his stomach knotted. "But think about it," he said, trying to cheer her up, "how many people get messages delivered by a very clever dog?"

It worked, because she smiled widely at the memory. "Hey, I could send messages with Cutter to Ali, then she could give them to you. Mother doesn't pay much attention to him."

"I'll talk to them about that. I can't go there, I don't want your mother not trusting Ali, but I think our new Foxworth friends will figure something out."

Grace seemed delighted with the idea that she could easily reach him. "I could write you a note every day!"

She was so entranced with the idea of communicating via Cutter that he didn't point out she could do that while at Ali's anyway. "And I would treasure every one," he said instead. "And what a cool way to do it."

Her brow furrowed thoughtfully again. "But if you write me back, she might find it. Where could I hide them?"

"Maybe Ali would keep them safe for you."

She brightened. "She would! I know she would."

When their time was up and he had to get her home, he felt better than he usually did, probably because Grace was happier. Even Liam noticed the difference, and teased Grace about not getting him one of the treats he also loved.

"Next time I will, promise," she said.

She clearly had come to trust the young man with the twang, just as he had. "I like how you play stupid and she believes it," she'd told him when she'd first gotten into his truck today, making Liam grin.

"Don't forget," she said as they arrived at Liz's door, three minutes early because he figured she'd have the sheriff already dialed in ready to call if he was one second late, "I'll be back Sunday afternoon."

"I won't."

Liz's only response to their arrival was to double-check her watch, then order Grace to her room. She didn't say a word to Colby, merely shut the door in his face.

"Chatty, huh?" Liam asked as he got back in the truck.

"I kind of prefer her that way," he admitted wryly.

"I can see why." He started the engine and backed out of the driveway. "That girl of yours is a pistol."

"She is."

"I'm glad Cutter found y'all, so Foxworth can help."

Colby looked at the man driving. "I never would have expected them to get involved in something this…small."

"It's not small, to us. Because what matters is what's right, not how big a case is. We're not in it for the headlines—" he grimaced and rolled his eyes "—even if we have been collecting them in the last couple of years or so."

What's right.

Colby took a long, deep breath, still not quite adjusted to the idea that he had these people on his side. That he just might be able to free Grace, even a little bit, from that chewing machine that was the Hollen family.

Chapter 19

Ali realized with a little jolt she'd been pacing the floor. She never did that. But the house felt so…empty.

She walked over to where Ziggy was wrestling happily with his stuffed owl. He hadn't managed to break the hooter yet, so the quiet sounds still emanated from the little thing, seeming to inspire Ziggy to keep pawing at it. She didn't mind the noise. She'd bought the toy specifically because she figured she'd be hearing a lot of it, and it was the least annoying sound of all the squeaking things she'd heard as she stood there in the pet store.

She leaned down and picked up the pup, who was surprised, but judging by the way he immediately began licking at her face, happy. Which was an improvement on this morning, when he'd spent an hour or so exhausting himself—and her—by searching every corner of the house repeatedly, looking for his missing playmate.

She understood. She missed Cutter, too. She adored her little imp, but she couldn't deny there was something about that dog, something special. When he was here she was petting him so often, just to prove to herself that she hadn't imagined that odd feeling of comfort, that gentle soothing, that he somehow managed to transmit. She'd noticed, when they'd been at the Foxworth headquarters, that Colby did it, too. And he got the same puzzled but smiling expression she probably wore every time she did it.

She missed Hayley, too. She was a little surprised at how wound up she'd gotten in all this, and above all how much she wanted to help Colby Kendrick somehow get out of this awful situation. Sure, the big mistake—marrying that harridan next door—was his, but how long should he have to pay for it?

And Grace, sweet, smart little Grace shouldn't have to pay for it at all. She hadn't chosen her mother.

Ziggy wiggled in her arms, demanding to be let down. She set him gently on the floor, and he scampered off. She didn't bother to follow him this time, because she knew the path. He'd be checking every room in the house just in case Cutter had been hiding, or had snuck in in the last ten minutes.

The house must seem as empty to him as it does to me.

She assured herself it was just going to take time to adjust. And Hayley's visit, in the guise of her college friend, was over anyway. She'd made her assessment of the creature next door, which had been even more severe than Ali's own, given Hayley had more experience dealing with the type. But while Cutter had gone home with his mom for the weekend, he would be back, Hayley had promised.

"Working undercover?" Ali had joked.

"Exactly that," Hayley had said, with a knowing look that said she wasn't joking in the slightest.

As Ziggy trotted busily down the hall toward her office, Ali found herself wondering if Colby had moved into the Foxworth headquarters. Maybe he'd be doing that this weekend, while Grace was gone. And—entirely unrelated, she assured herself— she had the thought that before she even broached the idea to Liz, she should find out exactly how long it took to walk from here to there, especially taking into account Ziggy's curiosity about everyone and everything, and his much shorter strides.

Decided now, she went back to the bedroom to change from her comfy sheepskin boots into some sturdier shoes for walking. The rain appeared to have abated for now, but as she well knew, it could return with a vengeance at any moment, so she grabbed her slicker with the hood from the rack by the front door. She stuffed a small towel in one pocket in case she needed to dry Ziggy off, put her phone and ID and keys in another, and they were off.

By the time they were two blocks down, she was laughing at herself. She had so underestimated how long it would take for Ziggy to walk even this far. When the time came she might have to carry the little one, and let the well-trained to keep pace with a human Cutter set the speed. Then Ziggy could walk all the way home. Colby and Grace wouldn't have quite as much time together as she'd hoped, but she was sure they'd both think it was better than nothing.

And if she ended up in trouble with the Hollens in case they discovered it had been not accidental but planned, then so be it. She'd count it as a matter of pride to have people like them mad at her. Legal trouble would be a little rougher but with— she still grinned inwardly at the thought—Gavin de Marco on their side, even the Hollens would think twice about starting that gear grinding.

In the end it took them just over twenty minutes. If she carried Ziggy and hurried, she thought she could cut at least eight minutes off that. That would give them that much more time together.

And you have to give it to them. No staying and hovering just because it makes you feel good to see them together.

She hadn't counted on Ziggy somewhat hysterically realizing, no doubt by scent, that this was Cutter's place. The little guy pulled on the leash until she was afraid he'd choke himself.

"He's probably not here, Ziggy," she explained. "He's home with Hayley and Quinn, not here."

But what about Colby?

She yanked her mind off that path, and tugged the pup toward the open meadow behind the building. She didn't think the Foxworths would mind, given it was their idea. And Ziggy seemed willing enough, since she wasn't pulling at him to leave. And he could apparently scent Cutter in the lovely open space as well, because he went back to sniffing madly. He was so excited, his tail wagging so fast, that if it had been longer and he lighter she thought he might lift off like the helicopter she assumed that pad on the other side of the building was for.

She laughed as Ziggy took a short tumble off the small rock he'd tried to climb over, rolled and came up on his paws, looking at her as if to say, "I meant to do that!"

"Very graceful," she complimented him.

"Ali?"

She spun around, startled. She hadn't heard a thing, she'd been so focused on Ziggy. Her heart gave another jump. Colby. He was here. Standing there, just a yard or so away, smiling at her. He had the best smile, and she wanted to see it more often.

She realized she was just standing there, gaping at him.

"Sorry," she said, flustered. "I didn't know you'd be here already."

But I hoped...

She raced on before she let that thought slip out. "I wanted to find out exactly how long it would take to walk here. Turns out with Mr. Little Guy, it takes longer than I thought, so I figured on the way here I'd carry him and then he can get his walk on the way back. We don't want *the mother* to get mad at how long Grace and I are gone, or worse, get suspicious about it."

He was staring at her now, and she thought she must have sounded like some wound-up idiot. She tried to think of something to say, something calmer, less jittery, but she couldn't. And she couldn't trust herself to deliver it calmly even if she did think of something, because he made her so darned...edgy.

"You sound just like Grace when you say that. 'The mother,' I mean."

"She does have it down," Ali agreed, able to smile almost normally now. "So, you're moved in here, temporarily at least?"

He nodded. "Didn't take much. Not like my place is too far away, for whatever I forgot." He hesitated, then said rather quickly, "I just put coffee on. Want to come in?"

She couldn't think of anything she wanted more just now, but only nodded because she was afraid of what she might blurt out.

"I still have trouble believing these guys," he said as they stepped inside, waving at the interior as if to indicate the Foxworths in general.

She bent to let Ziggy off the leash. He was fairly well housetrained already, although not perfect, but since he'd just spent a long time outside she figured it was safe enough. Just sniffing out where Cutter had been would keep him busy for a while.

"What really impresses me is how little they blow their own horn," she said as she straightened up. "You go looking and aside from brief mentions in some news reports—many of which the reports say they limit—the only things you can find are posts and comments from the people they've helped."

"I know." He shrugged as he poured coffee into the two mugs he'd gotten from one of the upper cupboards. Obviously they'd showed him around. "I did some looking, too. Mostly out of shock."

They took the coffee and sat in front of the fireplace. Ziggy, interestingly, immediately trotted over to Colby and nudged at his leg. Then he raised up and put his paws on the seat beside him. And Ali couldn't deny that she liked the fact that he immediately and very gently lifted the pup up onto the couch between them.

Ziggy circled a couple of times then plopped down. He let out a long sigh as if utterly exhausted. As perhaps he was, walking that distance on his short little puppy legs.

"Yep, I'll definitely carry him here," she said, reaching out to stroke his soft fur.

A moment of silence spun out, then Colby said, his voice sounding a little tight, "I really don't know how to thank you for this. For offering to do this, to take all that time to get Grace here."

"We don't have the mother's permission yet," she cautioned.

"I know. But that you'd offer to do it at all..." He trailed off, staring down into his coffee mug as if it held the answer to all the world's questions.

She only wished it were that easy, especially for him. He deserved it. Grace deserved it. And she was more certain of that than she had been of anything since Josh had died.

Chapter 20

Colby watched as the puppy snuggled up to Ali.

I get it, dog. I'd like that, too.

He yanked his gaze back to his coffee mug.

"Colby?" she asked, and he knew she'd seen his sudden jerk.

"I just…" He struggled for a moment, then blurted out the first coherent question he could think of, nodding at Ziggy. "Does he help?"

She smiled softly and reached to stroke the soft fur. "Yes, he does. He's so…interested. In everything. That was something I lost for a while."

"After your husband died?"

She nodded. "I didn't care about anything, for a long time. Then my neighbor's dog had puppies, and I met this guy. He was the littlest of the litter, and the quietest. His siblings kept knocking him down. It's silly, but I felt like we could…understand each other."

"Not silly at all," he said, his voice a little rough at the images she was putting in his mind.

"I missed my husband so much, I needed something, anything, to fill at least some of the hole he'd left. And once I had Ziggy, I started to remember things besides the awful ending. Like how Josh was the one who pushed me to start my business, who supported me trying. He always had my back, always told me I could fly if I'd just trust my talent enough to lift off."

He wondered what that must have been like, to have someone

so on your side, so encouraging…instead of someone telling you the work you loved was useless, pointless and something to be ashamed of.

"What did he do?"

She smiled. "He was a locksmith."

"Well, that's useful."

"It is. Do you remember when the automatic locks at the emergency room at the local hospital went haywire about five years ago, and nobody could get in or out?"

"I do. It was all over the news, nearly caused a riot." He knew where she was going then. "I read they called some guy out in the middle of the night and he had it fixed in like twenty minutes. That was your husband?"

"It was."

He thought he recognized her expression. "You were proud of him," he said softly, wondering what that would feel like.

"Very. And he of me. And that," she went on, "is how it should be. A marriage, I mean."

He looked at her then. "You don't have to remind me. I realize that now."

"I can't imagine purposely making someone I supposedly love feel the way she's made you feel."

"No, you couldn't, could you?" He had no doubts about that. Ziggy squirmed and let out a sleepy little woof. He reached out and petted the little guy. "Sometimes… I felt like a stray dog who got adopted, but then dumped because he wanted to hunt or herd instead of being a lap dog."

"To do what he was bred to do," Ali said, getting it immediately, not to his surprise.

"Exactly. And to me, her world was like trying to herd sharks."

Ali grimaced. "How on earth did you last as long as you did with her?"

He shrugged. It seemed foolish to him now, beyond foolish. But it was the only answer. "Because I promised forever."

"And Grace."

"Yes." He let out a compressed breath. "She deserved better than the hell she's gone through. She deserved parents worthy of her. With a marriage that wasn't built on…"

He really didn't have any words for that, and waved a hand in defeat.

"You mean a marriage like, say, Hayley and Quinn's, for example," she said.

"Yes. They are…remarkable."

"Did you know they met when, thanks to Cutter, he had to kidnap her?"

Colby blinked. "*Had* to?"

She nodded. "In the proverbial black helicopter. Have one of them tell you the story. It's pretty amazing."

He gave a slow shake of his head. "Seems everything about them is."

"Yes. It does my heart good to know there are good people like them still around these days. To help good people like you."

Colby looked at her for a long, silent moment. "What a mom you'd make," he finally said, his throat tight. "The kind Grace should have had."

He only realized what could be read into that after he said it, but Ali didn't jump onto the inference that he would have preferred her as Grace's mom, too.

Because that's not who she is, she doesn't take advantage of every stupid thing you say.

"Thank you," she said quietly. "That is one of the biggest compliments I've ever gotten." She lowered her gaze to the pup. "We wanted kids. In fact, we stopped any prevention a few weeks before he was killed."

He didn't know what to say to that, and for once managed to keep his mouth shut before he said something that would make it worse. So he did the only thing he could think of. He reached over and laid his hand on top of hers where it was stroking the pup.

Her hand went still but she didn't pull away. She stared down at his hand atop hers and then, to his shock, she turned hers over and wrapped her fingers around his.

"Grace may have one of the worst mothers on record, but she's got you, and that makes up for a lot."

He didn't mean for it to happen. It wasn't a decision he made any more than petting Ziggy seemed to be. He meant only to thank her with a kiss on the cheek, to make up for the words he couldn't find. But she turned her head just then, her lips brushing his, and it became something much more.

She was so warm, so soft, so comforting and thrilling at the same time, that he couldn't stop himself. And she didn't seem to want him to, which only kicked him into overdrive. He tasted the lingering zest of the coffee, but only for a moment before all was erased but the singular, fiery taste of Ali herself. Sweet and sharp, luscious and so very alive, all at once. It was nearly overwhelming and when he finally broke the kiss he had a brief moment of trying to remember how to breathe normally.

She was staring at him, looking a bit as if she were in shock.

Of course she is, you had no right!

"Ali, I'm sor—"

She put a finger to his lips, stopping his apology. "Don't you dare say you're sorry. Not for that."

"But—"

"I understand. It was impulse. Unexpected." He thought he saw a faint rise of pink in her cheeks. "I liked it." His heart seemed to take a little leap. "But right now...we have to focus on Grace, don't we?"

That easily, and so very gently, she brought him back to earth. Back to reality. He couldn't look at her when he nodded.

"So, we put…that on hold. But Colby?" He did look at her then, because he had to. "Just on hold, okay? Don't bury it."

She already knew him so well it seemed impossible. Because that was his gut-level response, kill it, bury it, because he had no right to even think that way let alone do anything about it. He wasn't sure he would even if there wasn't this huge, malevolent cloud hanging over him.

But there was, and Ali was right. Grace ever and always had to come first. And he would see to it that she did.

Chapter 21

"Ali said I had to ask you."

Grace was wearing the perfect respectful expression. The child was carrying it off as if she'd rehearsed it a dozen times. As, in fact, they had over the last couple of days, since she'd gotten home from the city. Grace had said it was awful, that her mother had made her dress up and say nice things to a bunch of people she didn't even know.

"Consider it a rehearsal for this, then," Ali had suggested, and the child had lit up at that idea.

"She said that, did she?" her mother replied now, shifting her gaze from her daughter to Ali.

"Of course," Ali said, with just the right tone of deference she'd practiced right along with Grace. "I wouldn't dream of assuming it was all right for her to come along on our walks without checking with you first."

Ali thought she saw a flash of something in the other woman's eyes. She was fairly sure it wasn't gratitude. Maybe pleasure? Satisfaction?

More likely acceptance of the obsequious manner and tone as her due.

Taking that as incentive, she went on, still with that practiced smile. "You have my number, so of course if you need us to come back right away just call or text and we'll come back at a run."

"And just where do you plan on taking these walks?"

"I've been staying fairly close, not leaving the general neighborhood," she promised, leaving the interpretation of neighborhood open. "I need to learn my way around a bit, find some open places for the dogs to play. Ziggy needs to learn how to be on a leash, and Cutter needs the exercise. That last won't hurt me, either." She tried to make her smile look ingratiating but not fawning. "And maybe Grace will sleep better if we work off some energy."

That seemed to register, and Ali wondered if the woman was thinking the child might be less recalcitrant if she was more tired. Ali also noticed the woman barely glanced at either of the dogs, and in Cutter's case that seemed a good thing. Especially since the dog was rather casually inserting himself between Grace and her mother. Or maybe she was just imagining that. The dog was so smart, maybe she was giving him too much credit. But somehow she didn't think so. When she'd brought the dog back a couple of hours before Liz's expensive car had arrived, Hayley had explained once more how Foxworth had never gone wrong by trusting the dog's instincts.

Ali and Grace waited for a decision, but apparently there was one more thing the queen had to be sure of.

"And if I said no?" Liz asked, as imperiously as if she truly were that monarch that kept popping into Ali's mind.

"Then that's the way it is," Ali said simply. "You are her mother, and what you say goes."

Again that look flashed in the dark eyes Ali couldn't help thinking of as shadowy, but that was likely her overactive imagination. Or maybe the memory of that story Grace had written. Colby had shown it to her the day she'd first walked with Ziggy to Foxworth—she fought down the memory of that kiss—and she'd read the couple of pages with interest that had gradually turned to dismay. No wonder this had been the turning point for him. It was a simple yet appalling tale, and it made her want to grab Grace and run herself.

But apparently she'd hit the right tone, the right amount of submissiveness, because the woman nodded.

"All right," she said. She looked at Grace. "You may go on these walks, as long as you check every day to make sure I don't have something else planned for you. Is that clear?"

"Yes, Mother."

Liz shifted her gaze to Ali. "You're awfully generous with your time, to spend it with a troublesome child."

Ali had to tamp down her reaction to that statement, made right in front of the child in question. That Grace barely reacted told her this wasn't an unusual occurrence.

"Just trying to be a good neighbor," she managed to say lightly enough.

"Thinking I might return the favor some day?" Liz asked, and Ali could almost feel the thunk as the woman slid her into one of her mental slots, that of someone trying to curry favor with the queen.

"I hope that never happens, of course," Ali said, "but it's nice to have friends close by, isn't it?"

And I'd run all the way to Foxworth before I'd ask you for the time of day.

"Hmm," was all Liz said.

Ali had had more than enough of the woman. She turned to Grace. "You ready to go?"

"Yes," the child responded instantly. Ali could almost feel the child's glee as she started toward the door. She put a hand on the girl's shoulder to warn her not to let it show. She added a little squeeze as a reminder, and Grace looked back.

"Thank you, Mother."

Liz looked almost startled. Her glance flicked to Ali, who gave her the best smile she could manage, wanting the woman to think she was pounding home to Grace the respect due to the woman in charge. It seemed to work, for the smile she got in return seemed more sincere than any she'd gotten from the woman yet. Not that that was saying much.

They were down to the sidewalk in front of Ali's house before Grace couldn't hold it back and giggled. They made it past the stand of tall evergreens, which masked them from the big, fancy house, then Grace turned and threw her arms around Ali in a huge hug.

"Good job, sweetie," she told the child. "Now, let's get going. I'm going to carry Ziggy, so we'll get there quicker. You take Cutter's leash." Grace gave the dog a wary look, given his size, but took the leather lead. "Hayley promised, he knows his job is to protect you, Grace. You have your very own guard dog."

As if he'd understood, Cutter tilted his head and swiped his tongue across the back of Grace's hand. The girl giggled again, and Ali thought she would do a great deal to hear a lot more of that lovely sound. She reached out to pet Cutter's dark head. Her hand stopped mid-stroke, and she looked up at Ali, wide-eyed.

"He makes me feel so much better!"

"I know. It's amazing, isn't it? He gives me that same, warm, everything's-going-to-be-all-right feeling."

"Yes, that's it."

"Now, let's get moving, m'girl, so you can get to the other guy who makes you feel like that."

This time it was a full-on laugh, and such a joyous one that Ali felt like she would do a lot more than merely invite a child on a walk with her to hear it. And tried to ignore the feeling welling up inside that that same guy made her feel the same way.

The walk did go much faster with Ziggy in the sling she'd picked up for that very purpose. And the pup seemed content enough for the moment, with Grace and Cutter to watch, although he squirmed around now and then.

"You can do all the sniffing you want on the way back," she promised him.

They were there in about half the time it had taken her with Ziggy on foot. Her own pace slowed, and Grace stopped dead, staring at the big, black helicopter that sat on the pad she'd noticed earlier. Quinn was next to it, leaning into the...cockpit? Cabin? She wasn't sure what it was called on a helicopter. Cutter let out a short bark and Quinn spun around. And only then did Ali see the man on the other side, who had apparently been also leaning in, looking at the interior.

Colby.

"Daddy!"

Grace took off at a run. Her father turned to her and did the same. He swept the child up into his arms, taking care, Ali noticed, not to yank on the leash she held. Quinn, smiling widely, came over and took it from her, then unclipped it from Cutter's collar.

"You take some time," he told Colby, "then meet us inside."

Cutter had greeted Quinn quite happily, but stayed close to Grace when he walked over to Ali.

"He really does know she's his job, doesn't he?" Ali asked the head of Foxworth.

"He does. And he'd take down anyone who tried to hurt her."

"I had the funny feeling today, when we were talking to her mother, that he was purposely putting himself between them."

Quinn smiled. "I'm sure he was. He knows who the threat is."

"Wow. That's beyond just smart."

"He's beyond smart. He's...inexplicable."

Quinn said it with a shake of his head and an expression that told her that hadn't been an easy conclusion for him to reach. Or at least, admit to. She'd learned a bit from Hayley about his background in the military, where he'd worked with some very smart dogs, and wondered when he'd realized this particular dog was even more amazing. She remembered how it had been Cutter who had apparently directed the assessment of Colby, how the dog had sniffed, assessed and then sat at his feet looking up at his humans. Given them his "fix it" look, as they called it.

Because Cutter had decided Colby was the good guy in all this. And they believed him.

With that, even though she'd only just met them all a few days ago, she agreed.

Chapter 22

Colby wished it could have gone on and on, this time with his precious girl. She was chattering so fast, so excited that this had worked and they were together, it was hard to keep up with her. She'd always been so quick, and seemed quite able to think in multiple directions at once. She'd been putting together four- to five-word sentences at just over two years old, which her doctor had said was a sign of how quick and smart she was.

He'd had a dream about her once, Grace as an adult, standing at some podium, receiving some big award. He'd been there with her, cheering proudly, but Liz had been nowhere in sight. He'd awakened feeling a bit guilty about that, given they'd still been married at the time. Maybe he'd sensed what was coming even then.

Or maybe it was just wishful dreaming.

"—gonna fly somewhere in that?" Grace was pointing at the helicopter.

He smiled. "I don't think so. But it would be fun, wouldn't it?" She nodded, a wide smile on her sweet face. "They have an airplane, too, down south at the airport."

"Wow."

"Yeah. They're a pretty big deal around here, these Foxworth folks."

"And they're helping us."

"Yes. Yes, they are. So I guess we should go in and talk to them, huh?"

"And Ali. She's helping, too."

"I know."

Ali was a woman going about her life, building her own business while recovering from a terrible loss. That was enough to consume most people, but yet she was going out of her way, spending time, effort and emotion to help them. And doing it well, given she'd been able to convince Liz to let Grace accompany her on the dog walks.

He was still pondering that when they rounded the corner of the main building. Cutter trotted ahead, raised up and batted at the automatic door switch with his front paws, and the door swung open. Grace giggled happily.

"He's so smart."

"He is."

"And Ziggy is so sweet and snuggly."

The memory of the dog snuggled between him and Ali on the couch rocketed through his mind, but it was seared away by the heated memory of that kiss. That kiss that had awakened feelings in him he'd never known, sensations he'd never felt before.

That kiss Ali had refused to let him apologize for.

"I really like Ali a lot," Grace said with finality.

"So do I." *Oh, boy, do I.*

As they followed Cutter into the Foxworth headquarters, he had to remind himself yet again that he had also agreed to put all that on hold. He knew it was the right thing to do, for Grace's sake in the main, but so many other reasons as well. But obviously the wall he'd built in his mind to keep those thoughts at bay needed a bit of reinforcement.

And he tried. He was going to head for one of the single chairs by the fireplace, but Cutter got in the way. And then Grace was tugging at him, and they ended up settled on the couch with Ali on the next cushion. Grace was beside him, clinging to him—or maybe it was the other way around—Colby found himself wondering what on earth Foxworth would come up with now. Liam came downstairs, nodded at both him and Ali, and grinned widely at Grace.

"How's my favorite child genius?"

She rolled her eyes at him, but she was grinning back. "You're funnier when you're playing stupid."

Liam laughed as he sat in one of the armchairs at the end of the big couch. He picked up the remote control from the coffee table and aimed it at the flat-screen. "Just some general research," he explained with a glance at Colby. "You know this guy?"

An image appeared on the screen. The man, who looked about sixty, with a beard and what hair he had left both dark in color, seemed vaguely familiar but he couldn't put a name to him.

"That's Mr. Wells. He's a lawyer," Grace piped up cheerfully. Every adult in the room turned to stare at her. Grace shrugged as if it were nothing. "He was at the meeting the mother dragged me to. At her father's office."

Her father. Not "my grandfather." No, Grace had never felt a part of that side of the family, and Colby couldn't deny the fact that it warmed him. She was indeed a smart girl. Maybe even the child genius Liam had called her.

"Your mother," Quinn said carefully, "met this man at the Hollen offices in the city?"

Grace nodded. "That's why she went."

"Why did she want you there?" Colby asked.

"She didn't," Grace answered with a shrug. "She just didn't want me here."

Colby looked at Quinn, whose gaze had narrowed, then back to his daughter. "Couldn't Irene have stayed with you?"

"She would have, but the mother said she didn't want us alone in the house overnight, without her there."

He reached the only conclusion he could think of. He looked back at Quinn. "She suspects it was me who broke that window."

Quinn nodded. "Looks like."

Grace was looking at them both now, puzzled. "Of course she does. She always says you might try to steal me. When she's pretending she cares about me."

"What else does she say, Grace?" Hayley asked gently.

Grace shrugged again. "Just that I'd better not be stupid and go with him." She shifted her gaze to Colby. "And that if you ever do, you'll be really, really sorry." Her brow furrowed. "But that the…undertaker? Is that a person? She said the undertaker will be happy."

Colby felt a chill ripple over him. "Well, that's a new one," he muttered. As bad as she'd been, Liz had never threatened to kill him before.

"She's escalating," Quinn said, and his voice was grim enough that even Grace picked up on it and looked worried.

"Daddy, what does undertaker mean?"

He didn't really want to tell her. But he didn't want to lie to her, either. She was too smart anyway, and she'd know. But then Hayley spoke, in that quiet, gentle way she had.

"What your mother said means she wishes your father would go away and never bother her again."

"Oh. She always says that." She looked from Hayley back to Colby. "But if you go away, you'll take me with you, won't you?" she asked anxiously.

"I'm not going away without you," he promised her.

"Okay," Grace said, smiling now, as if that were all she'd needed to hear.

"Trust," Ali murmured, just loud enough for him to hear. "A beautiful thing to have earned."

He liked the way she put it, not that it was a gift—which it was, to him—but that he'd earned it. But then, Ali always seemed to see things that way. That he deserved any good thing that happened. Like Foxworth being pulled into his life by her own little pup, via the apparently far too clever Cutter. Who was now acting like a well-trained guardian for his precious little girl.

The Foxworths, Cutter and Ali. He'd never had a run of luck like that in his life before. He supposed that was why he was a little wary of trusting it now.

That word again. Trust.

I trusted you! I trusted you would see the sensible path, that you would realize what you had to do, the only possible thing to do. Not that you would cling to your pitiful former life. I trusted you would see the enormity of the gift my family is offering!

Liz's long-ago tirade was etched into that part of his brain he tried not to visit. But he'd never really had much ammunition to fire back at her accusations. Because she'd been right about the size of the opportunity the Hollens were offering. He could become a mover and shaker, someone of importance, of influence.

What she'd been wrong about was thinking he wanted that.

He supposed that was the moment he'd realized where they were headed. Because it was the moment he'd realized that her shouted words about trust no longer meant much to him. That he didn't care anymore if she trusted him. In fact, he'd even resigned himself to not caring if anyone ever trusted him, not if Liz's kind of life was the price.

But now...

Grace trusted him. The Foxworths trusted him. Ali trusted him. If the value of trust was directly related to the value of the person offering it, then it meant something.

To him, them trusting him meant everything.

And he would do anything not to betray it.

Chapter 23

Ali watched as the girl and the two dogs romped in the meadow. Even this time of year there was lots of green, and the expanse out to the towering evergreens—even, she thought, a few redwoods—was dotted here and there with some maple trees she knew would have been brilliantly red just a few months ago in fall, and various shrubs she was willing to bet would explode with colorful flowers come spring.

And she thought the tree they were next to was a magnolia. She'd bet it would smell wonderful when it was in bloom, and knowing what she knew of Hayley, that that was probably the reason it was so close to the patio they were standing on. Colby was beside her, also watching intently, while Hayley was on her other side, enjoying the show along with them.

"What a beautiful space," she said to Hayley as Grace's laughter rang out.

"It is." She smiled. "We love it so much we got married out here. Which seemed to have started a Foxworth trend."

Ali laughed. Hayley had told her about the string of marriages both done and upcoming, all of which she credited to Cutter.

She watched Grace do a cartwheel that was nothing less than...graceful.

"She's well named, in several ways," she said to Colby.

"Grace is her middle name," Colby said. "I wanted it to be her first, but Liz insisted she be named after her father, Brian. So legally, she's Brianna." He couldn't help smiling then. "But when she got old enough to understand, which for her was about age two, she refused to answer to it. Would only answer to Grace. Even Liz finally gave in, since legally she's still Brianna."

"So you've already beaten her once."

Colby blinked. "I...never thought of it that way, but yeah, I guess so."

"We'll beat her this time, too," Ali said, very conscious of using "we."

And Colby's gaze seemed to heat slightly as she said it, enough that she was glad when Quinn stepped out and came over to them. He'd been inside looking for something, although he hadn't said what.

He stopped beside Colby. "Call in your girl for a minute, will you?"

Ali noticed he didn't even hesitate, but called out to Grace to come over. The girl did, still looking wonderfully happy as she told the two dogs to keep on playing, she'd be right back. Ali saw Hayley notice what her husband was carrying, and give a very slight smile, as if she understood. All Ali could see was that it was a small tubelike thing in silver metal.

Quinn asked Grace to go inside with him. Ali liked the way she looked at her father first, not taking another step until he nodded. Then he moved to follow her. He glanced back at Ali, questioningly, and she in turn looked at Hayley.

"Go ahead," Hayley said. "I'll stay out here for...demonstration purposes."

Now she was really puzzled. But she followed the trio inside, curious.

Quinn ushered them to one side, away from the glass back door. So they couldn't see? Or couldn't be seen?

"Hear how quiet it is inside here?" he asked Grace. "How you can't even hear Ziggy barking?" The child nodded, looking as puzzled as Ali felt. Then Quinn handed her the little silver tube. "Here. Take this end, and blow through it, three times quick and short."

And suddenly Ali knew. She waited as the child did as instructed. And as she now expected, Ali heard nothing. It was as quiet as before in the well-built headquarters building.

"It didn't do anything," Grace said, looking at the thing in her hand. "Did I do it wrong? I did just like you said—"

A sound came from the back door, and Ali felt a rush of cooler air from outside and knew it was open. A split second later Cutter was racing into the room, coming directly to Grace and inspecting her urgently.

"A dog whistle," Colby murmured.

"Yes," Quinn said.

"But Daddy, it didn't whistle," Grace said, looking at him for an explanation while she petted Cutter, who was calmer now that he could see for himself she was all right.

"Not so we could hear it, no. But Cutter could."

"How?"

"Dogs can hear much better than we can. And they can hear sounds we can't hear at all. Like really high-pitched sounds."

"And that," Quinn said, "is what that whistle is designed to do. Put out a sound so high we can't hear it, but dogs can."

Grace was smiling now. "That's cool! Like a secret signal or something."

Ali saw Colby give Quinn a startled glance, as if he'd realized what this was really all about.

Quinn nodded in affirmation. "You hang on to that. Keep it with you, all the time while Cutter's staying with Ali. And if anything bad happens, or you get scared, you blow it. Cutter knows what it means, and he'll do what he just did. Come running."

Grace's eyes widened. "He'll come to help me? And...she won't know I called him, because she can't hear it either?"

"Exactly," Quinn said with a smile. "And nothing will stop him. Like now, he ran right past Hayley, because he knows keeping you safe is his job."

"But if I'm in the house and can't get out," Grace began.

"He'll raise such a fuss it'll interrupt anything going on. And believe me, unlike that whistle, everybody within a mile will hear that boy bark if he wants them to."

"Which means I'll hear him and call for help," Ali said.

Quinn smiled and nodded. "You use that phone we gave you, and whoever's closest will head that way." He shifted his gaze to Colby. "You're the one who has to be careful. You don't want to give her any excuses, so unless there's physical danger to our girl here, you hang on until one of us gets there."

Ali saw Colby's jaw tighten. Clearly he did not like that idea of staying back when his girl was hurting or scared.

"Trust us." Hayley said it softly as she came up beside them.

"If she's in trouble or danger, we'll come in like a tidal wave, unstoppable," Liam said, the first words he'd spoken in a while.

"And let the chips fall where they may," Quinn said. "We'll deal. But you need to stay free and clear so our girl here will have a place to land."

Grace was starting to look a little concerned. Ali wasn't sure how much of what they were saying she fully understood, but even knowing her less than two weeks she wouldn't underestimate the child's quick mind.

And neither would Hayley, who quickly diverted the discussion. "Here's something else, Grace."

She held out another small metal cylinder, but this one was shorter and bigger around, about the size of a flashlight battery. It had what looked like a screw-on lid, and a clip device on the other end. She opened it, and Ali saw there was a strip of paper rolled up inside it.

"It's blank," Hayley explained, "ready for you or us to write on."

She closed it back up, and clipped it onto Cutter's collar,

next to the blue name tag in the shape of the boat from which Ali guessed his name had come.

"For messages!" Grace yelped.

"Yes." Hayley smiled at her. "Like we talked about before. It's easier for him than trying to hide it in his mouth—and drier." Grace laughed as Hayley went on. "It's a little old-fashioned, but kind of cool, huh?"

Grace nodded. Then she looked up at Ali, who saw the expression she'd come to know meant the girl's mind was racing. "So you can send one to me, but what if I need to... Wait! I can use the whistle, then Cutter will come, and I can put in my message!"

"Come see us in about ten years, Grace," Quinn said with a grin. "We'll hire you."

"Hire?"

"That means you'd get to work with them, doing for others what they're doing for us," Colby said, his voice level now, apparently resigned to his rather removed role in this. Oddly, she found herself liking him even more for hating being sidelined.

"Wow! That would be the best!"

She was so excited now that Ali was glad they would have the walk home for her to calm down a little. Unlike a normal mother, she didn't think Liz would be pleased to see her daughter so happy.

Chapter 24

Saying goodbye had been hell. It always was. It just felt so wrong, to watch his little girl leave him.

But at least he now had more opportunity to see Grace than he had had in over a year. He'd rather it be every day, but had to agree with Hayley's warning that if it became too regular, too routine, it also became more likely that Grace would inadvertently say something that would give them away. His girl was brilliant, and she knew how important it was to keep this a secret, but she was also seven years old.

He couldn't deny that he felt better that she was with Ali, for at least a bit longer. And Cutter, too. That little demonstration today had thoroughly convinced him of both the dog's cleverness and his awareness that his main job was to protect Grace.

When Quinn started to go outside to roll the helicopter back in its hangar, Colby leaped up to follow.

"I need to do something. Anything," he said.

"Not used to not working, huh? Careful or you'll end up building my new tool rack," Quinn said as they walked toward the helipad.

Colby's mood shifted almost instantly. "Tool rack? Show me what you need and I'll get on it."

Quinn laughed. "Somehow I thought that might be your reaction."

"Anything that'll keep me from thinking too much about... things I can't do."

"I know it's got to be hard taking a back seat. But for now, while things are still stable, it's for the best."

He waited until they had the aircraft back under cover—a job that was a bit easier than he'd expected—and Quinn had shown him where he wanted the rack and what kind of tools it needed to hold, before he asked what had been eating at him.

"What happens later? If Liz really does blow up?"

"Then we do whatever is necessary to protect Grace."

"I believe you. I just don't know what that might involve."

"Steps," Quinn said. "If it looks like she's escalating, we'll take advantage of Ali's offer and station people at her place, for a quick response." He gave Colby a wry smile. "Sorry it can't be you, because if she spotted you over there..."

"Yeah, I get it. Not happy, but I get it."

"If I were you, I'd much rather be with Ali too," Quinn said, with no trace of joking in his demeanor. Colby looked away quickly, wondering just how much he'd betrayed without realizing. Probably would be hard to miss how he kept...looking at her.

Quinn went on as if he hadn't noticed. "Next option, or maybe simultaneous, would probably be Gavin. He's already digging into all the custody paperwork, and letting her know he's connected should make her take care. Then if necessary, involving Carly."

"And if Liz goes completely off the rails?"

"Then it's all hands on deck, and no holds barred, and a few other metaphors."

"They own a lot of properties in a lot of places," he warned. "And she's always threatening to take Grace to one of them, where I'll never find her."

"But I will," came a voice from behind them. Liam was walking into the hangar. "I've already got quite a list. They're good at hiding things behind fake corporate names, but not that good."

"You're just better at finding than they are at hiding," Quinn said with a grin at his operative.

Colby stared at the two men. "You're already finding the places she might go?"

"Too bad their attempts to buy a piece of that island fell through. That would have been a good place to run to. With that nice private jet they've got hangared over on the other side."

Colby was staring at the guy now, who just grinned back at him. Was their access that good, or was he one of those hacker types who could get...anything online?

Liam went on. "But they've still got some properties that would be possible places to hide out." He shifted his gaze to his boss. "Only two on the list where we don't have someone who owes Foxworth to call on."

"All right," Quinn said. "Give me the locations and I'll see what I can find."

"Owes Foxworth?" Colby asked.

Quinn looked at him. "That's what we meant, before. When we help someone, the only payment we ask is that you help us help someone else down the line." He lifted a brow at Colby. "Which means when all this is done and settled and Grace is safe, we may be calling you some day."

He said it so confidently, as if it were a given, that Colby felt his throat tighten. *Grace is safe...* That was what had to happen, and he would do whatever it took to make it so.

"Anything," he said, meaning it.

"We'll make a note," Quinn said, smiling slightly. Then he turned back to Liam. "Anything else?"

Liam grinned at him. "I'm also finding some interesting financial hiding places. Things I'm guessing they wouldn't want publicly known, which could come in handy."

"Excellent."

Colby couldn't think of a thing to say at this display of reach and efficiency. But something must have shown in his face, because Liam turned to face him.

"Think of it as stockpiling ammo. We don't want to have to use it, but if we need it, for that brilliant kid of yours, we'll have it."

He watched the guy leave, no doubt heading back to collect more of that ammo. When he looked back at Quinn, he was grinning as he watched his tech expert go. Then he met Colby's gaze.

"Your Grace has charmed all of us, it seems."

"She's...a miracle," Colby said, his throat tight yet again. He hadn't felt this much positive emotion in a very long time. Enough to think that maybe, just maybe, they could do this. Not necessarily beat Liz completely, but at least make life better for both him and Grace. And once that was done, maybe, just maybe, he could think about him and Ali.

Just thinking the phrase, just linking the two of them mentally, caused a jump in his pulse rate.

If I were you, I'd much rather be with Ali too.

Quinn's too-observant statement rang in his mind, and he made himself face the truth of it. Yes, he would much rather be with Ali. It would mean he was closer to Grace. But that wasn't the only reason he'd rather be in that cute little cottage that was so much more appealing to him than the grandiose mini-mansion Liz had had built next door. No, the other reason would be its owner. The woman who had disrupted her life completely to help a child and a man she hadn't even known two weeks ago.

The woman who made him feel...different.

Why would someone who can do what you do want to become a paper pusher?

People like you who can build or make those things, now, they're worth something.

He didn't think he would ever forget the words she'd said, or the tone of utter certainty in her voice when she'd said them. He'd always loved what he did, taken a certain pride in it, but had never expected anyone else to. His clients approved, yes, and he got the occasional "Well done," or "Nice work," which he treasured, but that was from strangers. Not from someone whose opinion mattered…personally. And Ali Moran's opinion mattered to him on a level he didn't think he'd ever felt before.

And it had even before he'd kissed her.

Chapter 25

"Grace just sent me a message via Cutter," Ali said into the Foxworth phone they'd given her. Both Quinn and Hayley were on one phone, and Colby was on another. They were set up for a video call, which made the three images rather small, but visible. Ziggy was in her lap while Cutter sat at her feet, and she adjusted her phone so his head was visible, thinking he was as big a part of this as any of them. Maybe bigger.

"Is she all right?" Colby leaned in toward his own screen.

Ali hastened to answer. "She's fine. She's upset, but fine. The note says—" she unrolled the curled scrap of paper again to make sure she got it exactly "—'Daddy, she wants to mess up our day together. I heard her talking about going to the city again that day. On purpose.'" Ali set down the little note. "Can she even do that, Colby? Take her away on your visitation day?"

"She's done it before," he answered, and she knew she was right about the bitter note in his voice, because it was matched by his expression. "She always makes sure it's for some 'educational' thing, so it's hard to deny. Threatens to take us back to court if I say no, because there's some kind of override proviso in the agreement."

"What there is," Hayley's said, clearly angry, "is some kind of overreach. I think we might need Gavin to step in sooner than we thought."

"Agreed," Quinn said, sounding flatly irritated as well. "Ali, can you try and find out someplace public the mother—" they'd all taken to Grace's terminology, and it made Ali smile in spite of everything "—will be one day soon?"

"Of course I'll try," she answered instantly. "I'll have to watch for when she's home, but—"

"She'll be home tomorrow," Colby cut in. "She's always there when I pick Grace up, and there when I bring her back. She's probably got an alarm set so she can call the cops if I'm a second late with her, like she always threatens to do."

"So she'll already be edgy," Hayley said. "That could be good. Ali, if you pour on the empathy, how awful this is for her, having to hand her child over like that, she might open up a bit more. Be careful not to pour it on too thick, though."

"But thicker than you'd think you can," Colby put in. "Because she believes that of course everyone feels for her and wants to help her."

"Because she's just so darned special," Ali drawled out in her best imitation of Liam's accent, and had the pleasure of hearing Colby chuckle.

"Exactly," he said.

"To quote our old friend, 'The opportunity of defeating the enemy is provided by the enemy himself,'" Quinn said.

"Sun Tzu again?" Ali asked, grinning.

"There's a reason he's still relevant after over two thousand years," Colby said, and she was glad to see a trace of a smile on his face.

"I'll find what we need," she promised. "And I'll send her a message back with Cutter, saying we're on it."

"Tell her to act like she doesn't really care," Colby said. "To shrug it off."

"Because the more upset she is, the more her mother will know it's a good weapon?" Ali asked.

"And she won't hesitate to use it."

"All right. I'll tell her in the note. And tell her you'll explain more tomorrow, when you have your afternoon with her."

"And tell her she can't let it slip she's been in touch," Colby said.

"I think she knows that. She did a beautiful job the other day when we came back from our walk. She gave me the biggest wink then told her mother that the dogs made her almost forget about your day coming up."

She smiled when she heard Colby chuckle. "Sometimes my girl is downright scary smart."

"And the two of you together are quite a team," Hayley said.

Ali liked the sound of that. And it made her even more determined to get the information they needed out of Liz tomorrow.

And in the end she did, much more easily than she had expected. She waited until Colby and Grace had been gone for nearly an hour. She'd spent half that time pacing the floor, going over and over it in her head until she was afraid she'd be so wound up she'd blow it by being too obvious. Plus she had to quash the rather fierce desire to be with them.

This was their time alone together, and she needed to respect that. It wasn't like she had any right to intrude on that precious interlude. No matter how much Colby kept thanking her.

She decided to take Ziggy and Cutter out to play in the backyard, hoping that would stop her obsessing about the task ahead. And it did, because before long she was laughing at their antics. Ziggy because he was such a sweet, silly puppy, and Cutter because the difference between this playful, gentle creature and the protective guardian he could become in an instant never ceased to amaze her.

Then she steeled herself, put the not quite housebroken Ziggy in his playpen with several toys, gave the pup a treat, then leashed Cutter and headed next door. She figured the more Liz saw of the well-behaved canine the more she'd ignore him when necessary. Plus, to Liz it probably made her seem weaker, unable to even come next door without the support animal at her side. Which was exactly what Ali wanted her to think.

And in the end, it was easier than she'd dared hope. She had her pretext, a flattering question about where she'd gotten that lovely, elegant dining table—which Ali in truth thought overdone to the point of being grandiloquent—and that alone did the trick. Liz gave her the name of the custom shop down in the city that was the county seat, saying that it was across the street from the best restaurant in the county, where it so happened she would be meeting for lunch with a county official a week from Monday, about a new Hollen project.

She just can't resist pointing out how important she and her family are.

That evening, after loading up both Cutter and Ziggy to make up for abandoning the pup this afternoon, she drove to Foxworth to report in. She let herself enjoy for a moment that Ziggy greeted Colby delightedly, batting at him for more when he dared to stop petting him. She started to take a seat on the other end of the couch, but Cutter was in her way and didn't seem inclined to move. In fact, he nudged her with enough energy that she almost had to sit down or fall down. And so she ended up in the same spot she'd been in the other night.

When Colby had kissed her.

She had to yank her thoughts away from those vivid memories to face the Foxworths and lay out how it had gone with Liz.

"That'll do nicely," Quinn said. He looked at Colby. "We'll just arrange for you and Gavin to be at a nearby table."

"What if she doesn't recognize Mr. de Marco on sight?" Ali asked. "She seems self-absorbed enough to not be aware even of someone on his level."

"She'd know the name," Colby said, "but you might be right she wouldn't recognize him in person, especially unexpectedly."

Hayley smiled. "No problem. So happens the manager of that restaurant is one of those people we mentioned. We helped out his son a while back. He'll be happy to play the concerned host, personally making sure everything's all right at the important Ms. Hollen's table, and in the process mention how excited he is to have both her and the world-famous attorney in his restaurant."

Colby simply shook his head in wonder. Ali understood. The expanse and power of Foxworth was amazing, and she loved that it was built on a foundation of helping ordinary people in the right, and how all those people became part of fighting back against self-appointed royalty like Liz and her family.

"Can you bring Grace here tomorrow?" Quinn asked. "She'll need to know to tread carefully the next few days, so we should go over what's coming."

"I'll get her here," Ali promised.

Quinn and Hayley then went over to the office area to make some of those necessary calls, leaving Ali and Colby sitting in front of the cheerfully burning fireplace. She noticed he'd rolled up his shirtsleeves in the warmth from it, and that his arm was healing nicely.

"You won't even have much of a scar, if any," she said, nodding toward the mark that was down to a faint pinkish line now.

"I'll just add it to the list." He shrugged, still staring into the flames. "I've got a few."

"Outside and inside," she said quietly.

He looked at her then. "But now I've got hope," he said. "And that's in large part thanks to you."

She smiled, but shook her head. "All I did was happen to be next door."

"And help my girl. Even before you knew…anything."

"She's so cute and charming, how could I not?" Her nose wrinkled. "So very unlike her mother."

"Thank goodness," Colby muttered.

"I'd say it's more thanks to you than anything. You've kept her sane and real and good amid Liz's nastiness."

She saw something in those blue eyes, something warm and wondering at the same time. She hated that such a simple compliment could mean so much to him, but at the same time was glad that it did.

And let herself hope that part of it was that the compliment had come from her.

Chapter 26

Colby sat looking at the fire again, twirling the half glass of wine he held, wondering what it would be like if this were... real. If this was home, if the dogs sprawled in front of the fire were his.

If Ali was his.

The longing that boiled up in him was searing, in more ways than one. She was, by just being herself, showing him how utterly bankrupt his marriage had been. Even in the early days, when he'd been caught up in the fantasy, marveling at his luck that the gorgeous, rebellious Liz had wanted him, it hadn't been like this. And looking back now, he realized the clues had been there all along, he'd just been too blinded to see them. It should never have been a surprise that she would be drawn back into the Hollen web, and eventually insist he walk away from the work he loved and join the family cabal.

He wondered how much of her initial attraction to him had been part of that rebellion. A lot, he suspected, because nothing could offend their sensibilities more than having a lowly carpenter as part of the family. They'd been a united front from the moment Liz had, as they'd put it, come to her senses and come home. And it was a front he was not welcome in.

That he'd never wanted to be part of that world removed some of the sting, but not all. And most of what was left was directed inward, at himself for not realizing the obvious much sooner. But then Grace had come, and he'd had no choice but to stick it out as long as he could.

He took a sip of wine, hoping to pull himself out of the useless pondering. Ali had stayed after the Foxworths had left, of her own volition, saving him from making a fool of himself asking her to.

"Funny, isn't it? Cutter, I mean?" Ali said now, gesturing at the dogs.

He snapped himself out of the last of the painful reflections of the mistake his marriage had been.

"What?"

"I mean how he stayed here, even though his people left. The way he came over and sat by you and just looked at them, like he was saying his job was here."

"From what they've told me, that's pretty much how it works," he said, looking at the bigger dog who was lying with one paw thrown protectively over the puppy.

"He certainly is the politest of houseguests," she said. "And he's a great puppy sitter, too. I think Ziggy is going to be heartbroken when this is over and he leaves."

She shifted in her seat to look at him. He wasn't sure he dared look back at her, not when they were here alone, in front of a warm fire, sipping wine, dogs snoozing at their feet. It was too sweet. Too homey. Too much something he wanted so desperately he couldn't even put it into words.

"And it will be over, eventually," she said quietly. "I've been doing some more reading, and Foxworth definitely gets things done."

He steadied himself, staring at the wine left in the glass. "I'm realizing that. They seem to have every aspect covered."

"So...do you think you could stop worrying quite so much?"

He did look at her then. "I doubt it," he said wryly.

"Because you'll always worry about your girl."

"Always."

It was a moment before, with a soft smile that did that crazy thing to his gut again, she said, "You remind me of Josh."

He went very still. He wasn't at all sure how he felt about the comparison to her late husband. "Is that…a good thing, or a sad thing?"

"A very good thing. If he gave his word, it was golden."

"I… You must miss him."

"Every day. But I also know I have to get on with my life. It's what he would have wanted. And," she added, "why I moved here."

His mouth quirked. "And look what that got you into."

"What it did was give me a chance to help the most nearly perfect child I've ever met." She smiled, widely. "And Grace is going to be so excited, that something's actually going to happen. I get the feeling she's wanted to fight back for a long time, but was afraid to. Afraid of what her mother would do."

Colby sighed. "Rightfully so. If she argued with her, or worse, tried to get away, Liz would probably lock her in her room every minute she wasn't actually in school."

"I meant," Ali said softly, "afraid of what her mother would do to you. You're who she's protecting."

He stared at her. "Grace…protecting me?"

"Did you not realize that the love between you flows both ways? She would do anything for you."

He didn't know what to say. The thought of his precious girl protecting him, worrying that much about him instead of herself, was nearly overwhelming.

He realized his hand had tightened so much on the stem of the wineglass it was surprising he hadn't broken it. Not wanting another bloody mess to deal with, he carefully set the glass down on the end table. Oddly, Cutter's head came up, and he stared at Colby as if he'd sensed something.

"I'm okay, dog," he said, not even caring if it sounded silly.

"He's an observant one, isn't he?" Ali said. "And Colby, I

think you're a lot more than okay. And it's going to get nothing but better from here on."

He gave a slow shake of his head. "I don't know which surprises me more, you or that dog."

He winced inwardly, wondering if she'd be offended by the comparison. But she wasn't. No, Ali laughed.

"I'm honored to be put in his company. He's amazing."

He should have known. True, he'd only known her a couple of weeks, but he'd never been more certain about anyone. And certain in a deep, rock-solid way he'd never felt with Liz, or anyone else. Josh Moran had indeed been a very lucky man.

He's dead, you idiot. How does that make him lucky?

That thought sent him meandering off into other territory, specifically a poet and his famous line about it being better to have loved and lost than never loved at all. He wondered if Ali felt that way.

And if her husband had known how lucky he'd been.

"Colby? Are you all right?"

He snapped out of it. "Just...thinking," he muttered.

"About what?"

"Love," he said before he thought. "And loss. And if it really is better."

She looked oddly startled. "Been reading Tennyson?"

"Not lately." She was staring at him, and he frowned. "What, you're shocked a carpenter can even read, let alone poetry?"

She pulled back sharply, then jumped to her feet. She started to walk away, but just as quickly Cutter was there, blocking her path. Her escape?

"Ali, don't," he said, getting up nearly as quickly as she had. "That was...reflex."

"You mean all those lovely hardcover books in the library in Liz's house weren't yours?" she asked, a little too sweetly.

He couldn't help it, he snorted at that. "For her, books are wall decor. She used to get really irritated if I actually took one off a shelf and opened it."

The tension in her expression seemed to fade away. "No wonder she didn't like my house, the one time she came inside. To inspect, I'm guessing."

He remembered the cozy little house, and how much he'd liked it, not just the floor plan and the quality of the build, but the atmosphere it already held, even after the short time she'd lived there.

And he remembered the books. One of the first things he'd noticed when he'd stepped inside that day that seemed like both yesterday and a lifetime ago. All looking both read and cared for.

"She finds reading a waste of time," he said. "But she knows many of the people she deals with value it, so she pretends with all those volumes she's never touched, let alone opened."

"So we add total hypocrisy to the list," Ali said.

He grimaced. "It's a long list." He drew in a deep breath, and said what he knew he had to. "I didn't mean what I said. It really was just a reflex. Something I would have said…to her. I should never have said it to you. And I'm really sorry I did."

Ali looked at him for a long moment, then nodded. "Apology accepted. I think sometimes when a sore spot gets poked often enough, it gets to where it doesn't matter who does the poking, or even if it's really a poke at all. We just…react. And I reacted the way I did because I'd been thinking about that same poetic line just a while ago."

He couldn't stop himself, he crossed the short distance between them and pulled her to him. Hugged her, and tightened it when he felt her head come down to rest on his shoulder. He could feel the slight tug from that not-quite-healed spot on his arm, but he ignored it.

Because nothing was worth letting go of her.

And for a moment, just a moment, he let himself think of

a life after this, and Ali being a part of it. He quashed the thought. There was too much to get through first, and he had to stay focused.

But for now, until she had to leave, he held her.

Chapter 27

"I really like that they need to go for walks on the weekend, too," Grace said as they started their walk. "But tomorrow I can't come with you."

"Oh?" Ali asked.

"I have to go with her somewhere, all dressed up and silly-looking."

"You, my dear, could never, ever look silly."

Grace smiled, but it didn't last. "I hate when she's around all day and I have to hide in my room."

Ali considered what to say as the dogs led them down to the sidewalk in front of the big house. Cutter, as always, was polite on leash, and better yet, he was teaching Ziggy to behave as well. Stops to sniff were allowed, but pulling so hard Grace had to fight him was not.

Of course, as soon as they were out of sight—they had to be more circumspect when Liz was home—she would pick up Ziggy and hand Cutter's leash to Grace and they'd double their speed.

"I'm sorry you feel like you need to hide," she finally said.

Grace made a face. "I'm afraid she'll get mad and take away all my time with Daddy. I don't trust her."

"Then it's good that you can completely trust him."

The frown became a smile. "I do. And I think I trust the Foxy people." That made Ali smile. The child had started using the term when she decided the Foxworth Foundation was too long to say all the time. "And I really trust you," Grace added matter-of-factly, as if it were a given.

Ali stopped in her tracks. Grace stopped beside her and looked up, puzzled. She couldn't stop herself, she leaned down and gave the girl a rather fierce hug. "Thank you. That's one of the best birthday presents I've ever gotten."

Grace's eyes widened as Ali released her. "It's your birthday?"

"Well, tomorrow is."

"I didn't know. I should have got you a present."

"You just gave me a huge one."

"But there should be something else," the child protested, sounding almost upset.

"Tell you what," Ali said as they started walking again, "write me a story."

Grace looked intrigued. "About what?"

"Whatever you want. Maybe—" she gestured toward Cutter and Ziggy "—about two dogs who become friends."

Grace's face lit up. "Okay. But we're past the trees, so now you can pick up Ziggy so we can hurry."

Ali nodded and Grace reeled in the puppy. She settled him in the sling and he seemed happy enough, looking around with just as much interest as when he'd been on the ground sniffing everything within reach.

When they got to Foxworth, Grace let Cutter off the leash as they neared the front door to the big green building. He started toward the door; Ali was even looking forward to seeing him hit that auto switch and open the door himself again. But then he unexpectedly changed course and headed not for the main office, but for the building on the other side of the landing pad, where Colby had said they hangared the helicopter and stored other vehicles.

The dog looked back, as if to be sure they had registered the change in destination.

"I guess we follow him, huh?" she said.

"Of course," Grace replied.

The big doors were shut, but the human-sized one was open. And when they got a little closer she could hear the sound of hammering.

"Daddy!" Grace exclaimed, and started to run.

By the time Ali got there, Grace was up in her father's arms, both of them all smiles. She hesitated in the doorway, thinking that now she knew the child was safely with him she should leave them be. But then Colby turned to look, and the smile on his handsome face left her seemingly unable to move.

She'd never seen him like this, in work mode. It was warmer in the hangar than she would have expected, so he was down to just jeans and a T-shirt. A T-shirt tucked in, showing her just how built he really was. Not an ounce on him that didn't look fit and muscled.

"Come on in," he said.

"I... You two need alone time."

"Come in, Ali," Grace insisted. "Look at what Daddy's building."

She was curious, so with a silent promise she wouldn't stay, she walked over to them.

"Quinn said he needed shelves and a rack for the tools, for all the equipment they store in here. He doesn't like the metal ones. Too noisy, he said."

She looked around at the tools stacked up along the far wall. "Wow. That's a lot of stuff."

Colby nodded, still smiling widely. As if having his little girl with him and work to do was all he needed to be happy.

"With the helicopter, a couple of generators, an ATV and three extra vehicles for various purposes, they need a lot of different tools."

Ali gave a slow shake of her head as she looked around at everything he'd mentioned. Colby set Grace back down, and the girl proceeded to dart off to explore those same things.

"Sometimes," Ali said, "I have to remind myself what a big deal they are, they seem so...normal."

He nodded. "I didn't realize they have five different locations. Here, down in Southern California, one each in the Northeast and Southeast. Then what used to be their main headquarters in St. Louis."

"Used to be?"

He was smiling again. "Quinn said everybody seems to be migrating here. He started out in St. Louis, but fell in love with this region, then when he met Hayley decided to stay. His sister started there too—she's the financial genius who funds it all—but she's in love with the guy who keeps all this running." He glanced over to where Grace was looking at the ATV, as if to be sure she was out of earshot before adding, "Who also happens to be an extremely lethal sniper."

That made her blink. "What?"

"Former Marine. Famous for it, apparently."

"Wow."

He glanced over again, clearly keeping track of his girl. Which prompted Ali to say, "Is Hayley here?"

He looked back and nodded in answer. "She's over in the office, pulling strings, I think."

"Good. I want to go say hello." *And leave you two to enjoy this precious time.*

"Okay. Thanks for getting Grace here."

She smiled. "You don't have to thank me every time."

"Yes, I do."

"You don't. Besides, Grace already thanked me in the best way."

She told him about the child's declaration of trust as they'd started their walk, and how she'd been so moved she'd nearly crushed her with a hug. She couldn't quite put a name to his expression then, but it was happy and that was enough.

Colby watched Ali go. He found himself more than a little fascinated by the way she moved, that female way. When he caught himself utterly focused on the back pockets of her snug jeans, he tore his gaze away. He shouldn't be looking at her that way, shouldn't be feeling this way. He should be focused on being grateful, not on her backside. After all, the woman had rearranged her entire life to do this, to help them, and she would barely let him thank her for it.

He heard the rapid patter of running steps and spun around to see Grace headed for him at a trot, apparently finding the vehicles other than the ATV just boring everyday cars. Personally, when he'd seen them parked here, he'd realized fairly quickly they could help Foxworth present any image they wanted, from the worn truck Liam had driven to the sleek, expensive import that he had a sneaking suspicion might be put to use impressing people like Liz.

Quinn's sister must be quite the financial genius. Liam had told him she'd used the insurance payout from their parents' deaths in a terrorist attack to build Foxworth, and she'd clearly done an amazing job of it.

"Did Ali leave?" Grace asked.

"She went over to see Hayley in the office."

"Oh. Daddy, we need to do something special."

"Sweetie, every extra minute I get to spend with you is special."

She rolled her eyes, but she was smiling. "I know, but we get to do that 'cuz of Ali, right?"

"Yes. Did you mean you want to do something for her?" He liked the idea, and even more that his girl had had the thought.

"We have to. Tomorrow's her birthday."

He blinked. "It is?"

Grace nodded. "She told me that me trusting her was a great birthday present, but I wanted to give her more, so she said for me to write her a story."

That sounded so like Ali, to encourage his girl in that talent that was already obvious. "Are you going to?"

Grace nodded. "But Daddy, we need to give her something she has to unwrap."

He reminded himself he was talking to his little girl to get rid of the image those words planted in his mind.

"You have something in mind?"

Grace's brow furrowed. "She doesn't like all the stuff the mother likes, jewelry and fancy clothes."

"That doesn't surprise me." No, Ali was too genuine, too real for that. He had the feeling for her it was function over form, not the other way around as it was for Liz. "Have you ever heard her mention something she wants?"

Grace brightened. "Yes!" Her expression turned thoughtful again. He focused on her, thinking he wouldn't trade the challenge of keeping up with his clever girl for anything. "But I don't think we could wrap it up like a present."

"What is it?"

"She wants a…a greenhouse? You know, the glass thing you grow plants in." Well, having seen her garden, that didn't surprise him at all. "Just a little one, but big enough to walk into."

"She have a spot in mind?"

Grace nodded. "Out back, next to the deck. She says it gets the most sun. And she said the reason she didn't already have one was she wasn't sure she could put it together. You can do that, Daddy. You can build anything."

For a moment all he could do was let those words, spoken with such love and conviction, play in a loop in his head. Then practicality rose up.

"It would have to be a late present," he said. "I can't be at Ali's house while your mother's home."

"But she won't be tomorrow." Grace frowned. "Neither will I. She's making me go with her to some fancy thing down near the big mall. She even gave Irene the day off."

"Oh." He tried not to dwell on not seeing her tomorrow and focused on making this wish of hers come true. "What time is this thing?"

"We have to go at eleven, she said. And if it's like her other stuff it'll take forever."

Colby knew he had to take the exaggeration of time forcibly spent with her mother into account, but even driving time there and back would be over an hour. Liz had never spent less than a couple of hours at these things, doing what she called networking, which to him meant she was cataloging the people there according to their potential to be useful to her someday.

That would give him four hours. More than enough time to put a small greenhouse together. And just the thought of doing something for Ali, something she really wanted, made him feel useful again. Building this shelving for Quinn had kept him from going stir-crazy, but the thought of doing something for Ali...

His mind began to race, with as much energy and enthusiasm as if he were about to build a monument.

Ali had been focusing on work this morning, trying not to worry about how Grace was doing at the "grown-ups" party her mother had, in Grace's words, ordered her to. She'd been falling a bit behind lately, because that focus had been faltering. She couldn't seem to stop thinking about Grace.

And her father.

So now here she was, still a little stunned that that father had shown up shortly after Liz and Grace had left. And with a stack of boxes in the back of his truck, with a big, green bow on top.

"Grace wanted me to wrap it all for your birthday, but given the size..."

His voice trailed off, and she realized she was staring at him.

"Look," he began again, "if this isn't a good time or is a lousy idea—"

"No!" She shook off her shock. "I just... I only told her... you did all this since yesterday?"

He shrugged. "I've worked with a guy whose family makes these kits. So when Grace said you really wanted a greenhouse, I got hold of him."

She was still a little rattled by the unexpectedness of it. And the knowledge of how much this had to have cost. "I...wow. This wasn't cheap. Especially now, with people thinking about spring coming."

He shrugged and smiled. "I got a discount."

"Colby, I don't know what to say, except thank you."

"That'll do," he said, and she only realized how tense he'd been by how things changed now. "But I'd better get started if we're going to have it done before they get back. Don't want to blow all our efforts out of the water by having Liz spot me over here."

"Oh, no, we don't," Ali said, but she wasn't happy about it. Because if it wasn't for that, she'd happily have him over here anytime.

Maybe all the time.

He pulled off the big bow and went to toss it, but she stopped him. "No, I want to keep it, to put on it when it's up." She smiled. "A green bow for my new greenhouse."

He paused, then handed it to her. "It made me think of your eyes."

He looked away quickly then, and she was almost glad, because she could feel her cheeks heating up.

The process was fascinating. If she was honest, however, half of her enjoyment came from watching him work. He'd read the rather copious instructions thoroughly, then never looked at them again. He'd laid out the parts and pieces, using a tarp from his truck as a base for the smaller bits, screws and clips. Once it was all organized to his liking, he started the assembly.

He was so thorough it took a while, but in a much shorter time than if she'd tried to do it herself, she had the exact greenhouse she'd wanted, including shelves, lighting and a fan for air circulation to prevent mold in the rainy season. And mere steps from her back door.

And more importantly at the moment, out of view of her nasty neighbor's cameras.

"I could build you a covered walkway," Colby suggested. "It's only about six feet, so it wouldn't take much. And that way you'd never get wet."

Ali looked at him and smiled. "I'm Pacific Northwest born and raised, walking six feet even in a downpour is nothing." Then she couldn't stop herself from grinning. "Tomatoes! Peppers! Carrots! Maybe even a mini citrus tree! And maybe some dahlias for color, and—"

"And, and, and," Colby said, grinning back at her. "I get it."

The color flooded her cheeks again, and she turned back to look at her birthday present. "You probably think I'm silly."

"I think," Colby said, something deeper, huskier coming into his voice, "you're beautiful. Wonderful. Remarkable. And, and, and."

She couldn't help herself, she turned her head to meet his gaze. And what she saw there in his eyes sent her heart racing. She couldn't look away. It was as if something tangible, something physical, had connected them.

He crossed the space between them in a single step, and when his arms came around her she wanted to cry out at the joy of the contact. She hadn't thought she would ever, could ever feel like this. She thought this kind of heat, this kind of desire, had died with Josh, never to be felt again. Yet for the first time since he'd died, she felt completely alive. Alive and humming.

If anything ever happens to me, Ali, you have to promise me you'll miss me, but that after a while you'll move on. Remember me but don't live like you'd died with me.

Josh's words ran through her head now. And she realized that until now she'd pretty much been doing that, continuing with the business of life, but setting the emotion of it aside.

Until Colby Kendrick had kidnapped her dog.

And then he was kissing her, and her last sane thought was that promise she'd made, so casually when Josh had asked her all those years ago when they'd been so young and death had been a faraway thing. Now, for the first time since he'd died, she renewed that vow.

And she kissed Colby back, fiercely, feeling as if she had come alive again.

Chapter 28

Colby felt as if the world around him had stopped. As if all the problems, all the tensions, had vanished, as if the evil that was Liz had been boxed up, unable to escape to do her damage. Some part of his mind knew it was temporary, that reality would come roaring back, but right now he didn't care.

Right now, nothing mattered but the feel of Ali in his arms, and her lips against his, returning his kiss, stoking the fire, sending his heart hammering in his chest. It wasn't just that she was the sweetest of heart and taste, or that she was doing so much for him and Grace, it was that she wasn't faking this.

It was real, it was genuine, because he could feel it down to his very soul. She meant it, she wanted this, wanted him, and that quieted the part of him that hadn't believed any woman ever would. The part that had thought maybe Liz was right about how…useless he was.

He felt her hands on his skin, realized his shirt had come—or been—untucked. He wondered if she could feel the pounding of his pulse. She must be able to, the way he could both hear and feel it in his ears. That touch, her fingers stroking across his abdomen nearly made him gasp out loud.

He knew he had to stop her, stop this. If for no other reason than there wasn't time, not now. But he couldn't, he just couldn't, not yet. Not when he wanted to do the same to her, touch and stroke bare skin, more than he wanted his next breath.

But if he did, he was afraid what little control he had left would snap.

Finally, somewhere, he found the strength to break the kiss.

"Ali," he gasped out.

"You stopped," she murmured.

"I didn't want to. No way did I want to."

"Then why—"

A buzzing sound interrupted her. For a moment Colby couldn't move, even though he knew he had to, because he knew too well what that buzz meant. Then, reluctantly, he pulled the Foxworth phone out of his back pocket. He looked at the screen.

She's on her way back.

He closed his eyes and let out a breath, then showed the screen to Ali. Her brow furrowed. "They were watching her? Foxworth?"

He nodded. "I told them what I was going to do, and they jumped right on it." His teeth clenched for a moment before he could go on. "I have to go. I need to be gone before she gets here. If she sees my truck—"

"I know. I hate it, but I know."

"Do you? Hate it, I mean?"

"That you have to leave…now? Just when we were—" She broke off and looked down, a rather endearingly shy expression on her face. An expression he was certain Liz Hollen had never worn in her life.

"Yes," she went on, still looking down. "Yes, I hate it."

"Good," he said.

He gave her a final, ardent hug, then reluctantly pulled back. And when he started to gather up his tools and the packaging debris, she pitched in and helped him.

"I'll go the back way, just in case," he said, referring to the much more complicated path down some narrow lanes that would eventually land him on the far side of Foxworth headquarters.

She was steadier now, and made a funny face at him. "I feel like a kid trying to hide from my parents."

"I want to hear about them," he said suddenly. "And about when you were a kid. I want to know everything."

"Then we'll trade. Because I want that, too."

He winced inwardly at that. Because Liz had done so much damage there, too. But there was no time now, he had to get out of here, out of sight. For Grace's sake, and right now nothing mattered—nothing could matter—more.

"Call me," he said. "When they're settled in next door. Maybe we can—" He cut himself off. "No, damn, we can't. Because Cutter has to be here, in case Grace needs him."

"I know." He heard her take a long breath. "She has to come first, Colby. I know that. So we have to wait."

"The last thing I want right now," he growled out.

"Me, too. But if it's real, it will keep."

He stared at her for a moment. "It's real," he swore. "More real than anything I've ever felt. But I have to get out of here."

"I know," she said again. "Go. I'll let you know when they've arrived, then try and make contact with her. Say I want to show her the greenhouse I had put up today."

He wanted to grab her, to kiss her again, but he already knew if he did, time would spin out of control and he'd seriously risk being caught.

He got himself turned around a bit taking the unfamiliar back roads, and had to pull over to check a map on his phone and straighten himself out.

That's not the only thing you need to straighten out. Just because she makes you feel things you've never felt, solid, real, glorious things rather than the ridiculous fantasies your mind has spun about what life with Liz would be like, it doesn't change the main priority. Grace. Forever and always, it has to be Grace.

Once he was sure of his route again, he pulled back onto the road. And knew how close they'd cut it when a moment later a text came in from Hayley, saying Liz's car had just gone past Foxworth headquarters. He saw it was cc'd to Ali, so she'd know they were nearly there.

And just as he was pulling into the Foxworth parking area, another text came in.

They're here. Grace looks fine, just cranky. The mother looks more smug than usual, so it must have gone well for her.

He couldn't help it, he smiled at how easily she used Grace's term for Liz. And that she had already realized smugness was Liz's normal expression.

Just as he got inside, using Cutter's door opener, he saw Hayley jump to her feet over at one of the desks.

"Sorry. I should have knocked."

"No," she said, with a smile now, "it's just that when I heard the click of the opener my brain said Cutter. I miss that rascal."

He'd been so glad the dog was at Ali's to help he hadn't really thought about that part. "I'm sorry about that, too."

She shook her head. "Don't be. It's his call. He knows where he needs to be. And I'll tell you, he wouldn't leave even if we told him to, not if he's made up his mind."

"He's...a different sort of dog."

Hayley laughed then. "The tales I could tell you..."

At his request, since he seriously needed the distraction, they settled on the couch and she told him a few of those Cutter tales, until he was shaking his head in amazement.

"Are you sure he's just a dog?"

"Not at all," Hayley said blithely. "The only thing I'm sure of is that my whole life changed for the better the moment he wandered into it."

"You sure he just wandered in?"

That made her laugh. "Actually, no, not at all." Then sounding businesslike now, she gestured him over to the desk she'd been at when he'd come in. "I need you to take a look at some video, see who you might recognize."

When he realized it was security video from the front doors of the hotel Liz had dragged Grace to today, he blinked and stared at Hayley.

"I'm not surprised anymore that you were able to get it, but this fast? Somebody there must owe you big-time."

"A life or two, maybe," she joked. At least, he thought she was joking, but then this was Foxworth, so maybe not.

He settled in to watch, with Hayley pulling over another desk chair to sit and take notes.

"I probably won't be much help," he warned her. "It's been a long time, and I always felt so out of place at the few of these things I went to with her I didn't pay much attention to anything except where to hide, and when I could get out of there."

"Not expecting a roll call," she assured him. "Just a name, first only if that's all you have, a position, what deals they might be involved in, what she's said about any of them, anything at all."

She started the video rolling. He stared at the screen, and actually surprised himself a little, although the memories being stirred up weren't pleasant.

"That's Ben Owen. Runs a local ISP. That guy's named Conway, a local developer, used to be competition, so kind of odd he's there. I think those two are county officials, but I'm not sure. That's Chuck Jeffries, her father's right-hand guy...almost as ruthless. And there's her father."

"Is that Liz's mother?" Hayley asked, indicating the blonde on Hollen's arm.

"Yeah." He left it at that and kept watching. Until he realized Hayley was now watching him, not the video. And then she reached out to hit the pause button.

"Why do I get the feeling she was even worse about you than Mr. Hollen was?" she asked.

He shrugged. "Because you never miss a trick?" He let out a long breath. "If that woman ever said a civil word to me, it was because she didn't realize it was me until after she said it."

"Sweet."

"If it hadn't been for her husband's orders—he wanted the tool of having a grandchild—she would have wiped the marriage off the books, somehow." His mouth twisted. "But I'm actually glad about Liz's father. Otherwise Grace might never have been born."

He watched until Hayley shut off the video when the entrance slowed to empty, but only came up with a couple more IDs, and most of them sketchy.

"No," she assured him, "that's good. You confirmed a couple we weren't sure about."

"Looked like a pretty standard Hollen power meeting," he said. "Full of people they already own, and people they want to."

"So, tell me, what does Grace do during all this?"

"She gets paraded around in some dress she hates that her mother picked out, to show what a loving, family-oriented group they are, then stuffed in a hotel room with a sitter."

"Such fun," Hayley said dryly. Then with an entirely different expression on her face, she leaned back in the chair. "So, how are you and Ali progressing?"

He blinked. Swallowed. "What?"

Hayley laughed. "Did you think we wouldn't notice?"

He shifted his gaze away from her, not knowing what to say and afraid if he kept looking at her she'd read his mind. If she hadn't already.

"Ever notice Cutter getting in your way when you go to sit somewhere, or nudging you when you're standing?"

"Well…yeah, but…"

"Let me tell you about my brilliant dog's other talents," Hayley said, smiling so widely it was hard not to smile back.

He couldn't even guess at what was coming, but after a mere two and a half weeks of dealing with Foxworth, he thought nothing would surprise him.

He was wrong.

Chapter 29

Ali leaned back, stretched, took one final look and closed the file, satisfied. She'd been worried about this one, since it was for one of her most loyal clients, and she hadn't been able to really focus on it—or much of anything—since that day a bloodied, desperate Colby Kendrick had tumbled into her life.

But Grace had given her the inspiration for the project—a redoing of the client's daughter's bedroom. Ali had already redone their living room and kitchen, and that they'd come back a third time made them invaluable in her book. And like Grace, the child, who was a year older, loved to read. So Ali had taken something Grace had said—that she would love a secret place with her books so she could live in that story world—and designed it, raising the bed to give a cave-like spot beneath it, lined with bookshelves and pillows. The parents had been a trifle iffy, but the child had practically shrieked with delight when she'd seen the mockup, and that had decided it.

Unlike poor Grace, who had learned so young not to show enthusiasm for anything she truly wanted, because it would guarantee she would never get it. And if it was for something she already had—like her father—her mother would do her best to take it away. Ali couldn't imagine what it must be like, but to see clever Grace fight back however she could was... well, inspiring.

As for her father...

She sighed. Ran a hand over Ziggy's soft fur. The pup had been snoozing in her lap after a morning spent romping with the big dog who made such an excellent puppy sitter.

She stood up abruptly, feeling the sudden need to move. Ziggy woke, swiped his tongue over her chin, then made the tiny sound that she had a suspicion meant it was time for a trip outside. Cutter was on his feet the moment she was. She looked down into the dark, amber-flecked eyes. In a movement that was almost automatic now, she reached out and stroked the dark head. That same, soothing calm seemed to flow through her fingers to her heart.

"If you can teach him to be one quarter as smart as you, I'll be happy. Not as smart, mind you, because I'd be exhausted just keeping up."

Cutter's mouth opened and his tongue lolled out to one side, and he looked for all the world as if he were laughing.

"Hayley and Quinn must miss you like crazy, but I'm so glad you're here. And so is Grace. We're going to make her life better, aren't we?"

Cutter let out a sharp bark, echoed by Ziggy.

"I'm going to take that as two yeses," she said, laughing herself now.

As she sat watching the two dogs play and admiring her new greenhouse, she instinctively glanced over at the big house now and then, even knowing Grace was still at school. She'd seen Liz leave at about the right time this morning, so assumed she rather than the child minder had dropped her off on her way to the Hollen offices. Irene was here, though. She'd seen the woman arrive just as they were leaving.

Good timing. On purpose?

She wouldn't blame Irene if it was. If she had to work for that woman, she'd avoid direct contact as much as possible. Although from what Grace had said, her minder was almost as strict as her mother. Still, she had little choice. Grace had told her there were nanny cams all over the place, watching every move, every step. She wasn't supposed to know that of course.

I figured it out when she knew I ripped the new dress she bought me. But I did it in my closet, she shouldn't have known. So I did something else—not bad, just something she told me not to do, touch the books on the shelves—and she knew that, too.

In fact, now that Ali thought about it, she wondered if perhaps Liz had some of those outdoor "security" cameras aimed at Ali's house, to watch what happened when Grace was here playing with the dogs.

A chill came over her as a new thought struck her. Would she? Could she?

She pulled out the Foxworth phone. She hesitated, not wanting to hit the red button that indicated everything a red button should, an emergency. Instead she just hit the speed dial for Foxworth headquarters.

Quinn answered on the first ring. "Ali?"

"Yes."

"Everything all right?"

"As far as I know, but… I just had a crazy thought." She told him what Grace had said about the nanny cams. Then asked, "How paranoid is she? Enough to maybe…plant cameras in my house, for when Grace is here?"

Quinn didn't answer her. "Let's go to video," he said, then called out, loudly, "Colby! Question."

It took her a moment to remember how to make the switch to a video call on this phone. As she was doing it, she heard Quinn repeat her question. It was only a moment before she heard Colby's voice saying grimly, "More than paranoid enough."

The video opened just as he said it, soon enough for her to see his worried expression.

"There have been a couple of times when she's been there and I've had to leave for a client meeting," Ali said. "I haven't seen any sign, but…I wasn't looking, either."

"So she's had opportunity," Quinn said. Then, decisively, "Well, since she's already seen Liam as a coworker, it's a good thing Teague's freed up now. Ali, you just gained a boyfriend."

She'd been focused on Colby, which was the only reason she saw him wince at that last word. And crazily, it gave her a little thrill, that he didn't like even the word let alone the idea that she had a boyfriend. Even a fake one.

"How about a brother," she said. "I get the feeling Liz would react less to that."

"Agreed," came Hayley's voice the moment before her face appeared next to Quinn's. "Good idea, Ali. Here, take a look at your new brother. Think you can sell it?"

Quinn backed away and another face came into view, a guy who looked close to her own age, with sandy-blond hair and blue eyes that were a shade lighter than Colby's darker blue ones.

He was smiling as he said, "Hi, sis." He was cute, but had that same brisk, businesslike air Quinn did, and she'd guess former military. "Teague Johnson, ma'am," he amended.

"I liked 'sis' better." He laughed, and she knew they'd do fine.

"We'll need to work up a story," Hayley said. "Just in case."

"Been thinking about that," Teague said. "Understand Cutter's undercover as your support animal?"

"Yes," Ali said.

"Then how about my wife, Laney, found him for you? She's a groomer, and does a lot of volunteer work for programs like that. That way if she happens to see Cutter being friendly with me, it'll make sense."

"Sounds good," Hayley agreed.

"So I'll come by to visit and see how things are going with the dog, and in the process do a sweep for bugs and cameras. And show you how to do it, so you can check regularly."

"That would be great," Ali said, meaning it.

"All right," Quinn said. "And in the meantime, Liam can get

to work on trying to hack into that nanny cam feed, although with some it's tricky because it's completely localized."

Ali had noticed Colby in the background, and that his jaw was beyond tight. She thought she might know what was bothering him, but didn't want to bring it up in a crowd, as it were.

The security check was thorough, using some device Teague said their tech guy in St. Louis had developed. She let out a breath of relief when he pronounced the place clean. Then he quickly showed her how to use the handheld scanner, and pointed out likely places for someone to hide any devices. That part made her a little nervous, and she wondered how long it would take her to get that idea out of her head, how easy it would be for someone to spy like that.

He was as nice, and clearly as dedicated as everyone at Foxworth seemed to be. And when he noticed she was a bit antsy about all this, he entertained her with the story of how Cutter had brought him and his wife together. She couldn't help laughing at the tale of the usually fastidious Cutter rolling in every mudhole he could find, requiring a trip to Laney's grooming shop every other day. And how everyone else at Foxworth had magically been too busy to go and pick up the mischievous dog when Laney was done with him.

"If he's got his mind set you belong together, you might as well give in. And by the way," he said over his shoulder as he headed into her office to check her computer gear for any sign of incursion or spyware, "he's never been wrong."

In the time it took him to complete the scans, she worked on convincing herself that all the stuff about Cutter connecting couples who belonged together was just a teasing story they told to put people at ease in stressful situations. She even almost believed it.

The whole time she kept looking next door, warily. But as it happened, they didn't have to deal with Liz, only Irene, who noticed him getting ready to leave as she was preparing to go pick up Grace from school. Knowing it would be reported to Liz, Ali cheerfully dragged him over as if he truly were a reluctant sibling, introduced him as her brother, neatly dropped in that his wife had gotten her the dog sitting politely between them, and that he was just here for a short visit.

"Nicely done," Teague said with a smile when the woman had gone. "You sure you've never done this before?"

"Never."

He got back into his car, still smiling. "Well, you pulled it off like you've been performing all your life."

"Unless you count a school play once, I've never acted at all."

Except when I told people I was fine, after Josh died. That was the biggest fakery of all time.

As she watched him go, she pondered the memory that had just hit her. She hadn't thought about those days much at all lately. Well, since Grace had come into her life, actually.

And Colby.

That was the biggest shift. She had to admit it. She hadn't denied that from the first she found him attractive. Even when he'd essentially kidnapped her puppy, and they'd found him worried and bloody back in those trees. But when the full story had come out, when she'd realized what he'd risked, how much he'd put up with for the sake of the little girl he so loved, it had moved him way beyond just attractive.

Chapter 30

After a day of absolutely no progress, and a night spent more awake than asleep, Colby had finally laced up his running shoes just after dawn and taken off to get rid of some of this tension. He pushed harder than usual, thinking that if nothing else, his legs should be too tired for the seemingly endless pacing he'd done all day yesterday.

When he got out of the shower after the workout, he found that the Foxworths had been and gone, leaving a note saying they were checking out something their tech guy at the St. Louis office had found. They'd also thoughtfully brought breakfast, although the famous cinnamon rolls from the local bakery just reminded him of how Grace had wanted him to take one to Ali. And how much he would have enjoyed doing just that.

But no, he couldn't do that, he couldn't be seen at her place, or with her. And it was driving him crazy, this taking a back seat through all this. Not that he didn't think Foxworth was more than capable of handling this—they'd handled much, much bigger cases, after all—but he felt…useless. Useless and helpless. As he so often had when facing the Hollens and the power they could bring to bear.

But he had no choice. If he pushed, they would somehow take Grace away from him completely, and he didn't think he could bear that. And worse, he was terrified that Grace would do something desperate, something that would blow up everything and endanger her.

When he heard the tires on gravel, he thought maybe the Foxworths had forgotten something and come back. He was startled when the door swung open and he heard dog paw steps. For some reason all he could think of was Quinn explaining to him how with Cutter's toenail length they had to strike a balance between short enough to not cause problems but long enough to use if he needed to, like running over rough ground, or climbing. But that idle memory vanished when the reality of him appearing here hit.

If Cutter was here then so was Ali.

He spun around, nearly colliding with Cutter. The dog dodged him neatly, nudged his hand in greeting, but then started bumping the back if his knees, as if urging him to move toward the door.

"I was going, dog," he muttered, unable not to think about the tales he'd been told about the dog's other capabilities.

"Colby?"

Damn. Just the sound of her voice... Even over the phone it got him revved up. The sound of it here, in person, and saying his name...he had no words for how that made him feel.

And then she was there, a wide smile on her lovely face. Her hair was tied back, and the sight of it just made him want to free it, to see all the colors of autumn tumbling down her back. Those eyes made him think of the spring that was just around the corner, and the trees here in his beloved Northwest that never lost that green.

And when did you start getting...seasonal?

"I was just thinking about you." He hadn't expected his voice to be quite so rough, and he hastily cleared his throat and explained. Or tried to. "Quinn and Hayley brought cinnamon rolls, and I was remembering how the last time we were at the bakery Grace wanted to bring one home to you, in case you'd never had one."

"Are those the famous ones?" she asked, as if she'd noticed

nothing odd about either his voice, or what he'd said. She walked over to where he'd gestured at the white bag on the table. And once more he found himself fascinated—a bit too fascinated— with the way she moved, that slight sway, and the way her sweater clung to certain places.

He had to swallow again before he could even say just, "Yeah."

"I haven't had one, yet. Sure have heard about them, though."

"Then you'd better have one of these, or Grace'll never let me hear the end of it."

She chuckled, and he felt his tension ease a bit. Or maybe it was just that he loved the sound of her so much he couldn't stay tense in the face of it. He grabbed the stack of napkins that had come with the rolls, then dug into the bag and got out the delectable treats.

At her first bite, Ali closed her eyes. "Mmm. They are so *not* overrated."

"They really are good."

"Lucky for me they're a bit of a drive, or I'd weigh a ton."

"I was thinking if I ran there and back, it might be a wash."

This time it was a full burst of laughter, and everything, even his situation, seemed lighter. When they'd finished, and he'd gathered up the debris, wondering if licking the last of the frosting off his fingers would be too tacky, he almost reluctantly asked the obvious question.

"Did you need something? The Foxworths already left, but I could call them and see if—"

"I need you," she said. He froze. Stared at her, unable to quite believe he'd heard her right. "Well, that, too," she said, her cheeks pink now. "But I need some plants for my wonderful new greenhouse, and I thought who better to go plant shopping with me than the man who built it?"

He felt as if he were scrambling to keep up, after the shock of that "I need you." He seized on the one thing he thought safe. "You want me to go plant shopping with you?"

"I just thought you might like to get out a bit. We have a few hours while Grace is in school. Unless you think the mother is likely to frequent plant nurseries."

"Uh...no. Not likely."

"Good. Anyway, Irene is at the house, so I thought we should start from here." When he just stared at her, her expression changed. "If you'd rather not, that's fine, I just—"

"No!" *Get it together, Kendrick. Chance of a lifetime here...* "I want to go. I was just...surprised."

"No warning, I know. I'm sorry."

"Don't be. Let's go." He glanced at Cutter, who had settled into what was obviously his bed here, seemingly content to stay in the familiar place while the humans went about their silly business. But then it struck him. "Where's Ziggy?"

She smiled, as if pleased he'd remembered the squiggly pup. "He's with Teague's wife, Laney, getting introduced to actual grooming. She offered, said it's good to start them young. So, everything kind of fell together this morning." Her voice softened. "I thought maybe a couple of hours of not worrying might be nice for you."

He was smiling himself now. "You have—" He stopped himself, then started again. "I was going to say you have no idea, but obviously you do."

It was Ali who thought—of course—to leave a note of explanation for the Foxworths, should they arrive while they were gone. Then they were in her car, since whatever she bought had to go home that way, and on their way to the biggest local nursery. They were out on the main highway—which here meant a full lane and a bike lane each direction—when she spoke again.

"You're really doing all right, not working for this long?"

His gut knotted, and he fought back memories of Liz's denigration of the work he loved. "Yes. I'm not rich enough for Liz, of course, but plenty for me. I've got a nice cushion, so I can do this without going broke."

"Probably just as well it's not enough for her, because I have the feeling she'd go after it," Ali said dryly.

He couldn't explain why that made him smile, but it did. "I see you've got her number."

"Sometimes it's hard to keep it hidden," she admitted. "But I know I have to, for Grace."

She said it as if it were a given. As if she'd do anything for Grace. Just as he would. His throat jammed up again, as it did so often around her.

"Have I mentioned," he said when he could speak again, which wasn't until they were pulling in to park at the nursery, "how glad I am that it was you who moved in next door?"

"You might have, once or twice."

"Not enough. Thank you, Ali."

"Now that, you've done more than enough of. So come on, help me pick out some plants that will live happily in that new greenhouse until they're big enough to move outside."

He'd always liked this place. Surrounded by all kinds of trees and plants, with various habitats built especially for them. They were just getting to one of the more sheltered areas when he heard a shout.

"Hey, Colby! Good to see you. Need help with something?"

He turned to see the son of the owner and founder heading toward them.

"She might," he said, nodding at Ali. "Ali Moran, John Reynolds. His dad opened this place what, fifty years ago now?"

"Almost," John said with a smile. Then he looked at Ali. "And this guy—" he nodded toward Colby as he had to him "—has built about half of it for us. All the new outbuildings, and the shelters so we could carry more indoor plants, and things that need a more protected life than the Northwest usually offers."

"He neglected to mention that," Ali said, giving him a sideways look.

"That's Colby, never brag, just let the work speak for itself," John said. "So, what can I help you find?"

She explained what she was looking for, some of which was familiar, a lot not. But when she described a flowering tree she'd seen and had been wanting ever since, something registered.

"You mean the one outside the library?" he asked.

"Yes, that one. But I don't know what it is."

"I don't either, but I know someone who does. Haven't talked to him since I finished his patio cover last summer, but..."

He pulled out his phone, looked up a number and dialed.

"Jake? Colby Kendrick. Got a question."

"Hey, been meaning to let you know Kim loves being able to sit out in the rain on the patio now."

"Glad to hear it."

"So, what's the question?"

He asked about the tree, and got an immediate answer. He thanked him and was about to hang up when Jake asked, "How's your girl?"

"She's...okay." He flicked a glance at Ali. "Doing better right now, thanks to some help."

"Glad to hear it."

They ended the call and he looked at John. "Japanese snowbell."

"Ah," John said. "Yes, that's a good one. Stays fairly small, not a lot of maintenance unless you want a specific shape, and my wife loves the flowers."

"Sounds like a home run to me," Colby said, smiling now.

Ali was watching him, a rather different expression on her face. But before he could figure it out she turned to John and smiled. "Lead on," she said.

And I'll follow.

The quip that shot through his mind then seemed to have a lot more weight than it should have.

Chapter 31

Ali was happy she'd had this idea for more reasons than she'd ever expected. Not only did Colby seem lighter, happier out and thinking about other things, she was seeing a side of him she never had. She was seeing at least glimpses of the man he was when not all consumed with worry. The guy who had a reputation around here, the guy people thought of as a friend, the guy who could make a call to someone he hadn't talked to in months and not only be welcomed, but to have that person ask about his little girl.

And she couldn't help noticing he'd been looking at her when he answered. It told her she was part of that help he'd mentioned, and that warmed her yet again in that way only he seemed able to.

Once they were loaded up, and the back of her little SUV was full of things she was looking forward to filling her new greenhouse with—including a baby version of the library's tree—she headed for the rather winding exit from the parking lot.

"I'm sorry I can't go to help you unload," he said, brow furrowed.

"I'll manage. I've got a dolly in the garage to manage the bigger, heavier stuff."

It wasn't until they were at the one stop light on their route that he asked, "Could we...make another stop?"

"Of course," Ali said to Colby's hesitant question. "We have plenty of time, although I'm not sure we have room for much more."

"I didn't mean more plants… I meant my place. I need a couple of things. It's close," he added, gesturing up the hill.

"Oh, of course," she said quickly. She couldn't deny the spark of interest that flared. She was curious to see where he lived, how he lived, when he wasn't under the kind of stress he was now.

She followed his directions until they ended up on a small cul-de-sac with about a half dozen houses. All were what she'd call tidy-looking, cozy, welcoming. Fairly new, but not starkly so. Each one different, yet they all fit together, with enough in common to suggest the same designer, yet not cookie cutter.

"This is lovely!" she exclaimed.

"Thanks." He sounded pleased, but a little embarrassed.

"I can see why you chose this place. All of the homes here are just perfect. And this one in particular," she added as he directed her into a driveway leading to one of the two houses at the end of the loop.

This one was a bit more secluded than the others, but mainly because of the trees that sheltered it. The house was a single story, with a small yard and a welcoming covered porch. It was painted a light gray with dark gray trim, which could have made it a bit stark, but not next to all the greenery.

Once she'd parked the car, she glanced over at him. He was looking pleased again, which pleased her in turn. Funny how just seeing him react in any kind of positive way warmed her heart. But there was something even more in his smile this time. And after a moment she had it.

"You helped build these, didn't you?" she exclaimed.

He looked startled then. "How did you know that?"

"Because you looked proud. And the only other time I've seen that look on your face is around Grace."

That seemed to startle him, but his smile widened. "Do you

want to come in?" His mouth quirked. "I don't remember how big a mess it is, I kind of left in a hurry."

"I'd love to."

It didn't look messy to her, but then she'd been living half-unpacked for three weeks. Sure, there was a coffee mug in the sink, a pair of boots on the floor inside the back door and a jacket and shirt tossed over the back of a chair, but to her that just meant lived-in.

As was instinct with her, she noticed some things—very few—she would do, give him a drying rack for those work boots, maybe a bit of tile on the floor for wet and muddy days, and add a splash of color here and there, but all in all this felt like a place she'd finished with, not one she needed to work on. And down at the end of a hallway she saw a door open, to a brightly colored purple-and-pink room with toys and books strewn about, and stuffed animals and more books on every shelf.

Grace. There was no question. She thought about the cold, sterile room the child was relegated to in her mother's house, and felt another jab of sorrow and sympathy.

Then they walked through to the main room, which had more of the neat, functional feel. And the stack of books on an end table were a positive, even if they weren't exactly neat. But all of it barely registered when she saw the view out the large back windows. Not just the expansive deck but, in the distance and between more of the trees she loved, as if they were a frame, the water of Puget Sound. It was a lovely blue today under the clear winter sky.

"Colby, this is beyond wonderful," she said when she heard him come up behind her.

"Kind of plain, I know—"

"It's not plain, it's functional. And who needs fancy inside when you have that—" she gestured toward the sparkling water through the trees "—outside? This spot up on this hill is the perfect place, and I love that you didn't mow down all the trees to take advantage of the view."

"They talked about it, but I told them I was buying this one and to leave them. To me, they frame the view, not distract from it."

She turned around quickly as he used exactly the word she'd thought of a moment ago. She hadn't realized he was quite that close, and before she knew it she was up against him. She wobbled a little, and his hands instantly came out to steady her.

And then she was in his arms, looking up at him. She thought she saw something flash in those blue eyes, something hot followed by an effort to look away that was underlined by the tension in his arms, as if he were trying to let go but his arms wouldn't cooperate.

"Colby," she whispered, her voice coming out husky because of the tightness in her throat. And then he was kissing her.

It began almost harshly and definitely hungrily. Fierce, even. She let out a low moan without even thinking about it, because she couldn't have stopped it anyway. He broke the kiss, and she felt him start to back off.

"No!" she protested, and reached up to pull him back to her.

"Ali, I...can't do this."

"Oh." She felt a chill go through her. "I thought...you wanted to."

He let out a low, harsh laugh. "I do. God, do I. But I'm afraid you'll regret it."

"What is there to regret that I don't already know about?" she demanded.

He just looked at her for a moment, his expression softening. He let out a low, wry and short chuckle. "Point taken. You pretty much know it all."

"I want you," she said firmly. "*You*, Colby Kendrick. Who you are, now and from now on."

She saw the change come over him then, and before she could

even put a name to it heat rippled through her in response. Then she realized it was fierceness, the same kind she was feeling. Heat, want, need all billowing through her in waves so potent she even imagined she could see the reflection of it in his eyes. Or maybe it was his own need, finally cut loose.

She hoped so.

And then he removed all doubt by sweeping her up into his strong arms as if she were as light as a leaf from one of those plants waiting outside. His mouth came down on hers again, heat spiked again and she barely noticed they were moving. She didn't even register the room as he pushed open the door. All she saw, all she wanted to see was him, all she wanted to feel was his mouth on hers, and anywhere else he wanted to put it. Which had her thinking of all the places on him she'd like to kiss, to taste.

She wasn't sure who removed what clothing, thought she might have tugged at his jeans while he was pulling off her sweater, but it didn't matter. What mattered was within moments they were skin to skin.

He was as beautiful as she'd expected, strong, leanly muscled, powerful. They hit the bed, and the only thing she noticed about it was that it just might be big enough.

He reached over and pulled open a drawer in the nightstand and pulled out a small, clearly unopened box of condoms.

"Sometimes," he muttered, "I'm thankful for my smart-ass friends."

"If they provided those, so am I."

He laughed, and she felt it down deep where his abdomen was pressed against her. She also felt the prod of another powerful part of him, clearly ready and able. He fumbled for a moment, sheathing that part, telling her it truly had been a while for him. As it had for her.

He rolled back, half over her, cupping her face in his hands. "You're really sure?"

"So very sure," she answered. "Just…it's been a long time, so I'm not…used to this. Just don't stop."

"I won't." He almost growled. "But I'm going to go slow and easy until you tell me not to. And then, look out Ali Moran, because under all the chaos, I've been wanting this since the first time I saw you."

"Ditto, Colby Kendrick."

Then his mouth was all over her, finding places she'd forgotten existed, feeling sensations she'd forgotten she could. And when he finally slid into her, long and slow and deep, it was only a moment before she did exactly as he'd said, and told him not to be so careful.

And even in this it seemed they were in tune, because the moment she felt an incredible wave of sensation making her convulse around him, he groaned out her name and pulsed inside her. And there were no words she knew that could describe the wonder of it, of him.

Of them.

Chapter 32

Colby turned his head away from the clock on the nightstand, but it didn't change anything. It was still time.

"I know," Ali said quietly as she sat up in his bed. "We need to go."

The memories of the hour and a half they'd just spent exploring, discovering and, in his case, learning his body was capable of things he'd never realized, flooded him. The last thing he wanted to do was leave this unexpected bit of heaven.

To leave her.

He didn't dare watch her get up and start to dress. Just looking at her, at those curves, the soft, sleek skin, that glorious fall of red hair that he now knew was completely natural, made him ache all over again.

"I wish…" It was all he could say.

"Me, too. But Grace will be home from school soon, and Cutter and I need to be there."

"I know."

With an obvious effort at cheer, Ali said, "I think I'll ask Liz if she can go with me to pick up Ziggy at Laney's shop."

"Grace would like that."

He tried to put some enthusiasm in his voice but failed. Right now he wanted nothing more than to spend the rest of the day and all of tonight right here in his bed with her. And a whole lot of the nights after that.

But instead he was facing a yawning, empty hole.

"You sound…" Her words trailed off, but he knew what she meant.

"Yeah. Can't wait to get back to where you have to do everything, or Foxworth does. While I sit around and do nothing."

"Nothing but stay out of the mother's way, for Grace's sake."

He let out an exasperated breath. "I know."

"And I know it's totally unlike you to be a bystander when something critical is happening, and probably close to impossible when Grace is involved. But you've got one of the biggest forces around backing you up now, precisely so that you don't have to fight this battle alone."

He stared at her for a long, silent moment. Then, softly, as softly as he had whispered her name when he had been buried to the hilt inside her, he said, "With you on my side, I can fight anything. Even her."

She gave him a smile that made him want to pull her right back down on these sheets and start over. But he knew she was right, they had to get moving. His girl would be home soon.

They hastened through a process that went surprisingly well, as if they'd already learned how to coordinate. He gathered up what he'd actually wanted to stop here for—he'd never expected it to end up like this, never even hoped—and looked over at her. She glanced at the book in his hand, the one he'd been in the middle of when all this started, and the copies of legal papers Quinn had advised him to bring so they could turn them over to Gavin.

"Do me a favor?" she asked, her gaze locking on his now.

He wanted to say "Anything," and would have meant it, but he couldn't seem to get even the single word out. So he just waited.

"Grab that box of condoms, too."

She was out the door and headed back to her car, leaving him standing there barely able to breathe.

He was still processing as they headed back to Foxworth. His brain seemed to be careening in a dozen directions at once. Trying to analyze the implications of her wanting those condoms available. That there would be hours while Grace was in school when they could be together. That she would have to come to him, which made him nervous and oddly revved up at the same time. And which would also require explaining to the Foxworths, should they happen to walk in on them in his generously loaned living quarters.

He was still working on that last one when they arrived. The Foxworths' SUV was parked in its usual spot, making Colby remember the note Ali had left for them. Somebody's brain was working, at least. Cutter raced out the door to meet them—he still boggled a bit at the trust they gave that dog—before they were even fully parked.

Oddly, the dog skidded to a halt about a yard away from them instead of romping up demanding the usual pets and scratching behind his right ear. He stood looking at them, with his head tilted as if questioningly. As if he somehow knew or sensed something had…changed.

Okay, now you're buying into that alien-in-a-dog-suit thing Liam talked about, Kendrick.

And then Cutter covered those last few feet at a trot, head and ears up, tail wagging. As if whatever had made him stop in the first place had now met with his approval.

"That dog," Colby muttered.

Hayley wasn't far behind her dog. When she reached them Cutter had turned to face her, but sat down between him and Ali. His tail was wagging again, vigorously, and he had what Colby had to call a grin on his face.

Hayley stopped almost where Cutter had, and studied them for a moment almost as the clever animal had.

"Well, well," she said quietly. She shifted her gaze to her dog. "Another win, huh?"

Cutter let out a soft woof that sounded almost self-satisfied. And Colby was thrown back to that day when Hayley had explained about Cutter's most unexpected gift, that of simply knowing when two people belonged together. And when his gaze met Hayley's steady one, he knew she'd had the same thought. He rarely blushed, but he could feel his ears getting warm, and was very glad he'd stuffed that box of condoms deep inside his jacket pocket.

"Told ya," she said with a grin. Thankfully, before he had to try and explain that to Ali, Hayley went on. "Nice selection," she said, looking at the plants and the small tree in the back of Ali's car. "I gather the greenhouse install went well?"

"Perfectly," Ali answered before he could shrug and say his usual "Okay."

"Excellent," Hayley said, then glanced at her watch. Before she could speak, Ali responded to the action.

"I know. I need to get moving if we're going to be there by the time Grace gets home."

Colby felt a jab of disquiet. He knew she had to go, but he didn't want to let her leave without kissing her one more time. It felt awkward, here in front of Hayley. But then Cutter's mom laughed.

"Would it help if I said it would be no surprise to any of us that you want to kiss her goodbye?"

"Goodbye...for now," he amended, his voice more than a little rough.

Then he did kiss her, and thought that if the Foxworths hadn't been here, he would have wanted to carry her inside to resume their earlier joyous activity. And as he watched her drive away, with Cutter now secured into the front passenger seat, the only one not full of plant life, he marveled at how things had changed.

He'd assumed he would forever have to fight alone for Grace. He'd assumed someday he might lose that fight, and thus lose his precious girl. He'd assumed he would never again risk getting close to a woman, certainly never let her in to batter his heart.

But now he had the thought that life seemed determined to turn everything he'd always assumed on its head.

Ali had just slid the tree off the dolly in its selected spot when Cutter, who had been sitting and watching all the plant arranging with apparent interest—more than she would have expected from a dog, anyway—suddenly leaped to his feet, spun and headed for the door.

That she had almost expected. Because when Grace and the mother had arrived home about twenty minutes ago, she'd heard the girl's wailing "I hate you!" even from inside the greenhouse. It made her stomach knot, because her first instinct was to run to the girl and comfort her, but she knew she couldn't. She had to play this as if she didn't know a thing.

And she had to let Cutter do his job. Which included responding to the whistle she couldn't hear.

But that didn't mean she couldn't watch. And she did as the dog ran over to the back of the big house next door. Normally Grace would appear on the back porch, ready with a note to place in the tiny canister on the dog's collar. But this time there was no trace of the girl.

Cutter sat, waiting, for a minute or two. His head tilted, as if he were trying to figure out why she wasn't there. Then he moved back along the side of the house, stopping, to her surprise, at the window to Grace's bedroom. The same window Colby had broken that day, which seemed so much longer ago than just three weeks. The window where Grace now appeared, although she was looking back over her shoulder.

They'd warned her that the new cameras would show if she tried to open or climb out that window, warned her that everything on that side of the house was being watched, yet she seemed to be trying to slide the sash-style window up. But she stopped, turned and vanished back into the room, and Ali let out a breath of relief.

Then Ali saw something else. Something small and white falling to the ground. Something Grace had slid through the tiny gap she'd made at the window sill. Cutter was on it immediately, picking it up with his teeth. Then he spun on his hindquarters and raced back toward her. She stepped outside the greenhouse and shut the door behind her, thinking rapidly.

She tried to picture what that would look like on those cameras. She hoped it would seem the dog had come over to play, but when he got no response had given up and left. Would the thing the dog had seized be recognizable? Would it even occur to Liz or anyone else who saw the video that the dog could be this clever?

She had no more time to dwell on those questions because Cutter was there, offering the carefully folded note delicately.

She won't let me be with Daddy on Saturday and I can't come see you anymore at all. She thinks you're telling me bad things. I can't even play with Cutter or Ziggy. Tell Daddy I'm going to run away, I can't be with her anymore.

The knot in Ali's stomach tightened even more, making her faintly nauseous. Did the woman really think Colby would just take this lying down? Did she know so little of how much he loved his daughter? Of how far he would go for her?

Well, you're about to learn, mommy dearest.

She made herself walk back into her house at a normal pace although she badly wanted to run. Once inside and out of sight from next door she did run, to the counter where the Foxworth phone was. And this time she hit the red button.

Chapter 33

"You don't seem surprised," Quinn said.

Colby grimaced as he stopped pacing the Foxworth headquarters. "I'm not. I've been expecting this."

Hayley tilted her head slightly as she looked at him with that intensity he'd come to expect from the woman. The intensity that meant she was hearing much more than his actual words. Then she looked at Ali, who was sitting almost huddled in on herself, hugging Ziggy close as if the pup could ease the pain. As if she were hurting as much as he was.

"You answered her?" Hayley asked.

Ali nodded. Managed a small smile and a nod toward Cutter. "That dog of yours… I wrote that I was calling right away—I figured she would know who—folded it up and gave it to him. Not in the note holder, since Grace couldn't get to it without getting into more trouble. And darned if he didn't run over there, plop it on the window sill and nudge it with his nose until it caught in that tiny sliver of an opening she left, right where he picked up her note."

Colby had no words for the amount of amazement and gratitude he felt for this animal, so settled for a stoke of the dark fur on his head. And felt yet again that odd, calming sensation, as if somehow things would work out.

Ali let out a long breath before going on. "I thought I'd best stay out of sight, so I just watched on our monitors. It was maybe five minutes before she came back to the window and found it. Once I knew she had it, I headed here."

Hayley nodded, then she and Quinn walked over into the office area, and started to make calls. That was one thing he'd learned about the Foxworths, they didn't waste any time when the ball needed to roll.

Ali shifted her gaze from Hayley back to him. "You've been expecting this? That she'd clamp down like this?"

He nodded. "Ever since the day you hugged her outside, in the clear."

She drew back, her eyes widening. "You think she saw me do that?" He nodded. "And that…that's all it took?"

"For her to be wary of you, and of the influence you have with Grace, yes." He grimaced again. "No one, but no one, owns her child except her."

"'Owns'?"

"That's how she thinks of her. A helpful possession. Something to make her seem more human to the people she wants to manipulate. Same reason she allowed the dogs." For a moment Ali just stared up at him, her expression pained, as if she were feeling queasy. He shrugged one shoulder as he shook his head. "I can't explain her. Any more than I can explain how I was so stupid for so long."

"I should have thought," Ali said, her voice even more troubled now. "We always wait until we're past the trees to pick up Ziggy and start to head here fast. I should have thought first, shouldn't have hugged her out where she could see."

Colby sat down on the edge of the big coffee table directly opposite Ali. He took her hands in his, squeezed them. "You couldn't have known. You're sane, normal, your mind could never work like hers does. Thank goodness."

She managed a slight smile. She looked at their clasped hands. Then, with a tiny gasp, her gaze shot back to his face. "You don't think she knows, do you? About…us?"

Now, that hadn't occurred to him. He thought about it, trying to see from all angles, then said with some certainty, "I don't see how she could. Not already." She looked nervously over at the Foxworths, and his mouth quirked. "Oh, they know."

Ali drew back slightly. "What?"

"They've been expecting...what happened." She blushed. And he kind of liked it. "Remember what they said about Cutter's matchmaking?"

She blinked. "That was a joke, wasn't it? Or anthropomorphism?"

He shrugged. "I don't know. But Hayley insists he knows when people...should be together. And does what he has to do to make it happen."

"I know they say he brought them together, but..."

"And Liam and his wife. Teague and Laney. Even Gavin de Marco and his wife. Who is, by the way, your local librarian."

Her eyes widened. "Katie? I met her when I went in there right after I moved in, when I needed an internet connection and mine wasn't hooked up at home yet. She's married to Gavin de Marco?"

He nodded. "Hayley said his most extreme case was that sniper I told you about. He tried to walk away and Cutter literally put him on the floor. Now he's about to marry Quinn's sister. And that's just the Foxworth part of the list, apparently. All of it thanks to this guy," he said, reaching out to give Cutter a scratch behind the ears.

When he looked back up at her, she was staring at him, still wide-eyed. More than this amusing but silly idea warranted. Then her eyes darted away quickly, as if she felt...caught? Embarrassed? Simply upset?

The Foxworths came back to join them in front of the fire, interrupting his rather crazed string of questions.

"Let's get the dogs outside for a bit," Hayley said. "We have some planning to do. Cutter, outside?"

Ali set Ziggy down on the floor, and the moment the bigger dog headed for the back door, the black-and-white puppy scrambled after him, as if he remembered it led out into that expansive meadow.

"We need to know," Quinn said to Colby in a businesslike tone as the door closed behind the dogs, "that you're still up for going full bore on this."

"I won't let her steal Grace out of my life, if that's what you mean. No matter what it takes."

"You trust us to get it done?" Hayley asked. "Even if it means you may have to pretend a bit?"

He flicked a glance to the woman in front of him. "I trust you and Ali, yes."

Ali's head came up, and she was smiling now. And he had the thought that he would give a great deal to see that smile often, and for a very long time. But then he made himself focus.

Quinn nodded. "All right. We're going back to our old friend Sun Tzu, then. When in conflict, don't rely mainly on physical and material power, but on mental power."

Colby drew back, his brow furrowing. "Mental power?"

"They're not used to having people stand up to them, especially people they feel beneath them. So you convince her you won't…before you do."

"So…she'll be surprised. Off-balance maybe."

"Yes. You'll have to judge carefully, you can't roll over too easily or she'll be suspicious. But at the same time let her think she's won, that there's nothing you can do."

Colby dug back into the memories of those days when his father had read the philosopher strategist to him. "When we are able to attack, we must seem unable…"

"Exactly."

He nodded slowly, but with a wince. As if she'd read his mind, Ali said softly, "What about Grace? She'll think he's giving up, too."

His jaw tightened at hearing it put into words. Just the idea of his girl thinking he wasn't going to fight for her, that she wasn't worth everything to him, up to and including dying for her, made him even more determined.

"You still have your three hours tomorrow, right?" Hayley asked.

"Unless she tries to yank that, too," Colby said grimly.

"Then we need to decide if we're going to tell her anything about the plan," Quinn said.

"I think we have to tell her something," Ali said. "We can't just let her think Colby's given up on her. She already said she'd run away, and I think that might tip her over the edge."

She already knew his girl so well. Much better than the mother did. "Ali's right."

"That's putting a lot of weight on a seven-year-old," Quinn said, sounding wary.

"But a very smart, very special seven-year-old," Ali said firmly.

"All right," Hayley said, briskly now. "But we have to keep it to a minimum. The less she knows, the less she can give away under pressure."

"I'd say we should meet up here," Quinn said, "but if she's followed you on these visitation days before, she might be triggered enough to do it again now. We've been lucky so far, but..."

Colby nodded. "You're right. If she's edgy enough about Ali to tell Grace she can't even play with a couple of dogs next door, she's on guard and will be watching closely."

"So you'll need to take her someplace open, public, where people go," Quinn said. "She still hasn't seen Teague, or me, so we can be in the area without raising suspicion."

"I'm glad you didn't say without attracting attention," Hayley said to her husband, with a glance full of a very pointed kind of heat.

Colby might not be the most tuned in to nuances, but even

he didn't miss the twitch at the corner of the imposing former Army Ranger's mouth or the heat that flared in his gaze. Colby risked a glance at Ali, who had one of the sweetest smiles he'd ever seen on her face as she watched the couple. He couldn't blame her, they fairly reeked of "this is forever."

And suddenly, like a misguided hammer blow, it hit him. Why she'd looked so odd when he'd told her about Cutter's track record in the matchmaking department.

Every couple he'd mentioned had gotten married or was about to. Did she think he was implying that the same thing would happen with them? Was that what had had her so rattled?

The images that thought paraded through his mind were breath-stealing. And unexpected. He'd never really thought about getting married again, had thought himself a charter member of the "once burned, forever shy" group.

But this was Ali. And Ali was different. Special. Real. True.

He could have gone on for ages with all the things she was. And somewhere down deep he knew that he was as right about her as he'd been wrong about Liz.

And what better to build a life on?

Chapter 34

Ali thought she'd never seen a couple so in tune, so well matched. She and Josh had been great together, but they'd never had this sort of communication-without-words thing.

"—decide where you're going to take her," Hayley was saying, making Ali tune back in. "Someplace public, but not crowded, so you can talk without being overheard."

"And you'll have to convince her how crucial it is that this is kept secret," Quinn added. "She's been good so far, but this is the crunch. You'll have to tell her in a way she won't forget."

"The lighthouse," Ali said suddenly. They all looked at her. "She's talked about it, that it's so close but she's never seen it."

"I... She never said she wanted to," Colby said.

"I think when she's with you, she doesn't care about anything else," she said, trying to explain the idea that had hit her. "But if you take her there, she'll remember because it's the first time for her, and you can tie it to what you're telling her. That it's...it's the light in the darkness, and like it, you'll always be there for her."

They were all staring at her now. Surprisingly, it was Quinn who shifted his gaze from her to Colby, gave him a smile and said, "You're a lucky man, Colby Kendrick. Finally."

Colby looked at her, then answered simply, "Yes."

Ali felt a kick in her pulse. Maybe he had meant it, when he'd linked them to all of Cutter's apparent successes. Heaven knew she'd seen enough of the dog's uncanny cleverness to at least consider the possibility that it was true. All of it. The idea made her very hesitant to leave now, but she knew she needed to be home for Grace's sake.

When she got back home, Cutter immediately looked over to the big house, as if he knew it was out of the ordinary for them to have left while Grace was at home. There was no sign of the child now, through the window or anywhere else. And the dog didn't indicate he'd been called.

After a moment he made what she'd come to think of as his rounds, checking every bit of her house. He didn't react to anything, so she felt fairly safe, although she did the camera check that had become routine. Then she turned on her flat-screen to her own monitors, so she could watch Grace's room without getting caught staring out her window. Cutter went over to nose Ziggy, who had plopped on his bed, clearly tuckered out from the romp in the Foxworth meadow.

They'd discussed her possibly putting that red square of paper in the window, to indicate Grace needed to come over and play, but decided it was too risky until Colby had talked to her. They didn't want Liz to crack down even more, and maybe try and stop Colby from having his paltry three hours with her tomorrow. It would be his last chance before they started to move. Grace had to be clear on what was happening, on what to do, and more importantly what not to do. Ali had a lot of faith in the child, but she was still a child.

But the worst part of it was that she couldn't even be around. It made sense, if Liz or someone she'd assigned was spying on them, it could blow up everything if she was seen with them. But that didn't mean she liked it. She already felt so much a part of this, and had even before that afternoon when she'd discovered that hot, female part of her wasn't nearly as dead as she'd thought it was.

That afternoon when Colby Kendrick had shown her she could still fly.

But now she was relegated to pacing the floor, feeling worse than helpless, feeling useless.

She stopped mid-step when a memory hit her. Colby's words rang in her mind, and she knew she was truly understanding them for the first time.

Can't wait to get back to where you have to do everything, or Foxworth does. While I sit around and do nothing.

No wonder he was so on edge. It was driving her mad, she could only imagine how it made him feel to just stand by.

It also led to a sleepless night for her. Which in a way turned out to be a good thing, because she was awake when her phone chimed an incoming text. She knew who it was, who it had to be.

Going crazy. I wish you were here or I was there.

She thought of all the possible platitudes she could send back, that it would be all right, that he just had to hang on, they were on the edge of making their move.

In the end she went with the simple truth.

Ditto.

There was a long pause, as if he were thinking as hard as she had been. And in the end he, as she had, went the simple route.

This weekend?

She'd wondered about that. If Liz and Grace were both going to be gone, to whatever event Liz was using as an excuse to take Colby's full day with her away from him, then maybe they could...revisit. Discover if it really was as explosive as she remembered.

Please.

She'd typed and sent it before she thought much about it. It was time, she decided, to go with the truth. She felt a qualm after the "message sent" notification appeared, but then Cutter was there, nudging her hand. She automatically reached out to pet him, and at that first stroke of his head it was there again, that sense of calm, that reassurance.

Yes, it was time for the truth. She was where she never thought she'd be again. Looking at a future suddenly very different from the one she'd had just a few weeks ago.

She walked over and picked up Ziggy, needing to cuddle the little ball of fluff. He squirmed a little, but once she sat back down and he realized he was safe in her arms, he settled and went happily back to snoozing. And with her puppy on her lap and Cutter at her feet, she felt comforted.

But this weekend, with Colby, she would feel whole again. And that, she had never expected. That if he meant what he'd said, that wholeness would include the sweetest, smartest child she'd ever met, who would be the frosting on the cinnamon roll her life seemed like it could become.

Chapter 35

"Can we come back here, and bring Ali and Ziggy and Cutter?"

Just hearing her link them all reached a place in Colby's heart he'd only recently discovered existed.

The day Ali welcomed you, made you feel whole again.

He rested a hand on his girl's shoulder, trying not to think of how not so long ago he could only have reached the top of her head without bending over. She was growing up so fast, and these short interludes with her were just not enough. Which steeled his resolve to fight.

Helps that you have the best cavalry around at your back now.

He smiled at the thought, and at the certainty that Ali was included in that force to be reckoned with.

No sooner did the thought form than he heard Quinn's voice through the earbud in his left ear.

"Looks all clear. The two subjects out on the point are from the US Lighthouse Society, and the family that are out on the beach arrived in a car with Idaho plates."

He knew the man had them in sight, so he just gave a thumbs-up to indicate he'd heard.

"Can we, Daddy?" Grace drew him back to her initial question.

"I hope so," he answered. "And soon."

That made her smile. Then her brows rose sharply. "Oh! I almost forgot!"

She reached into her jacket pocket and pulled out what looked like a couple of folded pages torn from a notebook. It looked rather like that story he'd found, about the little girl and the monster.

"This is for Ali. I promised it to her, for her birthday. She said she didn't care if it was late, since her birthday was last Sunday." Grace expression shifted to a sad frown. "You have to give it to her, since I'm not allowed to see her anymore. And we're leaving in the morning anyway, to go over there. Again."

She waved her hand in the general direction of the city. He took the folded sheets, tamping down his anger at Liz's latest tactic. "I guess I shouldn't look at it, if it's hers, huh?"

"You can," Grace said, "if it's okay with her. But she should see it first, 'cuz it's her present."

He tucked the pages carefully into his own jacket pocket. "I'll see she gets it. But right now, Gracie-girl, we need to talk. Very seriously."

His girl's blue eyes, so like his own, looked up at him. "Is this about…fighting her?"

"Yeah. Yeah, it is."

"We better sit down," she said wisely, and looked around. One of the north-facing benches was empty, and she scampered that way. Colby ran to keep up, loath to have her anywhere outside of arm's reach, as if Liz could somehow swoop down and grab her.

Like the vulture she is.

Sending up a silent apology to the birds that were a necessary part of the system, he sat down beside his daughter. He'd thought a lot about how he was going to approach this, what he was going to say. He knew his girl, knew how she thought, even if she sometimes almost scared him with how smart she was.

"How would you feel if I gave up fighting for you?"

Grace stared at him for a long moment. He could almost hear her brain racing, processing. Then, finally she shook her head. "You wouldn't. You just wouldn't."

He couldn't help the sudden stinging of his eyes, and the tight, grateful smile that tugged at his lips. He blinked rapidly a few times, put his arm around his precious child and pulled her close.

"No. No, I wouldn't. And I won't. Ever." Remembering Ali's words, he pointed to the tall light behind them. "I will always be there for you, just like that lighthouse is there for the ships going by."

His girl looked at the solid, steady fixture, and smiled. "I know you will."

"But honey, I'm going to have to pretend that I'm giving up. Give up fighting at all over her taking tomorrow away from us. And more, I'm going to have to tell her that I'm not going to fight her anymore at all. No more arguing with her when I pick you up or bring you back."

Grace looked up at him, her brow furrowed. "Why?"

"So she'll think she's won."

"Why?" she repeated.

Although it wouldn't surprise him if she could totally grasp Sun Tzu, he went for a more modern explanation.

"Because if she thinks she's won, maybe she won't be so… careful. Maybe she'll get careless, overconfident." His daughter's brow furrowed again as she processed the words. He shifted to something he knew she'd understand. "I know she'll get smug, think she's better than anybody else, that nobody would dare challenge her."

Grace made a sour face. "She already thinks that."

God, he loved his girl. "I know. But now we're going to use it against her. Lull her, then come up from behind and shock her. But part of that is I have to act like she's won. Like I gave up."

Again he could almost hear that clever brain churning away. "How should I act?"

"How do you think you'd react...if it were true?"

She shook her head. "I wouldn't believe it."

"Then act that way. Like you don't believe it."

Grace went very still for a long, silent moment. Then she looked up at him, with an expression he could only describe as mischievous on her face. "Can I call her a liar?"

Despite his tension, Colby nearly laughed at her glee. "I don't think so, honey. That might tip her over the edge, and she might really lose it. Lose her temper, I mean. She might even try to hit you or something."

Grace shrugged. "She's done it before. It wasn't so bad."

Colby went rigidly still, all humor vanished. In his ear he thought he heard someone swear. "She what?"

"Well, she slapped me once, when I told her I wanted to go live with you. It hurt, but only for a little while."

"You never told me that."

"It was while you were gone, working up on that island."

His jaw tightened. Last year he'd been on a crew repairing storm damage on an emergency clinic on one of the San Juan islands north of here. He'd hesitated about being gone that long; it had been a monthlong job. But it was the only medical clinic on the island, so it had needed doing, and the money had been good and steady.

"You should have told me," he said, a little tightly.

Grace looked up at him, and for one of the few times in her stubborn life he saw actual fear there. "I was afraid you'd get really mad at her, maybe do something... She always talks about that, that someday you'll do something stupid and she can keep you away from me forever."

He pulled her into his arms, hugging his beloved girl tight. "You might have been right, if I'd known she dared to hurt you."

Then he pulled back enough to look into her eyes again. "Why did you tell me now?"

"Because now you're going to fight her anyway," she said simply.

He gave a wondering shake of his head. "What am I going to do when you're the genius out there saving the world and I'm just your dumb ol' dad?"

"I don't wanna save the world," she said, hugging him back rather fiercely. "I just want us."

"So do I, Gracie."

"Then so be it," came Quinn's determined voice in his ear.

"Amen," Colby muttered.

But hope was burgeoning, because he had the feeling that if it could be done, Foxworth could do it.

Chapter 36

Ali blinked rapidly, but it wasn't enough to stop the tears. One trickled down her cheek, then another, until she had to swipe at them before they fell onto the paper she was holding.

It was a simple story, in a child's simple hand.

It was also simply beautiful.

"Have you read it?" she asked Colby, not even caring that the powerful emotion she was feeling had tightened her throat and made her words a little shaky.

He put the mug of coffee he'd poured for her down on the counter in his kitchen, then sat on the stool next to her. She'd watched Liz and Grace leave early this morning, and confirmed that Irene was still in the house. That had started Foxworth moving. Quinn and Teague would be tracking them on the other side, keeping in touch, while Colby prepared for the engineered meeting on Monday. He had an appointment with Gavin de Marco tomorrow morning to go over the plan, but had asked her if she would come here today so he could give her Grace's gift.

"No," he answered now. "She said you had to read it first, since it's your present." He seemed to hesitate before adding, "After that, it's up to you."

"You should read it. I know how hard that was on you yesterday—this will make you feel better."

He grimaced. "You mean telling her I give up, I can't fight her alone anymore?"

"Yes. Even if it isn't true, it had to sting."

"Slash, more like," he muttered. But then he gave her a sideways look and an almost smile. "But it really isn't true, is it?"

She put everything she had into the smile she gave him then. "No, it's not. And boy, is she going to be surprised."

She got a much better smile back then, and it warmed her to the bones. She held out the story his little girl had written, a fairy tale of sorts, about a family who had come together in a different sort of way. A handsome prince who had fought bravely, a princess who had had sad times, and a little girl who wished more than anything for them to be a family. And a very smart dog who seemed to think they already were.

And they needed a dog of their own so a little black-and-white puppy came to live with them, and they were all happy forever after, and the evil queen went away because she didn't like being around people who were happy.

She remembered that ending word for word. She thought she always would. The assessment of the mother was razor-sharp, and Ali thought anyone who ever underestimated Grace Kendrick would soon learn the size of their mistake. But more important to her was the clear, simple certainty that the prince and princess and little girl would be happy, because they'd be together.

Forever after.

She watched him read it, saw his expressions change as he did, from a smile simply because it was from his precious girl, to his eyes widening as he realized who she had cast in the parts of her little story, to quickened breathing as he neared the end. And she saw his eyes were glistening in a reaction just like her own.

For a minute, maybe two, he just sat there staring at the end of the story. Then he spoke, without looking at her, but sounding as if his throat was as tight as hers had been.

"You ever read a fairy tale and wish more than anything that it was true?"

Ali's heart leaped with joy at his reaction. "Yes," she said softly. "Just now."

He looked at her then. "You mean it?"

"I mean it."

Colby looked like a man who had opened a door and found paradise. And also as if he couldn't quite believe it. And it made her love him all the more.

Her heart took another little leap as she acknowledged the truth. If you'd asked her a month ago she would have said she didn't think she'd ever love again, not the way she had loved Josh. Now...now she knew better. And somewhere deep down she knew that Josh would approve of her choice. They would have been friends, these two, had they ever had the chance.

Colby swallowed hard. "I mean it, too. I know this is...a crazy way to have met, and a crazy mess we're in, but...when things calm down..."

"After you win, you mean?"

A flicker of his old fear flashed in his eyes. "What if I don't?"

She let out an intentionally snorting bit of laughter. "Foxworth took down an evil governor and a crooked senator. Do you really think they're going to let the likes of *the mother* beat them?"

It worked. The fear vanished, and it was the Colby who knew he had a small but very effective army at his back who was smiling at her now.

"Then...can we try and make this—" he held up Grace's story "—come true."

"We'll do more than try. We'll plan out life after you've won," she said. "But for now...could we take advantage of being actually alone together?"

His smile became the one that she remembered, from the afternoon spent in his bed. An afternoon she wished to repeat.

And even as she thought it, he swept her up in his arms and proceeded to make the wish come true.

Colby settled the earpiece in his ear, more for something to do than because it needed it. It was in his right ear, facing away from the rest of the big dining area that was rapidly filling up, probably with a lot of government types given the county seat was just a couple of blocks away.

He was a little peeved at himself, because just the thought of being in the same room with Liz was bugging him more than sitting across a small table from a world-famous attorney. As if he'd read his mind—and given his courtroom abilities, Colby wouldn't be at all surprised if he could—Gavin de Marco reminded him of their rehearsal.

"You're happy. You know you're going to win. And when you spot her across the room—after she spots you—you're going to…?"

"Laugh," he said.

"Believably," de Marco suggested rather wryly. "Think of Grace, and being where you should be in her life." The man lifted a dark brow. "Or think of Ali. I gather that should put a smile on your face."

Not for the first time since Ali had come into his life, Colby was glad he wasn't a blusher. "Who told you that?"

"Hayley told me early on that Cutter had decided."

He hesitated, then asked, "He really got you and your wife together?"

"He did. And believe me, it wasn't easy. I was stubborn. My logical, fact-based brain did not want to even play that game with him, but he made it impossible not to. Thank goodness. Katie's the best thing that ever has or ever will happen to me." He tilted his head slightly, assessingly, before adding, "Just as Ali will be for you, I think."

He remembered last night, and the long, sweet hours they'd spent together. And smiled. "I love her."

De Marco smiled. "That's obvious."

"If you two are done, the play is about to begin."

Quinn's voice in his ear startled Colby, and considering what they had just been saying, he could only hope they hadn't been listening all along on the Foxworth end. Especially when he knew since Grace was in school Ali was there with them, no doubt hearing everything. But then, he'd already told her those words last night as he'd held her close, finally letting himself believe.

Good, because I love you, too. I think I have ever since I realized everything Grace says about you is true.

The joy ran deep, and he couldn't help smiling.

"Now, that's the happy Liz needs to see," de Marco said. Then, for the sake of the earpiece that was in his left ear so neither of them would be visible from what would be Liz's table, he said, "Ready when you are, Quinn."

"No changes," Quinn said. "She's with the Community Development guy we researched."

Colby remembered how they'd been happy to discover this was the first public engagement of the two, because it implied she was just beginning to try and reel the guy in. She probably needed some rules bent, and would offer to make it worth his while to bend them.

"We're on," came Teague's voice a moment later, from where he was stationed outside the door, wearing something Liz would be sure to overlook, a waiter's outfit. "They're on their way in."

"Rick is ready, too," Hayley said.

She was back in the restaurant's office with Rick Giles, the manager who was readying to step on stage. Colby had met him briefly, when they'd first arrived. The man was middle-aged, a bit round, and looked slightly nervous as he fiddled with the mic Foxworth had rigged him with, attached invisibly to the back of his name tag. They would be able to hear the entire exchange at the table, for as long as the man could manage to be there.

Oddly, his nerves had calmed Colby a little. This man, who didn't know him at all, was going to play a crucial role in his fight for Grace. And when that man turned to him and said, "Foxworth saved my life, and my son's. I'm honored to help them do the same for you," Colby had never felt more humbled.

Except when he'd first held baby Grace.

And last night, when Ali had said she loved him.

He'd spent so long afraid to hope. But now here it was, bubbling up inside him like the untouched glass of champagne on the table before him.

"We're celebrating, remember?" de Marco had said when he ordered it. "We've found what we need to take her down, and we're delighted."

Colby had stared at the face he'd seen in the news so many times. "How much of what you do is acting?"

De Marco had burst out laughing. "Oh, so much," he'd said.

And then they were there. Liz strode in as usual, dressed to the nines, head high, phone at her ear.

"You said she always does that, the phone thing?" de Marco asked.

Colby nodded. "Half the time, probably more, it's not even real, she's not talking to anyone."

"But she wants it to seem like she's so in demand that her guest should be grateful that she's allotted him some of her precious time."

He smothered a laugh. "You sure you haven't dealt with her before?"

"Yes. But I've dealt with her sort dozens of times. They're half the reason I went to work for Foxworth."

They stayed quiet after that, according to the plan. The food on his plate would have been appealing at any other time, under any other circumstances, but right now his gut was churning enough that putting anything in it seemed like a bad idea. But he tried not to let it show, tried to present the demeanor of a man who had found a solution to the biggest problem in his life, thanks to the man sitting across from him.

That it was possibly true was what got him through the next few minutes. And then it began, when he saw Mr. Giles stride across the dining area to greet his guests, doing an excellent job of appearing overjoyed that someone on the level of Elizabeth Hollen would grace his humble establishment.

And then he heard that painfully familiar voice in his ear. "Mr. Harkness here recommended it for our meeting. I'm glad to see he was right about the management appreciating the level of clientele."

Colby happened to be looking at de Marco at that moment, and seeing him roll his eyes as if she'd fulfilled his every negative expectation almost made him laugh. But it wasn't time yet, so he stifled it.

"I'm having quite a day here in my little restaurant," Mr. Giles said, sounding delighted. "First a world-famous attorney, and now you."

"World-famous?" Liz didn't snort, but her voice had taken on that tone Colby knew meant she would be the one to decide who was well known enough to rate that description.

"Absolutely," the manager gushed. "I mean, Gavin de Marco? Here, in my little place?"

Colby couldn't stop himself from risking a glance, figuring she'd be fixated on the man who'd just done that huge name drop. For no doubt one of the few times ever in her life, Liz looked taken aback. "Gavin de Marco? *The* Gavin de Marco? Here?"

"Yes," Giles said with just the right amount of pride. "He brought a client in to celebrate, something about having found exactly what they needed for their upcoming court action."

"I don't envy whoever they're suing," said the county official. "I mean, the guy took down our sitting governor."

Colby heard Quinn's chuckle through the earpiece. "Couldn't have written a better line for him than that."

"And rightfully so," Giles said enthusiastically. "But I agree, I don't envy his opponent, no matter who it is. He's lost what, one case in his entire career? And then won it in the end on appeal."

"Wonder what this one's about?" the official said.

Colby blinked as the man asked for the info Giles had been about to drop. It was hard not to look over there, but that wasn't the plan. "You sure you didn't arrange this guy, too?" he whispered. De Marco laughed.

The manager handled the shift perfectly, sliding in what he'd been going to say anyway, just in a different form. "I heard him mention a child custody case that was turning into a criminal one. Sounds exciting, doesn't it? I bet it will be all over the news soon. I mean, Gavin de Marco, in the headlines again!"

"Great job, Rick," came Quinn's voice. "Seeds planted, feel free to fire the last shot and then disengage."

"Please, enjoy your meal," he said with all the charm of a host. "I need to go make sure Mr. de Marco and his client enjoyed theirs."

Then, as planned, he walked over toward their table, staying in Liz's line of sight, blocking her from seeing Colby, who was intentionally turned mostly away from their table anyway.

"Great job, Rick," de Marco echoed Quinn's words to the man. "And by the way, the crab melt was great, too. I have a feeling you'll be seeing some Foxworth folks here more often."

"I would be honored," Giles said with a bow.

Then, at de Marco's nod, he turned and walked away. And Colby, as planned, shifted in his chair to where he could be spotted from that table across the room. In the same moment, de Marco lifted his glass of champagne. Colby did the same.

"A toast to victory," the lawyer said.

"I'll drink to that," Colby answered fervently, tipping his own glass to clink lightly on de Marco's.

"Now," Hayley's voice said in his ear, "would be the time for that laugh."

Think about how it will feel when she's beaten, and you did it. Think about the look on Grace's face when you tell her.

Ali's words echoed in his mind now. The pure delight on her face when she'd said it had made him laugh joyously then, and Hayley had immediately seized upon the sound of it as a weapon.

The memory of Ali saying it did it again now. And he let it out, not even trying to muffle it.

"That did it," de Marco said with satisfaction. "She looked, and I only wish you could have seen her face when she recognized you. Now drink that last bit down—happily—and let's decamp before she has a chance to get her bearings."

Smiling purposefully, he gave the famous face across from him a wondering look. "You're really enjoying this."

De Marco laughed. "I am."

He downed the last swallow and they both stood up. "I know it's tempting, but don't look," Hayley warned in his ear. "You'll get to see it shortly. Teague got some great video of her reaction. Ali is still dancing gleefully over it."

And that mental image alone was enough to enable Colby to stride out of the dining room, the famous lawyer at his side, looking as if he owned the world.

Chapter 37

"So," Quinn said as they leaned back on the couch after watching the video Teague had shot, "do you think we got to her?"

Ali watched Colby as he sat there, slowly shaking his head in wonder, staring at the now-blank screen. She had a feeling she knew just what had him so gobsmacked.

"Could we watch that moment when she spots Colby again?" she asked. "It just does my heart good."

Hayley laughed and rewound the video. The moment when Liz's eyes widened was wonderful, and the next instant when her jaw dropped, heedless of the fact that she was out in public, was even better.

But the best of all was the moment when fear flashed in her normally cold, gray eyes. That was absolutely priceless.

"As well you should be afraid," she murmured.

Colby heard her, because his head snapped around to look at her. "So... I'm not imagining that?"

She reached out and took his hand, squeezed it. "That scared look in her eyes? No, you are not. Isn't it wonderful?"

He laughed, then looked up toward the ceiling, biting his lower lip. He closed his eyes, and she wished she knew what was racing through his mind at that moment. When his eyes abruptly snapped open and he looked down, she saw that Ziggy was pawing at his leg, trying to climb up. But before the pup could do it, and even before Colby could reach down for him, Cutter was there.

He picked Ziggy up just like Quinn and Hayley had told them he had when he'd brought Ziggy to them, and plopped the wiggly bit of black-and-white fur in Colby's lap. Colby simultaneously patted Cutter and picked Ziggy up. He held the squirmy pup against his chest, and Ziggy reached up to swipe his chin with a pink tongue.

Even my puppy loves him.

For a moment she allowed herself to think beyond this crisis, to a time when things would settle and they could just be together. When this horrendous strain was behind him and Grace, and they could actually be happy. But then Quinn spoke, yanking her back to reality.

"We'll be watching her carefully. Teague's on her now. I suggest you remain here, Colby, so she can't corner you at your house. I have a feeling she's going to react rather strongly once she gets over the shock."

Colby nodded. Ali reluctantly glanced at her watch. Hayley noticed, and nodded.

"Yes," she said, "you need to be close by when Grace gets home from school, to make sure she doesn't take any heat from this."

She felt Colby stiffen, and reached over to grab his hand. "I won't let her hurt Grace. If I have to go kick down the door or make up a story and call the sheriff."

"We'll call them, if necessary," Quinn said. "We've already alerted Carly that things may be starting to move."

"Good," Colby said flatly. "Grace's safety comes before anything else."

"I'll come with you," Hayley said. "I think we can get away with another visit from your old friend."

"Thank you," Ali said, meaning it rather fiercely. She had

the feeling things might start happening fast, and if she couldn't have Colby at hand, Foxworth was the next best thing.

They only had a few minutes, so her goodbye with Colby was much shorter than she would have liked. But he blew all other thoughts out of her mind when, hugging her close, he whispered, "I can't wait until this is over and we can just be us together."

"All three of us," she whispered back. She felt a ripple go through him, and knew she'd found the right response. And she meant it with all her heart.

They made it to her place ten minutes before Grace usually got home. Irene was still at the house next door, which usually meant Liz herself was picking her up from school.

"I hope that's not a bad sign," she muttered.

"We won't assume," Hayley said. "She does pick her up frequently, and she was already out. But we won't assume it's nothing, either." She gave Ali a reassuring smile. "Now, show me this new greenhouse of yours. I've been thinking about one myself."

"I still can't quite believe he did it," Ali said with an almost embarrassed smile as she led Hayley to the newly installed—and filled—structure, Cutter at their heels.

"I can. Because I can see how he feels about you."

"Sometimes I can't believe it's even real," she admitted, not even bothered by the fact that Hayley clearly knew how close she and Colby had become.

"Then trust Cutter. He knows it is."

They walked around inside the small greenhouse, much warmer than the February chill outside, where her plants were already showing how much they liked it. It might be crystal clear and the sun might be bright enough to make you squint, but that didn't mean it was warm here in the Northwest. Sometimes February was one of the harshest months of all.

They'd gone back inside for some hot chocolate when Cutter alerted. He trotted over to the window and stood still, watching.

"Must be her car," Ali said. "I swear, he can tell even cars apart."

Hayley laughed as she went and turned on what Ali had taken to calling the spy cams, the ones that showed the house next door, including the driveway, at the edge of their broad visual field.

"I don't even question anymore," she said as the images popped to life on Ali's flat-screen.

And sure enough, a moment later when a car pulled into view, it was Liz's top-end luxury sedan. The garage door began to rise, and the car pulled straight into the garage. But not before Ali spotted the passenger. Definitely Grace, she could tell even though the child was slouched almost below the level of the windows of the vehicle.

"She didn't look happy," Hayley said.

Ali sighed. "She never does when the mother picks her up."

They watched until a light came on in Grace's room at the back of the house. Cutter finished making his rounds, interrupted by the arrival next door, then settled into the bed Ali had made for him from a soft throw. Ziggy, adorably, had begun to imitate his big companion, following him around the house as he checked every door and window, then plopped down beside him on the floor.

"You know, you could rent him out as a puppy trainer, along with all the zillion other things he's good at," Ali said.

"Now, there's a thought," Hayley said with a smile.

Ali watched the screen. "I wish she wasn't so careful about having the house checked for bugs or cams. I'd love to know what's going on in there right now."

"Agreed. We even thought about giving Grace something to record with, but the risk was too high that if her mother found it, she might hurt her."

Ali grimaced. "Even higher, now that we know she's hit her at least once," she said, remembering that moment when they'd been talking on the lighthouse bench. She'd felt a little uncomfortable, as if she was eavesdropping on something very personal, but it was all part of knowing what they had to know to rescue Grace.

And that particular bit of knowledge was well beyond infuriating, it was enraging.

Time passed and it was starting to seem like just another day next door when Cutter's head came up. He got to his feet and walked over to the window. Ali looked at the screen and waited, trusting the dog's incredible hearing. And about a minute later a car pulled into the driveway. It wasn't on a par with Liz's favored luxury model, but was the same make.

"A rideshare, maybe?" she suggested to Hayley. "We don't have much in the way of taxis over here."

"I'd agree, if the driver wasn't acting like that," Hayley said dryly, nodding at the screen.

Ali looked back at the man who'd gotten out from behind the wheel. Tall and burly, he looked around. Not at the house number as she would have expected if he wanted to be sure he was at the right address, but all around him, lingering long enough on her house to make her uncomfortable. Then he turned to look back the way he'd come, as if he were checking to see if anyone followed him.

"Security?" Ali asked.

"That would be my guess."

Ali grimaced. A Foxworth operative would likely know one when she saw one.

They couldn't tell who had come to the door, since they didn't step outside, but watched as the man went into the house. Quiet reigned again. Cutter was more restless, as if he'd somehow sensed the new arrival was…different. Or maybe she was just starting to believe the dog was as amazing as the Foxworths said he was. He'd certainly done nothing to disprove that. But finally he settled back into his old spot, and she went back to snuggling with Ziggy, who didn't have quite the calming effect petting Cutter did, but there was something about that soft fur and tiny body, and most of all the utter trust, that soothed her all the same.

Cutter suddenly scrambled to his feet. He raced to the back door and looked back at them, letting out an almost urgent bark. Hayley headed toward him while Ali grabbed up Ziggy to keep him from trying to follow. Playing together was one thing, but Cutter was obviously working now.

Hayley opened the door, but stayed inside. Cutter raced into the yard, leaped over the short fence in one scrambling bound, and headed for Grace. Hayley stayed at the door while Ali ran back to the screen, where she could see Cutter had already reached the window of Grace's room.

The window that was open.

She watched, with her heart pounding, as the child leaned out as Cutter reared up on his hind legs to reach her. Grace's hands went to his collar, and Ali guessed she was putting a message in the little canister.

The pounding in her chest became a wrench as Grace looked back over her shoulder every few seconds, as if she knew she was being pursued. Still the child took a moment to stroke Cutter's dark head, and even in the small image on the screen Ali could see her smile. So even at times like this—or maybe especially—the clever, protective dog could provide comfort.

And then Grace pulled back inside, slid the window closed and darted back into her room and out of sight of the camera's field. Cutter wheeled around and started back toward them at a dead run, head down and tail out straight as if he understood speed was of the essence. Which made Ali feel that painful twist in her chest again.

She spun around as fast as the dog had and hurried over to where Hayley was waiting, arriving in time to see him clear the fence again. Hayley murmured something soft and loving to the amazing animal as she opened the tiny container and pulled a tightly rolled piece of paper, larger than the previous ones had been.

Ali you have to help me!!! She pulled me out of class. Some stranger is here. She's packing stuff. She told me we're going away and not coming back. I asked her where and she said I didn't need to know. I asked her why and she wouldn't answer. I said what about Daddy, and she got really mad and said it's all his fault. Help!

"So she's going to run," Ali said.

"Or try to," Hayley said, with a hint of steel in her voice that calmed Ali a bit. She reached for the Foxworth phone. But before she even picked it up, the red light lit up and the urgent-sounding notification went off. Hayley hit the red button. Quinn's voice came through immediately.

"We think she's making a move."

"We know she is," Hayley countered, and relayed the contents of Grace's note. "What happened on your end?"

"Liam's been monitoring, and in touch with our contact over in Everett at the airport. He heard the pilot of the charter jet they use just filed a flight plan. Two passengers. And one of them is a child."

Chapter 38

"It was filed IFR," Quinn said.

Before he could ask, Colby heard Hayley explain it in her response.

"Instrument Flight Rules?" she asked. "But it's severe clear out."

Colby recognized the local term for this kind of day, when you could see from Mount Rainier to Canada. His brow furrowed as he studied the video feed from the cameras at Ali's house.

"Exactly," Quinn said. "Why not just Visual Flight Rules? So Liam kept digging. Turns out the only real weather anywhere close is some heavy clouds with potential snow later tonight hitting the Rockies, west of Denver."

Colby tensed and his gaze snapped back to Quinn. "Her family has an office in Denver, and a house in Beaver Creek. Near Vail."

Quinn looked at him. "Address of the house?"

Colby gave a disgusted shake of his head. "I don't know. I've never been there. Grace either. I only know about it because I overheard her father bragging about it to someone. About how big the house is, and what big wheels they are around there."

"Liam!" Quinn yelled toward the stairway.

"On it!" came a return yell from the second floor, reminding Colby all of this was going on live via those rather heavy-duty Foxworth phones.

Quinn looked back at Colby. "Her father bragged about it, but she never told you about it?"

"No."

He didn't even try to explain how typical that was, that once he'd refused to become part of their world, they shared nothing with him.

"So she has every reason to think you don't know anything about it?"

"Yeah, I—" Belatedly it hit him. "So it's the perfect place to hide Grace."

Quinn nodded. "Liam," he called out again, "you copy that part about her pulling Grace out of class?"

"Already called Ria," came the answer.

Quinn turned back to Colby. "Ria is his wife. She's also a local teacher, who knows several others who work at Grace's school. She's already reached out and they're checking for us."

Colby wondered if the Foxworth network had no end. Then Hayley's voice came over the speaker.

"Ali and I could go over there, see if we can find out anything."

"Put that on hold," Quinn said. "We don't know who that guy who arrived is yet."

Hayley sounded tense. "We need to be sure before we commit. If we guess wrong…"

"Maybe Grace could help." It was Ali, and Colby couldn't help the little jump of his pulse when he heard her voice.

"How?" Quinn asked.

"Maybe she could get a look at what her mother is packing. If she's taking heavy, winter-type clothes, or if she's overheard anything…"

"Excellent idea. If she and Cutter can pull it off."

They decided it was worth a try. Hayley had Ali write a

quick note, then sent Cutter off to deliver it. They watched on screen as the dog raced over to Grace's window. The child was there almost immediately, pushing the window open. Then she vanished, but was back in under three minutes, wrestling with Cutter's collar. So they had an answer much more quickly than they'd expected. And with more than they'd asked for.

Ali read it out loud for them all.

She got out her big pink puffer coat. She called somebody and said to get the house ready. And I heard that nasty guy say something about mountains. We're going now.

"It ends in a kind of scribble, like maybe she heard her mother coming and had to rush," Ali said.

"That's it, then," Quinn said. He looked at Colby. "I really would like to hire that girl of yours when she's a bit older."

Colby let out a sharp laugh. "I have a feeling we may all be working for her."

"Truer words," Quinn agreed.

"Quinn! They're leaving," Hayley said urgently. "Shall we try and stop them?"

Colby held his breath, hoping Quinn would say yes, but when he said no, he sadly understood.

"We need a plan in place first. And I think getting away will lull her, put her off guard."

Colby didn't like it, but he knew Quinn was right. They both turned as Liam came running down the stairs. He rattled off information at a rapid clip.

"Ria says she pulled Grace out indefinitely. Got the address, and pulled some info. Big place—figures—overlooking the golf course at the resort. My guy over at the airport says they're scheduled to take off in an hour. In this."

He handed Quinn a scrap of paper with something scribbled on it. Colby could just make out the word *Citation*.

"Fast. So we can't beat them in the air. Any idea if they're flying into Denver and then driving?" Quinn asked. "There's a county regional airport a lot closer, I think. With a nice long runway, because of the weather they have to deal with sometimes."

"He's checking," Liam said.

Quinn looked at Colby, who had to shake his head. "Depends. They've got a fancy limo there in Denver, but if she's in a hurry she might risk the short drive in a possibly grubby ride."

"But if you had to guess?"

Colby knew the "had to" part was true. This was Grace. "I'd say the luxury limo. She avoids us peons whenever possible."

"All right. Hayley, you get all that?"

"Copied. All of us?"

"I think so. We want max shock value."

"Good idea," Liam said. "I could—" He broke off as his phone chimed. He looked, sent a quick answer to a text, then looked at Quinn. "Denver."

Quinn gave Colby a nod for his accurate guess. "Excellent. That's at least a two-hour drive, maybe more this time of year."

"Cutter, I assume?" Hayley asked.

"Of course."

"Prepping now," she said, and Colby could almost hear her smiling as she ended the call on her end.

Quinn went to the office in the corner of the building, which Colby now knew was his. He was on the computer there in seconds, and was quickly reading the screen and tapping a thumb on the desk.

When he saw Colby in the doorway, he glanced up and said, "Figuring timing."

He went back to the screen.

"This model jet has a cruising speed of about three hundred twenty knots an hour." He glanced again at Colby. "Say three hundred seventy-five miles per hour. So an estimated three hours plus a bit flight time. It's got just enough range without refueling, but only if they don't have to dodge anything or wait in the air very long. Pretty risky."

"I think they'll stop," Colby said hesitantly. "She'll feel safe once they're on their way. That jet makes her feel…"

"Privileged? Special?"

"Yes."

"Then she has a surprise coming." Quinn said it with such cool Colby felt that hope battering down his qualms. "They're not leaving for an hour. With driving time from Denver, that gives us roughly six hours, probably more when you add in delays and ground transit. And a lot more if they do stop to refuel."

Colby stared at the man. "Why do I get the feeling I'm about to meet Wilbur?"

Quinn grinned, widely. "Won't be as fast—it'll take us two hours or so more flight time—but ol' Wilbur's steady. With a range of five hundred miles more than we need, and that's with a nice fuel reserve left over."

"And you can top the Rockies?"

"Max altitude is twenty-five thousand feet. Cabin's pressurized, rare for a small turbo prop. We're good."

"What about that weather?"

"Always the X factor, but like I said, we've got the range to go around a bit if we need to. Especially since we're not heading into Denver International's traffic pattern."

"So you think we can beat them there?"

"No, but we'll be close on their tail. If Mother Nature cooperates and holds off until tonight."

"You mean Foxworth doesn't have any pull there?" Colby asked in mock shock.

Quinn laughed. "Good to see you're able to joke."

"Hope," Colby said, solemnly now, "is a powerful thing."

"Yes, it—" He broke off as another call came in. Quinn looked at the screen and then put it on speaker. "Gavin. Go."

"Just saw the case update Liam sent. Thinking I should go along."

"We've got room," Quinn said. "You have a reason?"

"Two. I've got a former client in the area who happens to have some legal pull."

Colby didn't doubt that. Back in his headline days, Gavin de Marco handled nothing but people who had some pull. Or a lot of it.

"And reason two?" Quinn asked.

"If I was enough to scare her into running from here, imagine what me showing up there might do."

Quinn laughed. "Our own personal boogeyman."

"I've been called worse," de Marco said with a chuckle. Colby was sure he probably had been, in those years when if there was a lawyer all over the news, chances were good it was him.

Liam appeared in the doorway. "ETA on Wilbur ready for takeoff is forty-five minutes."

"Excellent. You copy that, Gavin?"

"I did. I'll be there just about then. And I'll have to play it by ear, but I may have something worth using."

Quinn ended the call and turned to face Colby. "What did that mean, something worth using?" Colby asked.

"Knowing Gavin, it means something that could turn the tables completely. Just like he used to do at court. We'll have to leave that to him," Quinn said briskly. "It'll probably be pushing an hour by the time everybody gets there and we get loaded up."

"How many people can Wilbur carry?" Colby asked, trying not to leap on that bit about de Marco having something and chewing it to death.

"Five, plus the pilot."

"Who I assume is you?"

"Yep," Quinn said, looking nothing less than delighted at the fact. "So Hayley, Teague, Liam, Gavin, and you."

"And Cutter?"

Quinn grinned at that. "Yeah, him too, but since he's only about seventy pounds, we don't worry about it."

"That'd be one of Liz's suitcases," Colby said dryly.

Quinn laughed. "Hope you pack lighter."

He did, grabbing up whatever clothes were clean, including some of his heavier work socks he was glad he'd grabbed, given the weather they were heading toward. Quinn apparently had a go bag ready at all times, because the only thing he grabbed was his laptop with all the details he'd just researched and a couple of heavy jackets off the rack by the door.

Thanks to the fact that his stay here was temporary, he didn't have a ton of things to include, so was able to be ready only a couple of minutes after Quinn.

"What about Hayley?"

"She's got her go bag in the car. Along with Cutter's."

"The dog has a go bag?"

"He does. Food, water, collapsible bowls and some of Liam's gear we sometimes use with him." Quinn grinned again. He was obviously looking forward to flying. "He's even got a coat and some traction boots, so if that snow hits, he'll be ready."

Colby was still marveling at it all as they drove south to the small local airport Wilbur was hangared at. And his first look at the sleek little airplane had him, oddly, thinking better this to tackle the Rockies than the helicopter, although he suspected Quinn wouldn't cringe at that, either.

All those thoughts vanished when Hayley's SUV pulled up and two women got out. And only one of them had a backpack slung over her shoulder, looking ready to get on that plane and fly.

Ali.

Chapter 39

Ali let Hayley do the selling, since her opinion would carry more weight with Quinn. And hopefully Colby, who had seemed a bit stunned that she was there at all, let alone ready to roll.

"I'll hate not being there, but Ali has some very good points," Hayley was saying. "Seeing Gavin will worry her, especially now that she knows he's working with Colby. And if she sees Liam she'll connect him to Colby."

"If she even remembers me at all," Liam drawled. "Me being one of those peons, and worse, a country boy."

"If she saw me," Hayley went on, "she might wonder, but I doubt she even remembers me from our brief interaction. But seeing Ali appear out of the blue will shock and startle her, because she'll have no idea what she's doing there." Hayley paused, then added quietly, "Maybe you won't need that moment when she's too stunned to react…but maybe you will."

Quinn looked from his wife to Ali consideringly before saying slowly, "And Grace trusts you."

"Yes, she does," Ali said, thinking she was prouder of that truth in this moment than she'd been of almost anything in her life.

"You're sure?" Quinn asked. "It could get messy."

"I'm sure I don't want Grace in her hands a moment longer than she has to be."

"All right, then."

The head of Foxworth turned to the business of loading up.

While Ali turned to look at Colby. He was still staring at her, but his expression was different now, looking not stunned but more…awestruck. Like a man who couldn't believe his luck.

His lips moved. "I love you," he mouthed.

She smiled at him. "And I love you."

She said it aloud, not caring who heard. And judging by his quick glance around, that she was willing to say it aloud in front of witnesses made a difference. Because she thought she saw him blink rapidly a few times as he turned to help Teague load some gear into the small cargo area of the plane. What on earth she didn't know, but knowing Foxworth, it could be anything.

And she laughed when she heard Teague say there was almost twice as much baggage space inside, but when they had a full complement of passengers a chunk of that was reserved for the comfort and convenience of their most important operative, the furry one.

After all these days spent with Cutter, she believed it.

And then Colby straightened abruptly and turned back to look at her with a worried expression. "What about Ziggy?"

That he'd even thought of her pup under these circumstances told her just how right she was about this man.

"Hayley's seeing to him until we get back. Until all three of us get back," she added with emphasis, which got her a flashing smile that somehow filled her with faith that this would somehow work out right in the end.

Teague, who apparently was in the process of getting his pilot's license as well, sat up front with Quinn. Liam and Gavin were in the two seats behind them, facing the tail of the plane, leaving the other two forward-facing ones farther back for her and Colby. She would have thought the arrangement coincidence had she not noticed the way Cutter had nudged people around as they boarded…and the way he settled down into his spot behind their seats with an expression she could only describe as smug.

As they prepped for takeoff, she also noticed Liam talking animatedly with the famous lawyer, who was grinning a lot. Funny, in all the video and photos she'd seen of him from back when him merely being involved in a case put the case in the headlines, she'd never seen him even smile much, let alone grin like that. From what she heard, apparently his wife, the librarian, and Liam's wife, the dog groomer, had become great friends.

She sighed inwardly, happily, envisioning a future like that for them, where happiness was the order of the day, even under stress. Or maybe they weren't stressed, maybe they just had so much faith in Foxworth they didn't worry. And why not? So did she.

Ali had always loved mountains. She admitted the waters of Puget Sound were gorgeous, and she loved the evergreens, but when it came down to it, no matter where she was, as long as she could at least see mountains she was happy. She put it down to being born in the flat heartland. Now she was headed for some of the most magnificent mountains in the country, although Mount Rainier could give even the tallest Rocky a run for its money.

She should be nervous, she supposed. They were, after all, headed for a confrontation with one of the few people she'd ever met whom she would actually call evil. But she had faith in Foxworth, and the need to stand up for both Colby and Grace was more than enough to keep everything else at bay.

Once they passed the rolling hills of the Palouse in eastern Washington there wasn't much that couldn't be called mountainous. But they reached the Rockies—the true mountains among mountains—much sooner than she expected. She'd known they ran from Canada all the way to New Mexico, but she hadn't quite realized how wide they were west to east in spots.

She heard Teague saying something about Class A airspace, which apparently meant over 18,000 feet. Somehow that made it more real to her. It got a little bouncy in a couple of places, and she couldn't deny it made her a bit nervous, never having flown in a small plane before. But as if he somehow knew, Colby reached out and took her hand, squeezing it gently. Then he leaned over, his mouth teasingly close to her ear.

"Quinn's still letting Teague take the controls, so it can't be that bad or he'd take over," he whispered.

What he said made perfect sense, but she was a little slow in processing it because of the shiver of sensation that having his breath tickle her ear caused. And then Cutter lifted his head and poked it between the seats, resting his chin atop their clasped hands.

"Yep," Liam said from his seat about four feet across from them, "just like I expected. You've got the Cutter seal of approval."

They both looked, and the young Texan was grinning widely.

"To be greatly valued," added Gavin, very solemnly. And Ali looked up at Colby, whose gaze was lowered to the dog, but who also wore the sweetest smile she'd ever seen.

She wasn't sure how the four and a half hours of flight time slipped by so quickly, but it seemed the next thing she knew they were prepping for landing. She had the feeling she should be thankful she knew little of flying in smaller aircraft, because this place, in this narrow valley with lot of snow still on the ground, seemed a bit hair-raising.

Quinn was back at the controls, his headset now over both ears as he talked back and forth with what she assumed was the controller in the tower she could see in the distance, and maybe other planes in the area.

Teague looked back at them. "They're hanging onto ski season, so there's a bit of traffic, but we're cleared for landing next."

They dropped rather quickly, or so it seemed to her. Then they were passing over a fence and went from buildings and small roads to empty space, with the runway ahead. It went smooth and quick, and only moments after they touched down they were taxiing off the runway and over toward the hangars on the side opposite the tower.

Liam had told them all angles were covered. There would be a car waiting, a crew to see to the plane and prep it for the return flight, the local authorities—particularly someone Gavin had made contact with, because he'd helped him out of a mess once—were apprised, and Liam had the video equipment ready to go. And once Cutter had the "protect" command, nothing would stop him from keeping Grace safe.

But now Liam was grinning at them as he said, "Is now a good time to mention this place is on the list of the ten most extreme airports?"

"Considering we have to turn around and take off again, perhaps not," Gavin said dryly.

"Why?" Ali asked. "There's no snow or ice on the runway. And that landing seemed really smooth."

"That's because you've got a pro at the controls," Liam said, nodding toward Quinn. "Unless it's actively snowing, the main weather you have to worry about is wind. And the simple fact that we're at six thousand feet and the thinner air makes approach and landing speeds 'a bit interesting,' as Quinn would say."

"Less drag," Colby said. "Never would have thought of that, but it makes sense. I helped build a place over in Steamboat Springs once, and I remember having to catch my breath a lot."

The were offloading before Ali got the chance to say, "I didn't know you'd worked nonlocal."

He shrugged. "It was one of the things that made Liz think I'd go along with her plan. Because I was known enough to get called in on jobs in various places, so obviously I must be ready to go higher."

"And here I'm thinking it's way more than enough that your reputation precedes you that much."

At that he leaned over and kissed her.

Chapter 40

The place was even more pretentious than Colby would have guessed. It was nestled on a hill above the golf course—at least as much as a house that size could nestle. Three stories tall, the bottom level of custom-hewn rock, and the upper two of wood pretending to be cabin-like, with views to forever, he was sure. Ironic, for a family who looked only inward.

If he had to guess—and given his occupation he was pretty good at it—Colby would put it at 10,000 square feet or better. He didn't know what prices were running around here these days, but he'd bet this one was into the eight-digit range. Liz would have seen to it. After all, a Hollen couldn't have an address less distinguished than that.

They drove around and parked out of sight from the driveway at the back of the house. It was situated so nothing faced the neighbors or the street. All the views were out toward the open side, so it probably seemed as if they owned the mountains around them. Liam had already had an aerial view ready, and from that Colby could see that it wasn't quite as isolated as it seemed. Good planning on somebody's part. He doubted very much it had been a Hollen.

But most importantly, the garage door was open. Colby didn't know if that meant they were already here, or if the house was just being prepared for their arrival.

"You three stay here," Quinn said, "until we get this scoped out."

The three Foxworth operatives—because that's what they were at the moment, geared up and ready to skulk through the woods—headed out and split up to circle the house. Liam, because he'd been seen by Liz before, took the most hidden path, through a thick stand of evergreens. Ali watched them go, looking a little anxious.

"They're really good at this," de Marco assured her.

Colby didn't doubt it. With both Quinn and Teague being ex-military, and Liam having learned from them both, he was sure they'd get this initial recon done without being noticed. And they did it much more quickly than he expected.

"Movement, lights on, but we can't see who," Teague reported when they got back to the car.

"I'm going to take Cutter for a little walk," Quinn said.

Colby blinked, but wasn't about to question the man. So he just watched as he and the eager dog took off, looking for all the world like just a guy and his dog out for a stroll.

Until they got to the driveway and Cutter alerted. Quinn edged a bit closer to the house, as if letting the dog pick the path. Then Colby saw that dark head go down to the concrete, nose twitching. He couldn't see from here, but he recognized the motion. The dog had started toward the front door of the house when Quinn pulled him back and walked quickly back to the road. Colby frowned, not sure why he hadn't let the dog continue. But then he saw someone jogging down the roadway, a woman who paused when Quinn said something to her. She answered him. He smiled, she laughed, and then continued on her way.

The pair were back to the car in moments.

"They're here."

Colby blinked. "How do you know?"

"First, the way Cutter alerted up near the door. He scented

Grace, and you said she'd never been here before. And second, that lady saw the limo arrive about twenty minutes ago."

It still amazed Colby how the dog could apparently focus, ignoring what had to be a lot of other new and interesting scents, to home in on the one he was here to protect.

"Liam, you have the comms set up?"

"Will have in less than a minute." Colby didn't doubt it. He'd started messing with the gear the moment Quinn had said Cutter had scented Grace.

"You gonna take the bodyguard, or should I?" Teague asked Quinn, as casually as if he were asking about the weather.

Quinn looked at Colby, as if asking his opinion. He had no idea why, until it hit him that whoever didn't take the bodyguard would probably be the one to confront Liz. And Teague was slightly less intimidating at first sight. Was that what they wanted? He had to assess, quickly. But it wasn't that hard. Dressed in his rugged gear, Quinn looked like what he was, a man able to take on anything. He had no doubt Teague was also, but he didn't look the part in the towering, fierce way Quinn did.

"We want her off guard until we move, right? Then it should be Teague."

Quinn smiled. "Points for figuring out what I was really asking."

Teague didn't take offense at all. In fact, he ran to the back of the rented SUV, pulled his duffel open and yanked something out. Then he shed his tactical jacket and pulled on the item of clothing that, to Colby's surprise, was nothing less than a well-tailored, expensive-looking suit jacket. He'd apparently had it rolled rather than folded, so it looked no worse than if he'd worn it on the plane. And when he put it on over the sweater he was wearing, he looked downright a successful businessman.

"Damn," Colby muttered. "Perfect. She'll think you've come to connect with the family on business."

They'd discussed at length on the flight the aspects of the

Hollen businesses, including some things Colby hadn't known about but Liam had discovered in his seemingly endless research. And then they'd gone over one last time the plan for the encounter. With more what-ifs than Colby could have ever thought of himself. But then, Foxworth had quite a history of cases to provide possibilities.

"Liam, you have those business cards?" Teague asked.

"Side pocket," the young Texan answered without looking up from his laptop.

Teague reached into another duffel bag and pulled out an envelope that held a small stack of business cards. He marveled even at that, because no one the Hollens would deal with would walk around with just one to jam in someone's face. Every meeting was a business meeting, and had to be put to some use.

"These folks are out of Denver, too. But the best part," Teague said when he saw Colby watching him, "is that the Hollens have reached out to this company and been brushed off. I've got the details on that, so I can drop some on her."

"So she'll think they've caved and now want to deal," he said, knowing that was exactly how they'd react.

"But what if she calls the company, to verify you're who you say you are?" It was the first thing Ali had said since they'd arrived.

"They'll say yes, I'm one of their main front men, the one who makes the deals."

Colby blinked, but Ali only smiled. "You helped them out before, too."

Teague grinned briefly. "We did."

Liam was fussing with what were apparently body cams now, one for each of them, so small he was amazed. He'd have to remember that, that it was all going to be recorded live. He knew what buttons to push that would get to Liz the most, if necessary.

"She'll be totally distracted while I take the bodyguard out of the equation," Quinn was saying. "Then Colby, you and

Gavin make your grand entrance and we take advantage of the shock. She won't know if or how Teague fits in. But his and Gavin's presence should make her think twice about doing anything stupid."

"She's many things, but she's not stupid," Colby said. "But she's also never been cornered like this."

"Point taken," Quinn said with a nod. He looked at Ali. "And you search the house with Liam, out of the target's sight, until we have control. And have Grace safe."

"Unless..." she said quietly, and Colby felt a gut wrench at her willingness to walk into this mess.

"Yes," Quinn agreed. "Unless." He turned to the lawyer, who was looking at his phone. "What you said you had..." he began.

"First," De Marco said, holding up the device, "as of right now I have an agreement to reopen the custody case, which is enough for us to rescue Grace. And we got that because of what I had before, now confirmed. The Hollens' attorney, Colby, is now under official investigation for accepted bribes, and various other offenses. And that judge is looking at even worse, as in immediate arrest." He glanced at his watch. "In fact, should have happened while we were in the air."

"I'll find some news video," Liam said instantly, and went back to his keyboard. An amazingly short time later he had it, the district attorney, the county sheriff and the mayor of the jurisdiction all there as the DA read the charges to the gathered media.

"They all look like they're at a funeral," Ali said.

"In a way, they are," de Marco said. "That judge has been around a long time. And unless I miss my guess, some of the dirty threads they've found will lead right back to the Hollens."

And Colby thought the odds of Gavin de Marco missing a guess were probably pretty darn slim.

He'd never expected to actually do damage to the Hollens. All he'd ever wanted was Grace, and he would have left them alone completely if they just would have been decent about it. But the name Hollen and the word *decent* were the biggest oxymorons he'd ever encountered.

And now, finally, they were going to pay the price.

Chapter 41

It was like listening to an old-time story podcast, and it required some focus. Colby couldn't tell exactly what the quietly speaking—and probably timid, knowing Liz—woman who'd answered the door said, other than something about Liz having just arrived and wasn't ready for visitors.

But Teague very politely, and with the same assumption of joyous welcome Liz always had, explained that she would be delighted to see and talk to him. And managed to provide them valuable information in the process.

"I'm more than happy to go to the third floor to see her, just tell her on that intercom that I'm here and who I represent. She'll want to see me."

Third floor and there's an intercom. Just like that we know where she is and something to be wary of.

The woman gave in, clearly unsettled. After a moment when Colby could only hear the woman's voice as a muted sort of sound in the background, Teague whispered into his hidden mic that the front door was now unlocked, and he would make sure she didn't think to go back to secure it.

"I imagine you should take me to her," Teague said normally, his tone firm but genial. "I wouldn't want you to get in trouble for letting a stranger roam the house."

"I... Thank you," the woman said, sounding surprised. "There's an elevator over here."

"Of course there is," Teague said in that same amiable tone. "Perfect."

"Indeed," Quinn muttered. He gave them all a quick glance, and Liam and Gavin both nodded.

"Who's that outside, over by the hot tub?" came Teague's voice. "I was given to understand Mr. Hollen wasn't here?"

"Oh, he's not, no one else is. That's just the security man."

Colby barely had time to register how good Teague was at this when he made a comment on the brand of elevator, indicating they were there and stepping inside.

Then Quinn left at a swift but silent pace toward the other side of the house, clearly knowing exactly where the target was. Colby listened tensely, half expected the sounds of some nasty fight. But all he heard was a low grunt and the sound of something—or someone—large hitting the ground.

"Guard down," came Quinn's voice. "We'll have half an hour before he wakes up. Liam and Ali, set Cutter on the search."

Colby hated seeing Ali leave, but trusted Liam as he trusted all of Foxworth now. Particularly that black-and-brown furry critter. It was going to take time to search the massive residence, and the dog would make it so much quicker.

"He'll ignore anywhere there's no sign of Grace," Quinn had explained, "unless he comes across something dangerous, like weapons or explosives."

Colby remembered his startled reaction at the idea of the Hollens hoarding such things, with all their public declarations about them, but they were hypocrites about everything else, so why not this, too? Besides, the laws never applied to them, and even if they did, they would, as they had, hire someone else to do the dirty work.

"This is it? Second door on the left?" Teague asked, as if merely curious.

"Yes," the woman answered. "It's the family gathering

room." She said that last as if she was surprised he was being allowed in.

Colby had sat in on a few business encounters with Liz early on, before he realized she wanted him there not in support as her husband, but to see his future path. Now he listened to Teague, talking as if he were exactly what that business card said he was.

But he listened more closely to Liz.

He pressed the button to activate his own mic, and said quietly, "She's fired up to pull this deal off. She wants to be the one to do it. To be able to tell her father he has her to thank for it."

He heard Teague work the word *copy* into his next sentence, and knew he'd heard. The wait resumed. He knew Quinn was circling the outside of the house, looking for signs of other people, security or otherwise. Meanwhile Liam and Ali, led by Cutter, searched for his precious girl, although she hadn't been here long enough to leave much of a trail. But at least they were looking.

While you sit here doing nothing.

He fought down the long-instinctive guilt. He had his role to play today, and it was crucial. He just wasn't used to having help, that was all.

"Clear outside," came Quinn's voice. "Coming around."

So there were no other guards outside. Inside, they couldn't be sure. The thought of what else Quinn had mentioned, that she might have brought a guard along solely to keep Grace in line, made his jaw tighten, and he clung to the fact that she'd done this in such a rush there likely wasn't time. But that didn't mean more armed help wasn't coming, especially since he was sure there were security people at the office in Denver.

They listened to Teague work the situation, so perfectly Colby would have sworn the guy was exactly who Liz thought he was. And then Quinn was there, looking exactly as he had when he'd left.

"That guy have any clue at all what happened to him?" Colby asked.

That brief grin flashed, and Colby had a sudden image of how deadly this guy must have been in a war zone. "I left him snoozing peacefully in one of the patio chaises. Hoping he'll wake up thinking he just dozed off."

"I wouldn't be surprised if—"

Colby cut himself off sharply as something changed in the feed coming in through his earpiece. It wasn't much, just a shift in Liz's voice, an undertone he recognized. He keyed his mic again.

"She's ready to close this. She thinks she's going to pull off what her father couldn't, and she's euphoric about it."

"I think that's your cue, gentlemen," Quinn said. "I'll follow and be right outside. Liam?"

"Still nothing. Second floor now."

"Then let's proceed."

Colby couldn't help it, he was looking forward to this. Looking forward to seeing the look on Liz's face, not just when someone dared to interrupt this crucial victory, but when it turned out to be him…

De Marco didn't even knock. He simply shoved the door open. Colby heard a click and whoosh as the automatic closer kicked into action. De Marco ignored that, too, just strode into the room as if it were his. And Colby realized he was now looking not at the caring, empathetic Foxworth man, but the firebrand lawyer who had made headlines around the world.

Liz stared in shock. But then she saw Colby, and the shock turned to fury. "What the hell are *you* doing here?"

Colby couldn't help himself; he grinned. Her expression was even better than he'd hoped. She seemed to have forgotten her business meeting altogether. Teague was on his feet now and, Colby suspected, ready to move in any direction in the large room. It was a nice room, Colby noted out of habit, with a fireplace over by another entry door, and French doors leading out onto a deck that probably had a fantastic view up here on the third floor.

Nicer than the Hollens, anyway.

"He's here," de Marco answered silkily, "for his daughter. The child you have smuggled out of state without notifying her father, after breaking the custody-sharing agreement two days before."

"She's my daughter," Liz retorted loudly. "And I have every right to bring her with me."

De Marco smiled, as if he knew that would only set Liz off more. "Not without notifying her father."

Liz gave Colby a look of utter disdain. "Avoiding any time with the likes of him is good for her."

"You might want to rethink your attitude, Ms. Hollen," de Marco said, his voice still smooth and unruffled.

Liz swore, loudly. Considering whom de Marco had come up against in the past—and beaten—Colby thought she ought to be a bit more careful. But he was very glad she didn't see it that way.

"So you lied," she spat out. "When you said you wouldn't fight me anymore."

Colby smiled. "I leave the lying to you, since you're an expert. I only said *I* wouldn't fight you anymore. Not that the fight was over."

"But it is now," de Marco said.

"I don't care how unbeatable you think you are, de Marco, you picked the wrong side here. Judge Boras will slap you down with fines and maybe more if you interfere with me."

Colby tried to stifle a laugh, then realized nothing would push her over the edge faster, so he let it out. De Marco's smile widened. "If you mean your bought-and-paid-for judge, you'll want to rethink that, too. He was charged with multiple rather salacious crimes just an hour ago, and his time as a judge is over, for good. And he's going to take you and your family down with him."

Liz's eyes widened. "I don't believe you."

De Marco shrugged. "Check. It's all over the news. We'll wait."

She did just that, picking up the phone that lay on the arm of the chair she'd been sitting in when they strode in. A few taps and a half scroll and she stopped. She paled as she read, and Colby knew she'd found the story.

She looked up at them again, and this time in addition to the fury, there was a touch of fear. Just the idea of being held to account clearly frightened her.

"Well," Teague said as if he were still that businessman, "obviously you're not the kind of person my company wants to be associated with. You can consider this discussion over, and the deal officially dead. And I'll make sure everyone we do business with is warned off."

She let out a little sound as she spun around to look at the man she'd clearly almost forgotten was here. She wasn't used to being afraid, and she did not handle it well. She let loose a tirade so loud it made Colby's ears ring.

A noise came from another entry door he'd noticed by the fireplace. Colby saw Teague spin around, then take a long stride to put himself in front of both him and de Marco. The assistant coming to check because of the noise? Or worse, more security they'd missed? Or—

His mind went blank and his every muscle went taut as the door swung open and the person on the other side rushed in.

Grace.

Chapter 42

Cutter was practically dancing, but Quinn held him back.

"Daddy! I heard her and I knew it was you. You're the only one who makes her so mad."

The joy in the little girl's voice made Ali's heart skip a beat.

"Shut up, idiot child."

The fury in the mother's voice made a chill go down her spine.

"You shut up," Grace retorted.

And then she heard a yelp from Grace, a shout from Colby, the sound of a door opening and a "Don't even think about it," from Teague.

Her first instinct was to charge into the room, but Quinn held her back. "Not yet. Timing is crucial. And evidence, to win in the end."

That reminded her this was all being recorded. It was an effort, but she stayed put.

"You take one more step toward us, you bastard, and she goes over!" Liz was shrieking now. And beneath that horrid sound, she thought she heard a tiny scream of fear.

"Boss?" Liam's voice sounded like she felt, and Ali didn't like that. The young tech wizard held out his phone for them to see.

Liz was out on the deck, had Grace in her grasp, and even as they watched, pulled the child up onto the railing.

"Take another step," Liz screeched, "and I'll drop her!"

Three stories up, nothing but rocks and a stone patio below. A fall would kill her.

Quinn looked at Ali. "I think we need that moment."

She nodded. Steeled herself. She knew what her goal was. Grace, and Grace alone. She pasted the biggest smile she could manage on her face. With Cutter at her heels she grabbed the knobs and pushed the double entry doors open and strode into the room.

"Liz? Oh, there you are," she said cheerfully. "They said I'd find you here."

The woman gasped and spun around, gaping at her. And in that moment Grace pulled free of her mother's grip. Ali saw her start to grin victoriously, but then she wobbled and started to fall backward. That fatal drop. She screamed in fear.

Cutter ran. The dog arrived just in time to catch the sleeve of Grace's jacket in his strong jaws, using the vertical bars to hold himself back from the drop. And in the next split second Colby was there.

Without hesitation he went over the rail himself. He hung on to the decking with one hand as he reached down with the other. He caught Grace's wrist just as her jacket began to rip. Ali wasn't sure how he did it, but knew she was seeing just how strong he really was as he pulled his precious girl to safety.

Only when she was safely back on the deck did he start to pull himself up and over the railing. There was an instant when he nearly slipped and Ali gasped. But then his strength overcame gravity, and he was safely back. Grace clung to him like the lifeline he was and he hugged her fiercely.

Liz had turned as if to run toward the doors, but the moment she realized the woman was going to run, Ali stepped in front of her.

"I don't think so," she said, letting all the contempt she was feeling show in her voice.

Liz tried to shove her aside, but froze as Quinn stepped between them. Liz gaped up at the man she'd never seen, but whose steady stare had likely made worse people than her back down.

Gavin spoke, and sounded just amused enough to put the icing on Liz's humiliation. "Lovely." He plucked the disguised mini camera from his shirt collar, and let her see it. "And now, in addition to the recordings the sheriff will obtain from your nanny cams, we have you on video for child abuse, assault and attempted murder. And investigations will be opened in the next few days into many of the Hollen financial dealings. Say goodbye to your luxurious life, Elizabeth Hollen. Oh, and you might call your father, when they let you near a phone, and tell him you've managed to destroy his life, too."

"Are we going to go home soon?" Grace asked hopefully.

"Very soon," Colby promised.

Quinn had had them all decamp to a meeting room at a resort lodge Foxworth had rented down the hill, based on the accurate assumption that none of them wanted to stay in that house any longer than they had to. Then he had told them he would be flying them, including Grace, home as soon as the weather made it possible. Liam was busy gathering all their gear, then he would fly back with Gavin, who would stay as long as it took to deal with the locals. Then the attorney would head back himself to deal with the fallout at home, including any government agency that might want to get their hands on Grace.

"Where were you in the house?" Ali asked the girl. "We searched the bottom and second floor, and Cutter didn't find any sign of you."

"I was hiding in the library. Down the hall from where she was in that room. She never goes in the one at home. I was figuring out a way to sneak out."

Colby was still holding her tight against his chest with one arm. Ali was next to them, and his other arm was around her. He felt a bit drained, but that didn't matter, not when the three of them were together. And having Cutter at their feet, Cutter who had essentially saved her life by delaying that fall that precious second so he could get to her, was beyond comforting.

"Then what were you going to do?" Ali asked.

"I saw out the window there were some kids playing in the snow down the hill, with a dog." She paused to stroke Cutter's dark head. "I thought I'd go to them, and ask for help." She looked up at Colby. "I know not all parents are like her."

"Thanks to your father," Ali said softly, "you know that some of them are wonderful."

Colby swallowed hard, his throat tight. He was still feeling a bit dazed. But Grace smiled widely and nodded at Ali. Then she shifted her gaze back to him.

"I yelled at her, when she put me on that airplane, that you'd come for me. She said you wouldn't. That you didn't love me, I was just how you got back at her. She's a liar."

"A big one," Colby agreed. Grace snuggled against him, clearly never having believed a word of Liz's propaganda.

"I'm glad you're too smart to believe that," Ali said.

Grace looked up at her. "I'm glad you're here," she said simply.

"As am I," Colby said, looking at Ali now. "More than glad. Delirious with happiness."

Ali didn't answer, but looked at Grace. "And there's something I've been waiting to tell you. How much I loved my birthday present."

The child smiled. "You did?"

"I did. So much."

"I wish it were real."

Only then did Ali look back to Colby. She saw him swallow, hard, then he looked at his precious child and said huskily, "Maybe we can work on that when we get home. Making it real."

"That would be good," Grace said, and lowered her head to rest against him.

For a while they just sat there. Together, holding on to each other. Ali thought she'd never been more tired, but also never more exhilarated. It was all over but the cleanup, and Foxworth would see to that.

Ali's phone chimed and she pulled it out. It was a text from Hayley, with a video attached.

I think he misses you!

She laughed and held it out for Grace and Colby to see. Ziggy, curled up sleeping on Ali's couch, burrowed into the very sweater they had used to give Cutter Grace's scent.

Grace laughed, and Ali saw Colby close his eyes as if to savor the sound of it.

"Will you miss Cutter, now?" the child asked.

"I'll miss him," Ali admitted. "But I won't miss trying to keep up with him."

"Story of my life." Quinn's amused response came as he arrived beside them, a smile on his face. "And speaking of life, would you like to get back home and start rebuilding yours?"

They all looked up at him. "Now?" Colby asked, sounding hopeful.

"Now," Quinn confirmed. "Just checked the weather and it's all north of here. Clear sailing, and if we head out now, we can be airborne before it gets dark."

One day. One day and Foxworth had undone Grace's short lifetime of damage.

"I'm for that," Colby said, almost reverently. But then he looked at Ali. "Unless you want to—"

"I'll beat you to Wilbur," she said fervently.

"Who's Wilbur?" Grace asked.

"You'll find out soon," Colby promised.

"Good," Quinn said, then added with a smile. "Not a bad day's work."

"Quinn," Colby began, but the man shook his head.

"Time enough for all that later. Cutter, on me. I think your work here is done."

Cutter scrambled up, gave one last look at her, Grace and Colby, and she'd swear the dog was grinning.

"Yeah, yeah," Quinn said with a chuckle. "You did it again. Now let's go home."

Ali liked the sound of that. Tried not to dwell on the clever Foxworth dog's apparent matchmaking abilities. But it did suddenly occur to her to wonder where exactly that home was going to be.

Grace yawned widely. Ali didn't blame her—the post adrenaline crash had to be close. She snuggled up even closer to her father, but she didn't let go of Ali's hand.

"Ali's going to stay with us, isn't she?" she asked her father as he got up, still holding her. "So she doesn't have to look at that house next door?"

Ali felt Colby go still. But as if now that he had Grace back and safe, nothing could daunt him anymore, he looked over and met her gaze.

"That's her decision, honey. But it sounds good to me. Really, really good," he said.

Ali thought her heart would burst, her chest felt so tight. "I'd like to be with you. We have a lot of things to work through, Gracie."

"But it's over now, right?" the child asked, a trace of the old worry back in her eyes. "I don't have to be with the mother anymore?"

"All over except the details," her father said.

"Details?" She shifted her gaze from Colby back to Ali, still looking worried.

Ali smiled at her. "It's like a big firecracker exploded," she said. "Now the big bang is over, but there's some junk to clean up."

"Oh." As if that made it all make sense to her, she settled back down.

"You know the rest of that unpacking you mentioned?" Colby asked.

"Yes?"

"Put that on hold," Colby said.

And that, Ali thought, answered her big question. They were going to clean up the junk, and then…well, Colby was an amazing carpenter, a man who built. And now, with the weight that had been dragging him down gone, Ali had no doubt he could build an amazing life for them. Because this time he wouldn't have an anchor weighing him down, but a partner. Her. So together they would build that most precious of structures.

A family.

A short time later they had indeed introduced Grace to Wilbur, and Colby made her laugh when he explained the name, which the child thought was exceptionally cool. And it apparently made her ask if she could please, please not ever be Brianna anymore, but be Grace forever.

"We'll work on that, too," her father promised.

At takeoff, the child's sleepiness seemed to vanish at the excitement of flying in this smaller plane, or perhaps it was just because of her companions. In the end it didn't seem to matter, as long as they were together.

Home. They were going home.

Ali looked away from the small window to find Colby watching her, with a smile that held so much promise it sent a thrill through her. With Grace beside them, they flew into the sunset, to prepare for the dawn of three new lives.

And behind them, Cutter yawned and settled in for a nap, his work done.

For now.

* * * * *

Get up to 4 Free Books!

We'll send you 2 free books from each series you try PLUS a free Mystery Gift.

FREE Value Over **$25**

Both the **Harlequin Intrigue®** and **Harlequin® Romantic Suspense** series feature compelling novels filled with heart-racing action-packed romance that will keep you on the edge of your seat.

YES! Please send me 2 FREE novels from the Harlequin Intrigue or Harlequin Romantic Suspense series and my FREE gift (gift is worth about $10 retail). After receiving them, if I don't wish to receive any more books, I can return the shipping statement marked "cancel." If I don't cancel, I will receive 6 brand-new Harlequin Intrigue Larger-Print books every month and be billed just $7.19 each in the U.S. or $7.99 each in Canada, or 4 brand-new Harlequin Romantic Suspense books every month and be billed just $6.39 each in the U.S. or $7.19 each in Canada, a savings of 20% off the cover price. It's quite a bargain! Shipping and handling is just 50¢ per book in the U.S. and $1.25 per book in Canada.* I understand that accepting the 2 free books and gift places me under no obligation to buy anything. I can always return a shipment and cancel at any time by calling the number below. The free books and gift are mine to keep no matter what I decide.

Choose one:
- ☐ **Harlequin Intrigue Larger-Print** (199/399 BPA G36Y)
- ☐ **Harlequin Romantic Suspense** (240/340 BPA G36Y)
- ☐ **Or Try Both!** (199/399 & 240/340 BPA G36Z)

Name (please print)

Address _____ Apt. #

City _____ State/Province _____ Zip/Postal Code

Email: Please check this box ☐ if you would like to receive newsletters and promotional emails from Harlequin Enterprises ULC and its affiliates. You can unsubscribe anytime.

Mail to the **Harlequin Reader Service:**
IN U.S.A.: P.O. Box 1341, Buffalo, NY 14240-8531
IN CANADA: P.O. Box 603, Fort Erie, Ontario L2A 5X3

Want to explore our other series or interested in ebooks? Visit www.ReaderService.com or call 1-800-873-8635.

---

*Terms and prices subject to change without notice. Prices do not include sales taxes, which will be charged (if applicable) based on your state or country of residence. Canadian residents will be charged applicable taxes. Offer not valid in Quebec. This offer is limited to one order per household. Books received may not be as shown. Not valid for current subscribers to the Harlequin Intrigue or Harlequin Romantic Suspense series. All orders subject to approval. Credit or debit balances in a customer's account(s) may be offset by any other outstanding balance owed by or to the customer. Please allow 4 to 6 weeks for delivery. Offer available while quantities last.

Your Privacy—Your information is being collected by Harlequin Enterprises ULC, operating as Harlequin Reader Service. For a complete summary of the information we collect, how we use this information and to whom it is disclosed, please visit our privacy notice located at https://corporate.harlequin.com/privacy-notice. Notice to California Residents – Under California law, you have specific rights to control and access your data. For more information on these rights and how to exercise them, visit https://corporate.harlequin.com/california-privacy. For additional information for residents of other U.S. states that provide their residents with certain rights with respect to personal data, visit https://corporate.harlequin.com/other-state-residents-privacy-rights/.

HIHRS25